Now you see him...
Now you don't...

Julia had almost finished her drawing when she realized they were no longer alone. Two men had appeared far ahead on the rough path leading to the waterfall, their figures mere black silhouettes against the sun behind them. Julia watched them for some time, weighing whether or not to include them in her sketch. Would the presence of human figures detract from the beauty of the scenery, she wondered, or would their addition actually improve the drawing by giving some sense of the height of the falls and the grandeur of the fells behind it? She decided in favor of the latter, and was about to put pencil to paper once more when there was an abrupt movement toward the cliff's edge, and suddenly only one figure remained.

It all happened so quickly, Julia would have thought she'd only imagined it, had she not just spent several minutes weighing the effect of the two figures on her drawing. But no, there had certainly been two where now there was one—one dark silhouette that was even now stepping away from the sheer drop.

"John!" Although she was much too far away for that anonymous form to hear her, she whispered as she shook Pickett by the shoulder. "John, wake up!"

"Huh—what—?" Although groggy from sleep, he nevertheless recognized the urgency in her voice and pushed his hat off his eyes. "What's wrong?"

"John, I think I've just seen a murder!"

THE JOHN PICKETT MYSTERIES:

PICKPOCKET'S APPRENTICE
(prequel novella)

IN MILADY'S CHAMBER

A DEAD BORE

FAMILY PLOT

DINNER MOST DEADLY

WAITING GAME
(Christmas novella)

TOO HOT TO HANDEL

FOR DEADER OR WORSE

MYSTERY LOVES COMPANY

PERIL BY POST

Peril by Post

Another John Pickett Mystery

Sheri Cobb South

Don't turn that page!

Not just yet, anyway. First, I have a bonus short story for you. (Consider it a little appetizer before you begin the main course.) "Tales out of School" is 5,000 words, or about 15 typed double-spaced pages. You can download it in EPUB, MOBI, or PDF format here: BookHip.com/RJGVZJ

And the best part? It's absolutely free! It's my way of saying "Thank you" for sharing in John Pickett's adventures. There are a lot of books out there, and you chose to invest your time, imagination, and, yes, money, in mine. I'm more honored than I can say.

1

In Which John Pickett Takes On a New Case

T he long-case clock in the hall struck seven, the descending tones of its Whittington chimes echoing up to the bedrooms on the floor above. Pushing back the covers, John Pickett sat up and swung his legs out of bed, yawning as he raked his fingers through his tousled brown curls. Behind him, a mound of rumpled sheets stirred, and a sleepy feminine voice purred.

"Mmm, you're nice to wake up to."

He turned to regard his wife of three months in some surprise. "Oh?"

Julia smiled sleepily at him. "You find that surprising?"

"I do," he confessed, then turned away to hide the mischievous smile he could not quite suppress. "I didn't think you woke up until noon, at the earliest."

While she sputtered in mock indignation, Pickett leaned forward to reach for the pair of breeches lying on a chair beside the bed. Herein he made a tactical error, for she seized the opportunity to swat him on his bare backside. Such uxorial impertinence could not be allowed to go unpunished, so he crawled back into the bed, determined to wreak vengeance upon his laughing spouse. As a result, more than half an hour had passed by the time he left the Curzon Street town house and set out for Bow Street at a run.

"Late, late, late," he muttered under his breath, around a mouthful of the roll he'd snatched from the breakfast room to eat on the way.

Alas, in spite of his best efforts, it was five minutes past eight by the time he entered the Bow Street Public Office, and any hopes he might have entertained of being able to slip in unobserved were dashed when Harry Carson, one of the newer members of the horse patrol, called out to him, "Cutting it a bit close, aren't you, lover boy?"

How did they *know?* Pickett wondered, blushing crimson at finding himself the object of a dozen knowing grins. Was it so obvious? Did it show on his face?

"So pleased you could join us, Mr. Pickett," said the magistrate, looking considerably less amused than his men.

"I'm sorry, sir—" Pickett began, but Mr. Colquhoun silenced him with a look. He finished giving instructions to the men and dismissed them to their duties, concluding with, "Not you, Mr. Pickett." As Pickett squirmed in anticipation of the coming rebuke, his magistrate waited until the group had dispersed. Once he could be certain of not being overheard, he regarded his most junior Runner with a baleful eye. "This makes the third time you've been late since your marriage, does it not, Mr. Pickett?"

Pickett bethought himself of several late nights and certain unscheduled morning activities, and could not deny it. "I am sorry, sir. It—it won't happen again." He considered this last statement. "Actually, it will, but I won't be late again. That is"—he thought of his wife's warm and welcoming embrace, and smiled in fond remembrance—"I'll try not to be."

Mr. Colquhoun's Scottish burr recalled him to the present. "You might try for a little less smugness, Mr. Pickett. You haven't invented anything new, you know."

"It's new to me," Pickett objected, thus confirming what Mr. Colquhoun had already suspected.

The magistrate sighed. "You didn't have much of a wedding trip, did you?" he asked, not without sympathy.

Pickett could not agree to this. "Two weeks in Somersetshire," he reminded his magistrate, "with pay."

"During which you not only found yourself saddled with a missing-person case and a murder, but you spent the entire time housed beneath your father-in-law's roof. And don't tell me the latter didn't put more of a damper on the honeymoon than the former."

Pickett recalled his uncomfortable first meeting with his horrified in-laws, and shuddered. "No, sir, I won't."

"That being the case, would you fancy a trip to the Lake District with the missus? Tell me what you make of this."

Mr. Colquhoun reached across the railing that separated the magistrate's bench from the rest of the room and handed Pickett a folded sheet of paper, a paper directed to *Patrick*

Colquhoun, Esq., 4 Bow Street, London. Pickett opened it and scanned the few lines it contained. The message was brief and to the point: *Please send one of your men to the village of Banfell in Cumberland. He can put up at the Hart and Hound.*

Pickett looked up at the magistrate. "It isn't signed."

Mr. Colquhoun nodded. "It's obvious that marriage has not dulled your razor-sharp wits."

Pickett acknowledged this verbal hit with a rather sheepish grin. "No, but it doesn't give much to go on, does it?"

"No, it doesn't. Truth to tell, I'm a bit scunnered at having been obliged to pay a shilling for the dubious privilege of accepting it. And yet whoever wrote it expects me to send a man on an expensive and time-consuming journey, without so much as hinting at what the purpose might be. I don't know whether to dispatch you to the Lake District, or this thing to the fire."

"But what if he couldn't say more?" Pickett suggested a bit desperately, seeing the proposed honeymoon slipping away before his eyes. "What if he hadn't the time to dash off more than a quick note for fear someone else would see? Or if he was afraid to be more specific, lest it fall into the wrong hands?"

"Aye, you might have a point," the magistrate said thoughtfully, drumming his fingers on the bench. "If I were to send you to Cumberland on so little information, Mr. Pickett, where would you begin?"

Pickett looked down at the uncommunicative message in his hand, and sighed. "I suppose I would start by taking a room at the Hart and Hound, letting it be known that I'd come from London, and waiting for our anonymous correspondent to identify himself."

"Aye, and in the meantime, you and your lady wife would merely be a newly wedded couple on your honeymoon, which shouldn't tax your acting abilities overmuch. I think it might work. You might even enjoy the change of scenery. It's a wild and beautiful country, the Lake District. Reminds me a bit of my native Scotland, the countryside around Loch Lomond."

Pickett could see only one thing wrong with this plan. "I'm not sure Julia should be traveling in her condition."

"How far along is she?"

It had been a shock to both Picketts, man and wife, to discover that Julia—who, after six childless years of marriage to her first husband, had believed herself to be barren—had conceived almost immediately after their own marriage was consummated. "About three months—certainly no more than that."

"John, in another month—two, at the most—her condition will become obvious, and she'll be confined to the house until after the birth. If you'll heed a word of advice from a man who's been through it seven times with his own wife, let her get out as much as possible while still she may."

For women of Pickett's own class, life went on very much as usual whether they were increasing or not, so he didn't quite understand the gentry's practice of hiding pregnant women away out of sight—did they think babies were found under cabbage leaves?—but he had no doubt that his wife, a lady born and bred, would expect to conform to a custom that no doubt seemed perfectly reasonable to her. Then, too, there was the fact that she had wanted to go with him the last time he'd been obliged to travel during the course of an investigation. He had refused to allow it, not realizing she'd had reasons of her own for being disinclined to remain in London alone. What followed had been their first (and only, touch wood) quarrel, and he had no desire to repeat the experience. Besides, once the baby came, he wasn't sure she would want to leave it with a nurse long enough to accompany him on an investigation. They might not have another chance.

"All right, you've convinced me," he said at last.

"Good man! As it happens, I have an old friend who lives in the area, a fellow by the name of Robert Hetherington. If you'll wait a bit, I'll write you a letter of introduction. Who knows but what it might prove useful to you, having a local contact in the area."

For some moments afterward, there was no sound but the scratching of the quill as the magistrate penned his letter. At last he returned the quill to its standish, shook pounce over his missive to dry the ink, then folded and sealed it.

"In the ordinary way of things, I would instruct you to take the stage, but given that you'll be traveling with a lady—and a breeding lady at that, who will no doubt need to stop at every necessary between here and Penrith—I'll stand the nonsense for a post-chaise."

"Thank you, sir," said Pickett in some surprise, unaccustomed to traveling in such luxury at Bow Street's expense.

"No servants, though," the magistrate added. "I have to hold the cost down where I can. Think your wife can manage?"

"I know she can," Pickett assured him with no small note of pride in his wife's unexpected versatility. In fact, he'd been surprised at how well his gently bred bride had adapted to life in his own Drury Lane flat during the two weeks they'd lived there, although he had no intention of asking her to make such a sacrifice on a more permanent basis.

"Excellent! It will take you the better part of a sc'ennight to reach Cumberland," Mr. Colquhoun continued, scrawling his acquaintance's name on the outside of the letter and handing it across the railing. "Add another for the return trip, and I shall expect to see you again in, say, three weeks. If you should require more time—time for your investigation, that is, not for your honeymoon—you may write to inform me of it. For that matter, if you should care to apprise me as to what you find there, I will be happy to accept any letters you might send."

"Thank you, sir." Pickett knew this was no small concession, as receipt of the letter would come from the budget of the Bow Street Public Office, if not from Mr. Colquhoun's own pocket. Nor would such a correspondence come cheap: a single letter delivered by the Royal Mail from so remote a location would cost the recipient no less than a shilling—four percent of Pickett's own weekly wages. "I promise not to abuse the privilege. If you receive a letter from me, you may be sure I have significant news to report."

"I doubt you'll have much time for writing in any case,

Mr. Pickett," the magistrate said, then added, with a twinkle in his eye, "after all, you'll be on your honeymoon."

* * *

Pickett returned to Curzon Street a short time later to find Julia in the dining room, cutting up lengths of white linen spread over the table.

"Back so soon?" she asked, looking up from her task with every appearance of pleasure. "Nothing wrong, I hope?"

"No, but—sweetheart, I'm sure you must have a very good reason, but why are you cutting up the tablecloth?"

"It's not a tablecloth, silly," she said, pausing in her task long enough to greet him with a kiss. "I'm making clouts for the baby."

"Clouts?" Pickett's bemused gaze took in the mounds of large white rectangles stacked on several chairs, as well as the length which Julia was in the process of converting into still more, and he formed a very fair estimation of the use to which these "clouts" would be put. "How many clouts does the average baby need?"

"My dear John, surely you don't mean to suggest that our child will be 'average'!"

"Let's just say there are some things I would just as soon it not excel at," Pickett said, wrinkling his nose at the prospect. "But you don't have to make them yourself, you know. I'm sure we can afford to buy them." It was still a bit of a sore point to him, that he could not provide her with the many little luxuries to which she was accustomed; he supposed it always would be, no matter how many times she assured him that it did not matter. Still, he could not imagine this expense would be beyond his ability to pay.

"Oh, but I want to! I'll have to have *something* to do during those last few months. I thought I would cut them up now, while I can still lean across the table without difficulty, and then later, when I must keep to the house, I can roll the edges and hem them to prevent fraying. But you were about to tell me why you're home so early," she reminded him.

"I need to pack."

"Oh?" Her scissors sliced through the folds of cloth without so much as a pause. "You're going away?"

He might have been disappointed, even hurt, by her seeming indifference, had he not noticed her determination not to look him in the face. He braced one hand on the table and leaned forward, making it all but impossible for her to avoid his gaze. "*We're* going away," he corrected her. "How would you like to go to the Lake District with me?"

The scissors clattered to the table, the baby and its clouts temporarily forgotten. "Oh John, do you mean it?"

"I do." Once again he felt a twinge of guilt that marriage to him had effectively banished her from the society of her own class. Mr. Colquhoun was right: he needed to get her out of the house as much as possible for the next month or two. And after that, if hiding her condition away from the world helped her reclaim some part of her lost status—to say nothing of allowing her to escape the public eye until the gossip surrounding their unequal marriage could be forgotten—well, who could blame her? "Mr. Colquhoun thinks we can put on a convincing pose as a newlywed couple—I can't imagine how he got that idea—while I do a bit of investigating on the sly."

"What sort of case is it?" she asked. "When do we set out?"

"First thing tomorrow morning, if you can be ready that soon. As to what sort of case, well, it's a curious thing." He took the letter from his pocket and handed it to her.

"Curious, indeed." She scanned the brief note just as he had done only a short time earlier, then turned it over, searching in vain for any sign of a frank that would have allowed the letter to be delivered free of charge. "And wasteful as well, to expect your magistrate to pay a shilling for no more than this."

"Yes, Mr. Colquhoun said he was a bit 'scunnered' about that, which I assume means he was displeased."

"I can't say I blame him." One of the few things—the *very* few things—she missed about her first marriage was the loss of Lord Fieldhurst's franking privileges. She supposed her husband's cousin George, the new viscount, would frank her letters if she asked—he could hardly do otherwise without looking like the nip-farthing he was—but she refused to give him the satisfaction of believing, quite correctly, that her second husband was incapable of providing the luxuries to which she was accustomed. Instead, newly conscious of the expenses of keeping house (and the need to balance these against the peace of mind of a husband whose income was much less than her own), she reserved her correspondence for when she had real news to impart—or, as she had become increasingly aware, a rather large favor to ask. "In fact, I'm surprised Mr. Colquhoun agreed to send you at all, on so little information."

"Oh, he was sorely tempted to consign the letter to the fire, but I persuaded him otherwise."

"You did? How? And perhaps more to the point, why? Unless, of course, you saw an opportunity for the two of us to steal away to a secluded and picturesque locale for a few weeks, in which case you're even cleverer than I thought."

"No, I'm afraid not, much as it pains me to disillusion you," he confessed. "It just seemed a bit, I don't know, desperate, I suppose. As if whoever wrote this—what there is of it—didn't dare say more for fear of its falling into the wrong hands."

"It all sounds very cryptic and mysterious."

"And may yet prove to be nothing but a chase after mare's nests—in which case Mr. Colquhoun won't be best pleased with me for persuading him to fund this little jaunt."

"I thought the person who sent for you would be the person to pay your expenses."

"Yes, but the letter is unsigned," he pointed out. "If I can't identify the sender, Bow Street will be left to foot the bill—which is bound to be substantial, what with the hire of a post-chaise to Cumberland and back. But Mr. Colquhoun reckoned that I would not want my wife traveling on the common stage. And he was right," he added, taking her in his arms and kissing her again.

Her expression grew solemn. "John, if you would prefer to go alone, I'll understand. Truly, I will."

He didn't have to ask to know that she, too, remembered that recent quarrel. "I want you with me, Julia, never doubt that. Besides"—his arms tightened about her, and he dropped yet another kiss onto her golden curls—"a pretty fool I would look, going on a honeymoon all by myself."

* * *

Having settled the matter to the satisfaction of both, Pickett dispatched Andrew the footman to the post office to arrange for the hire of a post-chaise; although still not entirely comfortable with the rise in the world which his marriage had brought him, he was learning how to instruct servants without appearing too timid or, in overcompensation for the aforementioned timidity, too autocratic. As the footman set off on this errand, Pickett joined his lady wife in the bedroom, where he found her issuing her own instructions to Betsy, her lady's maid, as well as to Thomas, his recently promoted valet, as to the packing of their bags.

"Oh, but here is Mr. Pickett," Julia said as he entered the room just in time to see Thomas removing his evening clothes from the wardrobe and laying them out carefully on the bed. "I'm sure he and I can finish up on our own. You may go now, both of you."

"I'll just go and pack my own things, shall I, sir?" Thomas offered eagerly.

Pickett shook his head. "No, thank you, Thomas. Mrs. Pickett and I will be traveling alone." Seeing his valet's crestfallen expression, he added, "Perhaps next time."

"Very good, sir." Thomas turned away, grumbling under his breath, "That's just what you said last time."

That the fellow was right in no way excused this insubordination. "If you are unhappy in your new position,"

18

Pickett said, with a hint of steel in his voice, "I'm sure I could speak to Andrew about trading places with you."

"N-no, sir. I didn't mean—"

"Oh, I think you meant it," Pickett said with a sigh. Thomas had been an invaluable ally on more than one occasion, and Pickett had no desire to lose him. Moreover, he could understand and even sympathize with the longing for adventure felt by a man very nearly his own age. "And I can't say I blame you. But this journey is costly enough already. I can't ask my magistrate to pay for your expenses as well as my own."

"Yes, sir." Thomas conceded the point readily enough, but his speculative gaze shifted to Julia, to whom the added expenditure would present no particular burden.

"No," Pickett put in quickly, "so don't even think it. Mrs. Pickett will be traveling without Betsy, as well."

"Yes, sir," Thomas said again, and returned to the servants' hall, where Pickett had no doubt he and Betsy would have a fine time exchanging grievances as to what a skinflint the new master was.

Still, there was no help for it, so he thrust the matter from his mind and turned his attention to the more immediate task of packing for the journey. He picked up the evening clothes so carefully laid out by Thomas and carried them back to the wardrobe.

"You don't mind, do you?" he asked Julia apologetically. "Traveling without servants, I mean. Besides the extra expense, I'm not sure I can rely on Thomas's discretion. The temptation to boast to the inn's staff that he was accompanying me on Bow Street business might be too great to resist."

"I don't mind," Julia said, watching in bewilderment as he began to stow his evening garments away, "but what are you doing?"

"Surely I won't need these," Pickett protested. "I'm going to investigate a case. Exactly what sort of case I don't know, but I'm fairly certain it won't involve going to a ball. At least, I hope not," he added in some alarm at this new and unwelcome possibility.

Julia took the clothes from his arms and returned them to the bed. "On the contrary, you will be carrying a letter of introduction to an old friend of Mr. Colquhoun. It would be a very odd thing if this friend did not invite you to dine with him. And," some demon of mischief inspired her to add, "if he and his wife should happen to be hosting a ball while we are in the area, you may be sure we will receive an invitation."

Pickett stared at her. "You can't be serious!"

"Well, perhaps not about the ball," she conceded with some regret. "But I am certain about the dinner invitation. For him to do otherwise would be a shocking snub to Mr. Colquhoun, you know."

As a matter of fact, Pickett had *not* known. He had assumed the letter of introduction would allow him to pick the man's brains for any pertinent information he might be able to glean from someone familiar with the area and its inhabitants; he was not at all certain he liked the idea of any social obligations, especially given the fact that he'd recently made a fool of himself in front of his in-laws after being placed in just such a position.

"I have no doubt you will acquit yourself very well, no matter what the circumstances," Julia assured him, pausing with her arms full of primrose muslin long enough to give him a quick kiss.

"If you say so," said Pickett, unconvinced. "In any case, I will console myself with the knowledge that Mr. Colquhoun's friend can't possibly be any more terrifying than your mother."

"And you managed to win her over, at least to some extent, so there you are," Julia pronounced, and turned her attention back to her half-empty portmanteau.

Pickett's own packing did not take long, as his wardrobe was not extensive (although Julia was doing her best to rectify this situation) and fit easily into a single valise. He had filled his bag and was just about to close it when Julia said, "Don't forget this."

He turned and saw her removing the pistol he kept tucked away at the bottom of one of the bureau drawers. "I hadn't forgotten." He took the gun from her and returned it to its resting place. "I'm not bringing it."

"*Not bringing it?* John, you'll want a weapon of some kind!"

He stared at her incredulously. "Sweetheart, why would a man bring a firearm on his honeymoon?"

"This isn't just a honeymoon," she insisted. "This case, whatever it is, might prove to be dangerous."

"If I thought I would be putting you in any danger, I would never have agreed to take you along—nor, for that matter, would Mr. Colquhoun have asked it of me. But if anyone should discover I was armed, it would—well, it would raise awkward questions, to say the least."

"You could keep it out of sight in our room—"

"Rooms can be searched, you know, should anyone become suspicious or merely overcome with curiosity. Besides," he added, seeing she was not convinced, "if it's hidden away in my room, it wouldn't be much use in any case, unless the miscreant should be so obliging as to knock on our door and declare his intentions."

"It isn't funny," she protested, then cast an appraising eye over his person. Alas, the current fashion for long-tailed coats cut short in the front left very little room to hide anything— including, at times, what her husband was thinking. "I don't suppose you could tuck the pistol into the band of your breeches in the back, beneath your coattails?"

"That sounds like an excellent way to shoot myself in the bum," Pickett said in a voice that brooked no argument. "I'm sorry, Julia, but no."

"But you don't know what you may be walking into!"

Seeing the distress in her blue eyes, he drew her into his arms and kissed her lingeringly. When at last he raised his head, a hint of a smile lit his brown eyes. "If I find myself in any danger," he promised, "I'll hide behind you."

Their courtship (if one could call it that) had been conducted with a dead body or two in the vicinity, and against such a background of murder and mayhem, it had been a considerable surprise to Julia to discover that her young Bow Street runner possessed a rather appealingly self-deprecating sense of humor. She was not, therefore, deceived by this craven pledge.

"That might be rather difficult, considering that you're fully a foot taller than I am," she retorted. "Furthermore, I suspect you've never hidden from anyone or anything in your life."

"Only because you never saw me at fourteen with a stolen apple in my pocket and the constable on my heels." He added, in a more serious vein, "Don't think that in marrying me you've got some sort of hero, Julia, with or without a pistol in my hand. Nothing could be further from the truth."

"I don't *think* I've got a hero—I *know* I have! I confess myself curious, though: how would *you* describe a man who, finding himself trapped in a burning theatre with the woman he loved, fashioned a makeshift rope from the curtains and climbed down it while carrying her on his back?"

"That wasn't heroic," he protested. "It was the only way out. Believe me, if there had been a less dramatic exit available, I would have gladly foregone the rope. Besides, a real hero would have contrived to do the thing without getting himself coshed over the head."

Julia, quite naturally, could not agree with this assessment, and there followed a very pleasurable debate as to Pickett's heroic qualities or lack thereof. It was not until the next morning, long after they had left London behind, that she realized he'd got his own way after all.

The pistol was still in the Curzon Street town house, resting in the bottom of the bureau drawer.

2

In Which Mr. and Mrs. John Pickett
Pursue Very Different Quests

T hey arrived at the Hart and Hound in late afternoon of the sixth day, by which time Pickett was convinced he had, as his magistrate predicted, become intimately acquainted with every necessary to be found along the way. Pickett could not hold these frequent stops against her, however, as he was responsible for the condition that compelled them. As for Julia, she smiled so sweetly and so gratefully at the much put-upon post-boys (who had been privately warned in advance by her devoted husband of her interesting condition and exactly how that condition might manifest itself) that they, too, were quite won over, and treated Julia with respectful courtesy and Pickett with transparent envy. Still, passengers and post-boys alike breathed identical sighs of heartfelt relief when the yellow-bodied post-chaise swept down a hill and around a curve into the village of

Banfell and lurched to a stop in the yard of a neat two-storied structure of flat gray stones on its ground floor and whitewashed plaster on the one above.

Pickett did not wait for the post-boys to dismount, but opened the door himself and climbed stiffly from the carriage, stretching his limbs before turning to assist Julia to disembark. Taking stock of his surroundings, he found the Hart and Hound occupied a position of prominence at the heart of the village's commercial center, as evidenced by the shops surrounding it. Aside from the usual livery stable, linen-draper, and greengrocer that might be found in any village—to say nothing of a rival inn directly across the street, rejoicing in the name of the Golden Feather—there were several businesses better suited to London, or at least Penrith: a stationer's shop whose windows also displayed a selection of paints, brushes, and other artists' supplies; a bookstore large enough to rival Hatchards in London; and a china shop whose bow window boasted a number of porcelain plates featuring painted representations of mountains and lakes. The explanation for these rather rarefied establishments was not far to seek, for beyond the inn yard lay a breathtaking backdrop of rounded fells, the nearest of which had given the village its name. Clearly, Banfell was home to a thriving tourist trade.

"Mr. Colquhoun wasn't lying about the scenery," Pickett remarked.

"Indeed, not." Julia, who had grown up among the Mendip Hills of the West Country, appeared equally impressed by these much higher peaks. "Shall we have time to hike, do you think?"

Pickett, who spent much of his workday hoofing it from one part of London to another, could think of few activities that held less appeal. Still, the prospect of exploring these dramatic surroundings at close range held an undeniable attraction. "I suppose that will depend on—on what we find," he said, careful not to mention within hearing of the post-boys the case (if one could call it that) which had brought them northward.

He paid off one of the post-boys while the other untied their bags and hauled them down from the luggage platform at the front of the vehicle. As the post-chaise rattled away, Pickett hefted the bags (his own valise under his arm, and the handgrips of Julia's two larger portmanteaux, as well as the strings of her hatboxes, in his hands), thankful for the five years of hauling coal that had left him stronger than his slender frame suggested.

"You don't have to carry them," Julia protested, seeing what he was about. "We can ask the innkeeper to send someone—"

"Just open the door, will you?" Pickett asked somewhat breathlessly, jerking his head in the direction of the entry.

She hurried ahead to obey, and a moment later they were inside, blinking as their eyes adjusted from the bright sunshine outside to the dimmer light within. Pickett identified the counter directly opposite the door and made his way to it as quickly as his burden would allow. Upon reaching this destination, he dumped the bags at his feet, panting slightly as he addressed the stout, middle-aged man behind the counter.

"I'd like a room for myself and my wife."

Over the course of two decades of running a posting house, the innkeeper had developed a talent for sizing up at a glance the social and economic status of the various travelers who availed themselves of his hospitality. The pair who now stood before him, however, had severely taxed his powers of discernment. The woman was obviously a lady, but he hadn't known quite what to make of the man. A gentleman wouldn't deign to carry his own bag—much less five of them—and yet his demeanor toward the lady, and hers toward him, was too familiar to be that of a servant and his mistress. At Pickett's words, however, mine host's brow cleared. If he was the lady's husband, he must be a gentleman, albeit one of those eccentric specimens of the breed who found it amusing to ape their inferiors. Well, if the fellow wanted to carry his own bags, let him; he wouldn't find it nearly so entertaining if he had to do that sort of thing on a daily basis.

And so the innkeeper greeted him with civility, if not warmth, and pushed the inn's register across the counter with instructions to "sign here."

Pickett, seeing the opportunity to make his first move in identifying the unknown correspondent, promptly picked up the quill and handed it to Julia.

"Would you care to do the honors, sweetheart?" he offered, making no attempt to lower his voice. "You might as well get used to writing your new name: 'Mr. and Mrs. John Pickett, number four Bow Street, London.' "

They had agreed beforehand to list Bow Street's direction rather than their own residence in Curzon Street, and as Julia signed the register, Pickett glanced around the room to gauge the effect of this speech on the room's other occupants.

There was no shortage of these, for the inn also served the village as a pub, as evidenced by the various spigoted kegs and barrels behind the counter, and visitors and locals alike had descended upon it to refresh themselves. At one table, an apple-cheeked damsel serving ale from a pewter tray flirted with a curiously dressed young man with flowing black locks and an unstarched cravat tied in a floppy bow. A young blond giant in homespun, obviously a farmer, sullenly watched the pair from a table on the opposite side of the room. In a shadowy corner, a trio of men lifted foaming mugs to their lips and wiped the excess on sleeves so filthy that their wearers could only have come straight from one of the lead mines which dotted the mountains. Nearer at hand, a pious gentleman in an old-fashioned bag-wig sat with his eyes closed in prayer, one hand resting on the large Bible that lay closed in front of him, as if he were in so rapt a state that he could discern the words through the worn leather binding. A visitor of an artistic bent had claimed the table positioned directly beneath the window, presumably taking advantage of the light it afforded, and now neglected the tankard at his elbow in favor of a sketchbook and charcoal. At the table opposite his, two women of early middle age, dressed for exercise rather than fashion in sturdy twill pelisses and stout leather half-boots, collapsed wearily with much scraping of chairs and called for the pretty young barmaid to "leave that fellow alone, and fetch us some cider!"

If the address of the Bow Street Public Office meant anything to any of them, they gave no sign.

Pickett turned back to the counter, where Julia had finished signing the register and was now laying aside the quill. "If someone could help with these bags—" he began.

He got no further before the innkeeper came around the counter, professing himself all eagerness to take over this task. Clearly, his opinion of his newest guests had undergone a rapid transformation. There were, Pickett decided, certain advantages to having an aristocratic bride, quite aside from the obvious.

"Ever been to the Lake District before?" the innkeeper called back to them as they followed him up the stairs, Pickett carrying his valise and one of Julia's portmanteaux while his host carried Julia's other bag and both of her hatboxes. "No? Beautiful country, but then, I was born and raised here, so I would think so, wouldn't I? Here we are, just down the hall to the left, and then it's the last door on the right. Best room in the house, I always say, because of the view of the fells. Now, if you plan to do any what they call picnicking, my good wife's rheumatism says the fine weather will hold for a bit longer, and I can direct you to a likely spot."

They had reached the room by this time, and the innkeeper deposited the bags on the floor at the foot of the bed. Pickett followed suit, while Julia crossed the room to draw back the curtain and look out the window.

"You can see the path from here," the innkeeper told her, still puffing slightly from his burden. "It leads to a spot overlooking the river. You can see the waterfall upriver, and just a glimpse of the lake in the other direction."

"Oh, John, let's!" exclaimed Julia, raising shining eyes to his. "Tomorrow, perhaps?"

"Better make it the day after," Pickett amended. "I might have to pay a call tomorrow."

The innkeeper addressed himself to Julia. "I'll tell my wife to make up a basket for you, if that's agreeable."

"That would be lovely," Julia assured him warmly. "Thank you."

The man shook his head dismissively. "Never let it be said that Ned Hawkins don't take care of his patrons—unlike some I could name, who think a flute, a fiddle, and a bottle or two of home-brewed are any substitute for well-aired sheets, good English food, and a—"

"Tell me," Pickett said, cutting short an incomprehensible diatribe that threatened to run on for some time, "do you know of a man by the name of Hetherington?"

"Aye, it's an old Cumberland name. You'll find no shortage of Hetheringtons hereabouts. Do you know his Christian name?"

"Robert. Mr. Robert Hetherington."

The man's eyes widened. "Oh aye. It's Mr. Robert Hetherington what lives up at the big house." He jerked his thumb in the general direction of east.

"Is there someone here who can take a letter to him?"

"I'll have my son do it," the innkeeper promised, and it seemed to Pickett that a note of uncertainty had crept into his voice. "When do you need it delivered?"

"Today, if possible." Pickett withdrew the letter from the

pocket of his coat and handed it over.

"I'll tell Jem to take it over at once." He took the letter and headed for the door, then paused at the threshold and turned back to Pickett. "You need anything else, you just ask."

Pickett promised to do so, and fully expected the innkeeper to return to his post downstairs. He lingered so long in the doorway, however, that Pickett began to wonder if he should offer the man payment in coin. He glanced at Julia for some unspoken message that might advise him, but found her regarding her host with a polite smile no less puzzled than Pickett's own.

And then, just as the moment was stretched to the point of becoming awkward, the innkeeper tugged his forelock in Julia's direction and betook himself from the room.

"Well!" exclaimed Julia. "What do you suppose that was all about?"

"I wasn't supposed to pay him, then?" Pickett asked, relieved at having not—again—done the wrong thing.

"I don't think so," Julia said, considering the question. "One can never be quite certain of local customs, but I should have thought any vails would be given to the inn's servants, not the proprietor himself. Unless, of course, he thought you might give him something to pass along to his son for carrying out your errand."

"I suppose it's possible," Pickett said doubtfully. "If he should bring me a reply, I'll be sure to reward him for his trouble. And yet, I wonder if perhaps I should have agreed to that picnic tomorrow, after all."

"You think our host might be the one who wrote the letter

to Bow Street?"

Pickett shrugged. "At this point, I don't have sufficient evidence to form an opinion either way, but it could be that he'd thought to send us out on a picnic as a way of arranging a private meeting, away from the crowd in the public room." He sighed. "If that's the case, I may have missed my best chance."

"So what do we do now?" Julia asked, not without sympathy.

"We wait for someone—if not Ned Hawkins, then someone else—to identify himself. Until then, I suppose we act like we're on our honeymoon."

She looked coyly up at him from beneath her eyelashes. "We shut ourselves up in our room and only come out for meals?"

He grinned appreciatively at her, but shook his head. "Oh, you'll get no argument from me, but Mr. Colquhoun might be displeased, to say the least."

"In that case, may I make a suggestion?"

"Please do."

"You may depend upon it that word is already spreading in the village that a couple from London is putting up at the Hart and Hound—"

"What, already?" asked Pickett, taken aback.

"Being a native Londoner, you don't understand the fascination which outsiders hold for country people," she said. "When one sees the same people day after day, the prospect of seeing new faces—and, perhaps, hearing of goings-on beyond one's own sphere—is well-nigh irresistible."

"All right, I'll concede the point that I'm irresistible," he said with a twinkle in his eye. "So, what is your suggestion?"

"If they want to see us, we should give them an opportunity. I think it's safe to say that if whoever sent to Bow Street has heard of our arrival from London, he—or she—already has an idea that it might be you—"

"Very likely."

"So let's go for a stroll along the High Street before dinner. Then, if anyone wishes to reveal himself to you, at least he'll know what you look like."

Pickett could find nothing to dispute in this plan, and so after unpacking their bags—a task that would have been left to Thomas and Betsy, had they been allowed to make the journey—they set out on a walk up and down the main street through the village, gazing into shop windows and admiring the dramatic backdrop of rugged peaks. Although Pickett was conscious of more than one curious gaze leveled in his direction (and still more directed at his beautiful wife), no one made any attempt to approach him. At last they turned back toward the Hart and Hound and the dinner the innkeeper's wife would have ready for them.

When they reached the inn, they discovered more than roasted chicken and potatoes: Ned Hawkins's son had returned with a reply from Robert Hetherington, informing Pickett that he might call the next morning at eleven o'clock.

* * *

The following day, Julia kissed her husband fondly and closed the door behind him, then began counting under her breath. She could not observe his departure, since the window

33

offered a view of the fells rather than the inn yard, so she waited until she reached one hundred just to be sure he was well and truly gone. Having reached this number, she opened the hinged lid of her portable writing desk and withdrew paper, pen, and ink, then settled herself at the table before the window to craft a letter to Mrs. James Pennington of Greenwillows, Norwood Green, Somersetshire.

The first few lines were dedicated to inquiring after her sister's health and that of her husband and daughter, and giving assurances as to Julia's and John's own health. These niceties having been completed, Julia came to the point of her correspondence:

I am writing to request a Favor, she confessed. *You may not be aware—Women rarely are, I find, even though it concerns Us the Most—that should I die in Childbirth, my widow's Jointure from Fieldhurst would end with my Death. (You are no doubt at this moment mentally composing the Letter you will write me in return, assuring me of the unlikelihood of so Grim an Outcome. Be that as it may, I shall face the coming Event with more Fortitude if my mind is settled on this Point, so pray indulge me by reading to the End before penning your Rebuttal.)*

As I was saying, the Termination of my Jointure would mean John would be left with very little Money on which to support a Child. He would, of course, still have the House on Curzon Street, but without sufficient Funds on which to run it, I fear he would soon be put to the Necessity of selling it; thus, Father and Child would be reduced to whatever hired Lodgings might be had for his Wages.

And here we come to the Favor I must beg. If such an Occurrence should come to pass, please promise me that you and Jamie will give my dear John any such Assistance as he might require—or, more to the purpose, that he might be Persuaded to Accept. I would ask Mama and Papa for such a Pledge, but any Assistance they might offer would come in the Form of removing the Child entirely from John's Care, and this Eventuality must be avoided, whatever the Cost. (Note, if you will, the Ease with which I dispose of Jamie's Inheritance!) I know I can trust you and Jamie to do Right by your precious Niece or Nephew and its beloved Sire.

And if you don't, you may be sure that I shall come back from the Grave and haunt you.

Yr Loving Sister,

Julia Pickett

Post Scriptum: You know, of course, that I am only roasting you about the Haunting, but you must own that it would be no more than you deserve after the shabby trick you played on us all last March.

Having finished this epistle, she fanned the crossed sheet back and forth to dry the ink while she looked about the room for some means of sealing it. The window afforded sufficient sunlight to render the necessity of a candle superfluous, at least until later in the day. If she were to light one in order to melt wax, she could not be at all certain her husband (whose success at Bow Street owed much to his possessing a keen eye for detail) would not notice the burned wick and wonder at it. No, she would fold her letter and put it away to seal it later— perhaps tonight, after he was asleep. He was well accustomed by this time to her getting out of bed during the night to seek recourse to the chamber pot, so he would not wonder at it.

Satisfied with this decision, she tucked the letter into the bottom of her writing desk and settled down to await Pickett's return.

* * *

While his wife engaged in clandestine correspondence, Pickett followed the innkeeper's directions to the "big house," which, true to its name, proved to be a large residence of the same flat gray stone that adorned the ground floor of the inn. Upon presenting his card to the butler who answered his knock, Pickett was shown to a study furnished according to masculine tastes in shades of brown. A pair of nail-studded armchairs upholstered in leather worn to a buttery softness were drawn up before the fire that was necessary even in summer, as the sun's rays (those that could penetrate the heavy brown velvet curtains) would not reach this western side of the house until well past noon.

Left alone to await his host with no other companionship save the ticking of the clock on the mantelpiece, Pickett sank into the chair that faced the wide mahogany desk and surveyed this imposing piece of furniture for whatever clues it might reveal of its owner.

This is a social call, not an investigation, he reminded himself, although if truth be told, he would have been more comfortable conducting an investigation than paying a social call. In any case, he could not fail to notice the large Bible that held pride of place in the center of the desk, its leather cover so worn that it sagged in the middle. Even as the thought occurred to Pickett that he had seen this particular book before, the door to the study swung open. Pickett rose from his chair as a man entered the room, a man of about sixty-five who wore an old-fashioned bag-wig.

"I know you!" Pickett blurted out, taking the man's proffered hand. "That is, I don't exactly *know* you—we've never been introduced—but I saw you yesterday. At the inn." Painfully aware that his manners were hardly a credit to Mr. Colquhoun's patronage, he broke off abruptly, only to recall with some indignation his conversation with the innkeeper only a few minutes later. "I asked Ned Hawkins how I could send you a letter. He might have told me you were in the public room at that very minute!"

"Did he tell you how you could send me a letter?"

"He said he'd send his son with it."

"And so he did, for young Jem brought it to me that very day. Country people can be very literal-minded, Mr. Pickett."

Pickett, aggrieved, could not help feeling that he'd been played for a fool. "Do you mean to tell me that if I'd asked where you were, he would have said you were downstairs?"

"Very likely. If you want the right answers, Mr. Pickett, you must ask the right questions." He gestured for Pickett to be seated, while he himself took the chair behind the desk. "But I'm sorry I didn't hear your questioning of Ned, or I might have saved you a great deal of trouble. Nor do I recall seeing you, for that matter."

"The conversation didn't take place until Mr. Hawkins had shown my wife and me up to our room. As for your seeing me, I believe you were occupied at the time," Pickett said, glancing at the Bible on the desk. "To tell you the truth, I assumed you must be the vicar."

Mr. Hetherington chuckled. "No, no, just a humble country squire. But I do look in at the public room two or three times a week, and often take my Bible with me."

"It seems a rather noisy place to pray."

"By which you mean I should 'go into my closet and shut the door,' as the Good Book says."

"I—I meant no disrespect, sir—"

"You're quite right, of course," Mr. Hetherington assured him, dismissing Pickett's stammered protests with a wave of his hand. "It *is* noisy at times, especially when the stage coach arrives from Penrith. Still, I like to set a good example for the locals, you know. Visitors, too, for that matter."

"Do so many people come here, then?" asked Pickett in some surprise, recalling the shops along the High Street that obviously catered to the tourist trade. "I should have thought it would be too remote for many visitors."

Mr. Hetherington's shoulders shook as he laughed. "And you'd hoped to have a bit of privacy with your young bride, is that it? Patrick Colquhoun tells me you're on your honeymoon." He patted the left breast of his coat, where Mr. Colquhoun's letter of introduction no doubt resided in an inside pocket. "Oh, you'll find it's much quieter here than in London, but I'll not deny we have more visitors since those poet fellows started settling here. Never saw the point in that sort of thing, myself. Poetry, I mean. Seems to me that if a fellow can afford to sit in a cottage all day penning dismal meditations on Death while other men are obliged to clerk, or farm, or go down the mines in order to keep food on the table and a roof over their heads, he hasn't much cause for complaint."

Pickett, whose own reading tastes ran toward newspapers and the occasional novel, was inclined to agree—although the irony did not escape him that this opinion was being voiced by a man who had very likely never labored a day in his life. Then again, if Robert Hetherington was an old friend of Mr. Colquhoun, who had certainly worked his own way up in the world, he might well have earned his fortune rather than inherited it; thus Pickett himself, who had merely married into money, was in no position to cast stones.

"But enough about these scribbling fellows," his host continued. "I understand you're a young friend of Patrick Colquhoun. Tell me, how do you know him?"

Pickett was momentarily at a loss. He wished he'd thought to ask the magistrate exactly what he'd said in his letter. If Mr. Colquhoun had explained Pickett's connection with Bow Street, Mr. Hetherington would surely have made some mention of it—wouldn't he? Unless, of course, he had some reason for doubting the man's discretion, and wished to preserve Pickett's incognito—in which case, he would be wise to refrain from volunteering the information himself.

"He did me a kindness many years ago," Pickett said at last, choosing his words with care. "I had recently—lost—my father, and Mr. Colquhoun was good enough to take an interest in me. He still does, for that matter."

It was vague enough, but it had the advantage of being

true, so far as it went. Thankfully, Mr. Hetherington appeared to accept this explanation, such as it was, at face value.

"Well, any friend of Patrick Colquhoun's is a friend of mine. My wife and I would be delighted to have you and Mrs. Pickett to dinner—shall we say tomorrow night? In the meantime, there are other ways for a young couple to amuse themselves—the beauty of the fells begs to be explored, of course, and Jedidiah Tyson, him that owns the Golden Feather, hosts assemblies on Wednesday nights—you'll have seen it when you arrived, as it's just across the street from the Hart and Hound. The company is not exclusive, mind you— we haven't the luxury of being particular, so remote as we are, and so we'll admit anyone who's willing to pay half a guinea for the price of admission—but it's congenial enough if one cares for an evening of dancing. There's a subscription book you'll want to sign—aye, we're setting ourselves up as a resort for the fashionable set, just like Bath or Tunbridge Wells. Mind you, Ned Hawkins, your host, won't be best pleased to see you crossing the street to the Feather to put your names down in Tyson's book—great rivals they are, the pair of them."

Pickett's heart sank at the prospect of standing against the wall and watching his wife dance. Julia had never uttered a word of reproach, but it seemed cruelly ironic that a lady who loved to dance should fall in love with a man who didn't know how. Still, he accepted the dinner invitation with alacrity, hoping this would compensate her to some degree for the loss of the society she had turned her back on when she'd married him.

"Excellent! We'll expect you at, let us say, eight o'clock. My wife likes to keep Town hours, and the sun sets so late this far north that I can promise you'll be back at the inn well before dark."

Pickett agreed to this plan, and recalling from something his wife had once let fall that morning calls should not exceed fifteen minutes, took his leave. He had found nothing of particular use so far as the case was concerned (unless an invasion of poets might be considered cause for summoning Bow Street) but he hoped he had established cordial relations with a possibly useful source.

So pleased was he with his morning's work that when he returned to the inn (where he was warmly greeted by his wife, who was all too aware of the incriminating letter resting in the bottom of her portable writing desk), he told Julia that, if she was still interested in a picnic, he was more than willing to accompany her.

"Oh, let's!" she exclaimed eagerly. "If you'll go downstairs and ask Mr. Hawkins to have his wife make up a basket for us, I shall change my shoes for something better suited for walking."

Pickett readily consented, then, after a moment's hesitation, confessed, "Mr. Hetherington says the Golden Feather across the street hosts assemblies every Wednesday. If you'd care for dancing, we can sign the subscription book on our way out."

"Poor John! And so you shall be obliged to attend a ball, after all! Unless you don't like to—"

"No, no," he lied gallantly, hoping for something,

anything, to occur that might spare him the ordeal.

He could not have guessed with what irony this hope would very nearly be fulfilled.

3

In Which a Pleasant Outing Takes a Tragic Turn

D escending the stairs to inquire after the promised basket, Pickett found the space behind the counter empty; Ned Hawkins had apparently abandoned his post. Now that Pickett thought of it, he didn't remember seeing the man when he'd returned from calling on Robert Hetherington, either. He glanced about the public room (not so busy now as it had been when he and Julia had arrived the day before), but saw no sign of the innkeeper among the few patrons.

A noise behind him made Pickett turn just in time to see the pretty young barmaid emerge from a back room, eyes flashing and cheeks flushed with some strong emotion.

"Oh, it's you," she said, twisting her apron in her hands. "Can I help you?"

"I was looking for Mr. Hawkins," Pickett said.

"Papa's gone out."

"So I see. May I talk to your mother, then?"

"She's *not* my mother, only a 'step'! And if you want to talk to her, you're welcome to her, for I'm sure *I* have nothing to say to her!" She flounced away with a swirl of skirts, and paused at the door through which she had come. "Well? Are you coming to talk to Stepmama or not?"

Pickett muttered something halfway between a thank-you and an apology, and followed her through the door that led into a kitchen.

"Someone wants to talk to you," the girl curtly informed her stepmother, a woman in her forties who stood before a scarred deal table, stirring something in a large bowl.

Pickett had assumed the girl would beat a hasty retreat, wanting as little to do with her stepmother as possible, but to his considerable surprise, she took up a perch on a nearby stool and, in spite of her avowed reluctance to speak to this maternal surrogate, apparently picked up the threads of the conversation he'd interrupted, announcing, "Percival wants me to be his Muse!"

"I suppose that's one word for it, but I could give you another," said the woman, clearly unimpressed with this plan for her stepdaughter's future. "Now hush, Lizzie, and let the gentleman talk."

Pickett, equally flustered by finding himself in the middle of a mother-daughter quarrel—rather, a stepmother-stepdaughter quarrel, as he was sure Lizzie would have been quick to point out—and hearing himself described (quite erroneously) as a gentleman, stammered, "I only wanted to ask—I wondered if—your husband said you might be willing to—"

"My husband?" she asked sharply. "Is Ned back already, then? Mayhap he can talk some sense into this foolish girl of his, for I'm sure *I* can't!"

"No, I'm afraid not. Er, that is, I haven't seen him today," Pickett amended hastily, not wanting to cast aspersions on Lizzie's intelligence. "But when my wife and I arrived yesterday, your husband suggested you might be willing to make up a basket, should we wish for a picnic."

"Percival took me on a picnic last week," Lizzie said with a reminiscent sigh. "He spread a blanket on the ground, and after we'd eaten, he read me the poem he'd written about me. And then he suggested we lie down on the blanket and rest a bit, but I'm not such a fool as *that!* I told him I had chores to do, and I'd better come back home."

"About this basket—" Pickett put in.

"Aye, you'll come home by Weeping Cross if you're not careful, my girl," the older woman said, wagging the spoon at her stepdaughter.

"I'm *not* your girl—Percival says I'm *his!* His poem called me"—her face assumed a beatific expression, and she recited soulfully—" 'thou shy lady's slipper fit to clothe the naked feet of a goddess, that is to say, thine own.' "

"He called you a shoe?" asked Pickett, momentarily distracted from his purpose.

"It's a flower," she explained contemptuously, as if anyone with the slightest claim to intelligence, to say nothing of artistic sensibility, would have known this. "That's just the way poets talk."

"And how does he know what your naked feet look like,

I'd like to know?" asked her stepmother, eyes narrowed in sudden suspicion.

"If Papa likes Percival, I don't see that *you* have any right to object!"

"Speaking of Mr. Hawkins," Pickett said, trying again, "he told me you might—"

"Your papa likes the money that fellow is paying to stay here while he writes his wretched verse, but as for letting some rhymester give his daughter a slip on the shoulder, well, you'll find he holds a very different opinion there." She cast a fretful glance toward the door. "Can't imagine what's keeping him so long. I wish he'd come back."

"So do I!" Lizzie cried hotly. "Then he'd tell you—but no, you'd rather I married Ben Wilson and—and spent the rest of my days as a—a *farm wife!*"

"And how you think that would be a worse fate than being some poet's fancy-piece, I'm sure I don't know," Mrs. Hawkins retorted. "Ben Wilson farms his own land, and that's nothing to cock a snoot at. You could do a lot worse for yourself."

Pickett, feeling he was rapidly losing control of the conversation (if in fact he'd ever had any control of it at all) decided it was time to remind the women of his presence. "Er, about this basket," he said, "I would be glad to pay you something for your trouble—"

Perhaps it was the mention of money that did the trick. Whatever the reason, Mrs. Hawkins was instantly recalled to her duty. "Oh, I'm sure that won't be necessary," she assured him, although her tone suggested that, were he to insist, she would allow herself to be persuaded to accept. "I've a bit of chicken left from last night's dinner I could give you, or there'll likely be roast mutton after tonight. When was you wanting it?"

"This afternoon, if possible."

"Chicken it is, then, if that's agreeable."

"Quite agreeable," Pickett said and after promising to pick up the basket on their way out, left the women to debate uninterrupted the relative virtues of farmers versus poets.

He reached his own room to discover that Julia had changed her morning gown for a walking dress topped with a spencer of gold lutestring, and traded her soft kid shoes for a pair of sturdy jean half-boots.

"Very nice," Pickett said, eyeing his well-dressed bride appreciatively. "Have I seen this before?"

"No, for it came from the dressmaker only a few days before we left London," Julia said, then added contritely, "I should not have ordered it, of course, but I didn't yet know about the baby, and by the time I found out, it was too late to cancel the order." She tied the ribbons of a matching bonnet over her golden tresses, and Pickett no longer wondered at the number of bags she had deemed necessary for the journey.

Still, he could not argue with the results. They left the room and locked the door behind them, then descended the stairs to the kitchen, where they found Mrs. Hawkins waiting for them with the promised basket and a woolen blanket which she insisted they take with them.

"For Mrs. Pickett won't want her pretty dress spoiled by grass stains," she explained, leading Pickett to wonder exactly what the woman thought they would be doing on this picnic. Given Lizzie's recollections of her picnic with her poet, he could hazard a reasonably accurate guess. He didn't bother to disabuse her of this notion, but tucked the blanket under one arm and hefted the basket with the other, and they left the inn.

"Oh!" Julia exclaimed when Pickett would have circled the building in search of the path Ned Hawkins had indicated. "We were going to sign the subscription book at the Golden Feather!"

"How could I forget?" Pickett wondered with a marked lack of enthusiasm.

They crossed the road and entered the rival establishment. Unlike the Hart and Hound, which boasted a broad yard in front where carriages might disgorge their passengers and take up new ones (and did, as Pickett had already discovered, at all hours of the day, making him doubly thankful for a room at the rear of the building), the Golden Feather sat flush against the road, with no more than a three-foot pavement between its front door and the High Street.

Still, it soon became apparent that this inn offered amenities which Ned Hawkins would be hard-pressed to duplicate. Its entry was wainscoted in rich linenfold paneling that an eye more knowledgeable than Pickett's would have readily identified as oak, and cornices of egg-and-dart molding traced the perimeter of its plastered ceiling. Directly opposite the front door, access to the upper floors was provided by means of a curved staircase whose elaborately carved banister was polished to a sheen and scented faintly of beeswax. Pickett felt a pang of regret that his instructions had specified the Hart and Hound; it seemed to him that its competitor was more deserving of his lady wife's patronage. Then again, his anonymous correspondent might have assumed that the Golden Feather would have been above a Bow Street Runner's touch; a scant three months earlier, it would certainly have been above his own.

All these observations passed through his brain in less time than it took Julia to step up to the counter and ask for the proprietor. The man at the counter, a fellow as gaunt as their own host was stout, identified himself as Mr. Jedidiah Tyson, and subjected the Picketts to just such an appraising look as the one they had endured from Ned Hawkins upon their arrival at the Hart and Hound.

"Ah! Welcome to the Golden Feather," he said in an ingratiating tone, having apparently arrived at the same conclusion as had their own host. "What may I do for you? You'll require a room, yes?"

"No, thank you," Julia said. "We're staying at the Hart and Hound across the street. But we were told that you host assemblies here every Wednesday, and we should like to sign the subscription book, if we may."

"Of course, of course!" In anticipation of filling one of his establishment's rooms, Mr. Jedidiah Tyson had already been withdrawing the inn's registry from beneath the counter. If he was at all disappointed by the realization that he was mistaken in this assumption, he didn't show it; he merely shoved the registry back into place and left his position behind the counter, waving a hand toward the grand staircase. "If you will follow me?"

This they did, and soon found themselves in a room on the floor directly above, a large room boasting a raised dais at one end, yet devoid of furnishings save for a lectern positioned just inside the door and a dozen or so straight chairs ranged along the walls. Pickett viewed them with the lowering conviction that, should the letter prove to be of sufficient importance to require his continued presence in Banfell, it would be his fate to occupy one of these chairs for the better part of every Wednesday evening until they returned to London. Mr. Tyson reached behind the lectern to extract a second registry from the shelf built into it.

"We also host the occasional improving lecture or poetry reading, but these are not as popular as the assemblies," Tyson said, apparently feeling some explanation was called for as to the presence a lectern in a room set aside for dancing. He flipped through page after page of signatures until he found the one he sought, the first one with blank lines. "Ah, here we are! Tickets for this week's assembly are half a guinea each."

Pickett, seeing his duty clear, set the basket down and fumbled in his pocket for the necessary coin while Julia wrote "Mr. and Mrs. John Pickett" on the line Mr. Tyson indicated—an operation which the ambitious innkeeper observed with delight, rubbing his hands together in glee at the prospect of stealing well-born patrons (one well-born patron, anyway) from his rival across the street, if only for one evening.

"The dancing commences promptly at eight, and ends on the stroke of midnight," Tyson informed them, then cast a sidelong look at Pickett. "Of course, if it should happen that

50

the gentleman partakes a bit too freely from cellars that are held to be excellent—though I say it as shouldn't—I always keep a few guest rooms vacant for just such an eventuality."

"You have to hand it to him, really," Pickett told Julia after they had left the Golden Feather and set out along the path Ned Hawkins had pointed out from their window the previous day. "The Hart and Hound gets its custom from the mail coaches and the stage from Penrith, so Tyson has found a way to attract patrons to his own place, right under Mr. Hawkins's nose. Still, I don't think I'll drink whatever happens to be on offer from his cellars, no matter how 'excellent' they're held to be."

"Oh?" Julia asked. "You're not thinking of Lady Washbourn's peach ratafia, are you?"

"No," he said, shuddering a little at the memory of his last case and the toll it had very nearly taken on his marriage. "But our friend Tyson was a bit too quick to mention those conveniently reserved rooms. While I have no reason to suspect him of wanting to poison the Hart and Hound's patrons, I wouldn't put it past him to slip something into the drinks that would incapacitate them just long enough to oblige them to spend the night."

"Very well then, we shall delay the satisfaction of any need for liquid refreshment until we return to the Hart and Hound," Julia conceded. "Speaking of which, I don't think we should mention the poetry readings to Lizzie's poet, do you?"

"No, but a word in Ned Hawkins's ear might not go amiss. He might want to mention them to the fellow himself."

Julia nodded sagely. "Judging the loss of the poet's

custom a small price to pay for the preservation of his daughter's virtue. Yes, I see your point."

The village of Banfell was situated in a long, narrow valley, with Ban Lake at its southern end and the River Ban marking its eastern boundary. The footpath they now followed curved around a stand of trees and out of sight of the inn, eventually giving out onto where the valley ended abruptly at the top of a cliff overlooking the river. The rushing of the water could be heard far below, and an arched footbridge of gray stone had been erected across the ravine, giving access to the steeply rising ground on the other side and a rougher path that led upward to, presumably, the summit of the fell that gave both river and village their names. Nearer at hand, less hardy souls could continue along the path to the left, which continued along the cliff's edge, following the twists and turns of the river, or take a narrower track to the right, which rose as it approached the waterfall.

"Shall we stop here?" Pickett suggested, unwilling to subject Julia to further ramblings until they could learn a bit more about the difficulties this might entail. He recalled the two middle-aged ladies with their stout half-boots, and thought they might prove a useful source for this information.

"Yes, this is a lovely spot for a picnic," Julia agreed. "We can see the falls from here without having to shout at each other to be heard over them."

Pickett set the basket down so they could spread the blanket beneath a tree nearby. Once this task was accomplished, he placed the basket on the middle of the blanket, whereupon Julia dropped to her knees and began

unpacking bread, cheese, the promised cold chicken, and—
last, but by no means least—a bottle of wine and two glasses.
It fell to Pickett to open this last offering with the corkscrew
Mrs. Hawkins had thoughtfully provided, and he stepped
away from their picnic cloth to perform this task, not wanting
to risk getting it wet. This proved to be a wise decision, for
the cork had no desire to relinquish its post, and when it finally
yielded to a superior force, the contents of the bottle spewed
out, soaking the sleeve of Pickett's coat to the elbow and
sending Julia into whoops of laughter.

"Oh, so you think it's funny, do you?" he retorted, his
indignation belied by his own rather sheepish grin.

"Yes," was her unapologetic reply. "If you could have
seen your face—!"

"You won't be laughing when word gets out at the inn
that your husband is a sot," he predicted, trying without much
success to wring the liquid from his coat sleeve.

"At least you may be sure of finding accommodation at
the Golden Feather," Julia observed playfully. "And it might
help to preserve your incognito, for no one would suspect you
were with Bow Street. At least, I shouldn't *think* there were
too many Bow Street Runners with a penchant for
drunkenness."

"No, we leave that sort of thing for the Charleys in the
watchmen's boxes."

"I am relieved to hear it. When we return to the inn, we'll
ask Mrs. Hawkins to see what she can do to clean your coat,
but in the meantime, you can always take it off and spread it
out to dry. There's no one here to see you in your

shirtsleeves."

This much was certainly true, for their surroundings were as isolated as any pair of lovers might wish. Pickett shrugged off his coat and laid it out on the grass, then sat down in his shirtsleeves to dine. After they had finished all of the food and made serious inroads into the wine (or as much of it as had escaped the deluge), Julia produced a sketch pad and pencils, while Pickett rolled up his damp coat to cushion his head and, pulling his hat down over his eyes, stretched out on the blanket to enjoy the unaccustomed luxury of an afternoon nap. They spent the better part of an hour in companionable silence, with no sound to break the quiet save for the gurgling of the river below and, nearer at hand, the scratch of charcoal against paper.

"Julia," Pickett said thoughtfully, shattering the stillness, "what are we going to tell it?"

"Tell who?" she asked, although she already knew. When they had married in defiance of every tenet of the world in which they both lived, they had told themselves that, since she could not conceive, no innocent child would suffer for their decision. The discovery of her pregnancy, welcome though it was, had disabused them of this notion. And while Julia might count the world well lost for love on her own account, she wanted her child to be raised in such a way that it could perhaps eventually re-enter the society she had chosen to leave behind. Thus her furtive request of her sister and brother-in-law.

"The baby," Pickett said. "Someday it's going to notice the difference between its parents—and if it doesn't, you can be sure some other child will point it out. Children can be cruel to each other, you know." A shadow crossed his face, and she wondered again what his life had been like before Mr. Colquhoun had intervened. "So, what will we tell it?"

"We shall tell it"—she paused long enough to pluck the hat from over his face and lean down to kiss him—"that its parents loved each other enough to give up everything in order to be together. I assure you, many an aristocratic child would envy such a heritage, no matter what he might say to the contrary."

" 'He'?" echoed Pickett. "You sound very sure it will be a boy."

"Not at all. But I assume a boy will be sent to school—where he might very well run up against the sort of cruelty you fear—while a girl may be sheltered, at least to some extent, by being privately educated at home. Still, I should actually pity a girl more."

"Because she'll have no dowry," Pickett observed.

"No," she said, torn between exasperation and amusement. "Because she'll never be able to find a man who will live up to her own Papa."

Pickett regarded her with mingled hope and fear. "You don't think it will despise me, then?"

"Good heavens, no! It will grow up hearing all about how Papa saved Mama from the gallows. I daresay that will become the bedtime story of choice, and will become so embellished over the years that eventually you will scarcely recognize yourself."

"Hmm," said Pickett, pondering this vision of his

paternal self with surprised satisfaction.

"Now, if that has been worrying you, pray set your mind at ease and go back to sleep," Julia said, plunking the hat back over his face. "I want to finish sketching the waterfall before it is cast into the shadow of the fell."

It was not long before the steady rhythm of his breathing told Julia that he had followed this advice, and she had almost finished her drawing when she realized they were no longer alone. Two men had appeared far ahead on the rough path leading to the waterfall, their figures mere black silhouettes against the sun behind them. Julia watched them for some time, weighing whether or not to include them in her sketch. Would the presence of human figures detract from the beauty of the scenery, she wondered, or would their addition actually improve the drawing by giving some sense of the height of the falls and the grandeur of the fells behind it? She decided in favor of the latter, and was about to put pencil to paper once more when there was an abrupt movement toward the cliff's edge, and suddenly only one figure remained.

It all happened so quickly, Julia would have thought she'd only imagined it, had she not just spent several minutes weighing the effect of the two figures on her drawing. But no, there had certainly been two where now there was one—one dark silhouette that was even now stepping away from the sheer drop.

"John!" Although she was much too far away for that anonymous form to hear her, she whispered as she shook Pickett by the shoulder. "John, wake up!"

"Huh—what—?" Although groggy from sleep, he

nevertheless recognized the urgency in her voice and pushed his hat off his eyes. "What's wrong?"

"John, I think I've just seen a murder!"

4

In Which John Pickett Examines a Body
and Julia Makes a Sacrifice

A ll traces of sleep vanished. Without raising his head from his makeshift pillow, Pickett turned in the direction she was staring. Some hundred yards ahead, the dark silhouette of a man bent and picked up what appeared at this distance to be a long stick, then stood upright, braced it against his shoulder, and—

"*Get down!*" Pickett grabbed Julia by the wrist and yanked her down. She fell across his chest with sufficient force to knock the breath from his body, and in the same instant a shower of splinters exploded from the tree behind them.

"John—was that—did he—?"

"Yes—no, stay down," Pickett said, still gasping for breath. The man had not waited to see if his ball had found its mark, but hurried up the path toward the waterfall, presumably in the direction whence he and his companion had come.

"He—he pushed the other man off the cliff," Julia said, trembling with delayed reaction. "There were two of them, and I was trying to decide whether to include them in my drawing, and suddenly he was standing on the edge and the other one was—gone. It happened so fast—it was almost as if there had never been another man at all, as if I'd imagined the whole thing."

"That shot wasn't imaginary," Pickett said, glancing up at the trunk of the tree, whose bark showed a pale, jagged scar that hadn't been there before.

"So what do we do now?" Julia asked.

"I suppose I'd better find a way down to the river," Pickett said. No one stood on the path near the waterfall now, so he eased himself out from underneath her and cautiously stood up. Confirming that they were alone—at least for the nonce—he took her hand and pulled her to her feet, then picked up his coat and shook it out. One sleeve was still wet and smelled rather strongly of wine, but he shrugged it on nevertheless. "First, though, I'd better get that ball out of the tree to hold as evidence. I don't want him—whoever he is—to come back and tamper with the scene."

Julia cast a nervous glance up the path. "Do you think he will? Come back, I mean?"

"I don't know, but I'm taking no chances." Using the tip of the corkscrew, he prized the spent ball out of the tree trunk—an operation that seemed to take an unconscionably long time, exposed as they were to any murderer who might choose to return to the scene of the crime.

"I don't understand," she said unsteadily. "If he had a gun, why did he push the other man off the cliff? Why didn't he just shoot him?"

Pickett looked up from his task long enough to chide her gently. "Think, Julia. If a body is found with a ball in its chest obviously fired from point-blank range, it's a clear case of murder. But I expect when we find the body at the foot of the cliff, there will be no injuries that couldn't be the result of an accidental fall—and those, I'll wager, are frequent enough in these parts that no one would think to question it."

"And yet he shot at me," she pointed out with some asperity.

"Only after he realized he'd been seen."

She raised a shaking hand to her forehead. "Of course. I should have known—I'm afraid I'm not thinking very clearly."

"And who can wonder at it? I am a bit puzzled by the gun, though. It isn't yet hunting season, is it?"

She shook her head. "Hunting doesn't begin until the twelfth of August, so two months yet."

"Could they have been poachers, then? Or perhaps the man with the gun was poaching, and when the other fellow objected, he was killed for his pains?"

Julia cast her mind back. "It would seem to make sense, and yet—and yet they looked so—so *companionable*, the two of them! There was no trace of animosity in their bearing, and certainly no sign of a quarrel—at least none that I could tell from a distance."

At last the tree trunk surrendered its captive. Pickett dropped the slightly misshapen ball of lead into the inside pocket of his coat and stepped back to inspect his handiwork. His operation had done nothing to improve the scar of pale splintered wood marring the bark of the tree, but there was no help for it; he would just have to trust no one would notice or, if they noticed, would not wonder at it. For now, though, there was a body somewhere at the bottom of the cliff that required his attention.

"I'm afraid you're going to have to come with me, sweetheart," he told Julia apologetically. "I don't dare leave you alone here; for all we know, he might be lurking around the bend, waiting for a chance to come back and make sure any witnesses have been eliminated."

She shuddered at the prospect. "Believe me, I have no desire to be left behind!"

"Yes, but it may be rough going," Pickett cautioned. "It's a long way down, and the path is bound to be steep."

"You forget that I am country-bred," Julia said, pale but resolute. "I'll keep up, I promise."

She proved to be as good as her word. The only path down the face of the cliff was every bit as rough and steep as Pickett had feared, being more suited to the walkers and trout fishermen who no doubt constituted the majority of its traffic than it was to an aristocratic lady in a delicate condition. Julia's West Country childhood stood her in good stead, however, and with Pickett to help her over the worst patches or hold back the gorse that snatched at her skirts, they both made it safely to the foot of the cliff, where the water rushed past on its way to the lake farther downriver.

"It is beautiful, isn't it," Julia remarked, when they paused for a moment's rest. "What sort of person looks at such scenery and sees only a means to commit murder?"

"Perhaps when we find the body we'll have a better idea of that," Pickett said. As if concurring with this suggestion, a trout suddenly leaped from the water, a flash of spotted brown scales that vanished as suddenly as it had appeared. Recalling that his magistrate was an enthusiastic angler, he remarked, "Mr. Colquhoun will wish he were here."

Julia grimaced, her thoughts clearly dwelling on the act of violence she had witnessed. "I would be happy to yield my place to him."

"I thank you, sweetheart, but no! Much as I respect him, I have no desire to go on a honeymoon with Mr. Colquhoun."

She gave a shaky laugh, and Pickett took her hand and drew it through his arm, glad to have distracted her, if only for a moment.

Alas, greater difficulties lay ahead. The path had taken them some way downriver from their picnic spot, and the place where Julia had seen the two men was farther still, which meant they would have to follow the river upstream for some distance before reaching the body. But the bank was very narrow, so narrow that in places the water lapped against the side of the cliff itself.

"Stay here," Pickett said, stripping off his boots. "I'll be back as soon as I can."

"John, you will be careful, won't you?"

"I promise." He stepped barefooted into the water and

gasped. "Brrr! That's cold!"

"I'll warm you up when we get back to the inn," she said, and although she smiled bravely, there was little of the flirtatiousness that would ordinarily have accompanied such a promise.

"I'll hold you to that," Pickett replied, and began making his way against the current.

He had no idea how long he waded—fifteen minutes? Twenty?—but at last he came upon a rounded shape of brown and gray, half in the water and half on the narrow riverbank. Pickett might have mistaken it for a boulder, had it not been for the skirts of the old-fashioned frock coat that swayed in the current—and the broad shoulders that rose and fell in quick, shallow breaths. Somehow, miraculously, the man was still alive. For how long, however, was anyone's guess. Heedless of the splashing he made, Pickett increased his pace and soon stepped up on the bank beside the man. From this vantage point, he could see a leg stuck out at an unnatural angle.

"It's all right," Pickett said soothingly, realizing even as he said the words just how absurd they were. It was anything but "all right"; even if it were possible to get a stretcher down to the man, the chances of his surviving the trek back up to the top of the cliff without either succumbing to his injuries or being tipped out by his bearers was somewhere between slim and none. Still, Pickett knew better than to point out this probable outcome to a dying man.

"It's all right," he said again. "You're not alone."

"What—who's there?" The voice was the merest wisp of

sound, but the man seemed to be fully conscious.

"John Pickett. I'm visiting from London. I'd like to move your head a bit farther from the water, if I may. Will it hurt you if I turn you over?"

"Don't—don't think so. I can't—can't feel my legs."

This was a very bad sign, Pickett knew, but one glance at the twisted limbs told him it might actually be for the best. The man would very likely die in any case; at least he would be spared the agony of pain that must otherwise have been excruciating. The fellow no doubt outweighed Pickett by a good five stone, but he eased the man onto his back as gently as he could, being careful to keep his head clear of the water. When he saw the bruised face, he suffered a shock.

"Mr. Hawkins?" he said. "Ned Hawkins?"

The innkeeper acknowledged him with the briefest flicker of his eyelids. "John Pickett of Bow Street."

"Yes, sir." Was he just repeating the information Pickett had given as he and Julia had signed the inn's register, or did he mean something else entirely? One look at Ned Hawkins's ashen face told Pickett he had not long to find out. "Was it you who sent for me?" he asked urgently.

"Let her—" He broke off and took a rattling breath.

"Did you send to Bow Street for a Runner?" Pickett reiterated.

"Let her—" The words trailed off to a whisper.

"Let who what?" asked Pickett, his voice rising on a voice of desperation.

"No—in my—in my pocket—let her—let her—" The voice faded away, and the pale blue eyes grew unfocused. Ned

Hawkins was gone.

Let her, he'd said. *Let her.* But who was she, and what must she be allowed to do? Whoever and whatever, it had been important enough to Ned Hawkins that he'd spent his last breaths trying to communicate it. *Her*, then, must refer to Mrs. Hawkins, but that would presume she was doing, or intended to do, something which Pickett had the power to prohibit. Or perhaps he meant his daughter, and was giving his blessing to Lizzie and her poet—although what influence he imagined Pickett might exercise in such a case left the latter mystified. Hawkins had also referred to his pocket, however, and in a way that suggested this might shed some light on the puzzle.

It seemed somehow wrong to rifle a dead man's pockets while the body was still warm, but the dead man in question had given him permission, in a way. Besides, once the death was reported, he was unlikely to have another chance. *Nothing ventured, nothing gained*, thought Pickett, and reached inside the man's coat. His nimble pickpocket's fingers located the breast pocket and slipped inside. Paper crackled beneath his fingertips, and he withdrew a folded sheet sealed with red wax into which was pressed a crest bearing the image of a curiously shaped harp. He turned it over and found that it bore the name (slightly smudged) of one James Sullivan, along with an address in Dublin.

Not "let her," then, but "letter." It still didn't explain much. Was Hawkins asking him to make sure that the letter was delivered, or urging him to intercept it? He glanced down at the dead man, but there was no answer in the glazed eyes.

A quick search of the other pockets yielded nothing but a few copper coins and one silver shilling, none of which interested Pickett in the slightest. Meanwhile, Julia was waiting for him, and Pickett wasn't at all certain that, if he were to linger too long, she wouldn't come in search of him. Resisting the urge to close those staring eyes—it would not do to let anyone know that someone else had seen, let alone tampered with, the body—he tucked the letter into his own inside breast pocket, and stepped back into the cold water. Turning back toward the dead man, he made a cup of his hands and scooped water up onto the bank to eradicate any footprints he might have left behind. Finally, satisfied that he'd left no trace of his visit behind—no trace, that is, except for the absence of the letter— he waded back down the river to find Julia.

"Well?" she asked urgently. "Did you find him?"

"Yes," he said tersely. "It was Ned Hawkins, our host."

"Oh," she said faintly. "Was he—was he dead?"

He shook his head. "Not at first. He is now."

"Oh," she said again. "I can't help thinking it would have been better if he had died immediately. One hates to think of him lying there suffering, knowing it unlikely that anyone will come along to help—" She broke off, shuddering.

"It wasn't like that at all," Pickett said quickly, not wanting her to dwell on imaginary horrors. "I believe he must have sustained some spinal injury. He said he could not feel his legs, and so he did not suffer as much pain as he otherwise would have done. As for his being alone, I was with him at the end. Not that I could do much, but he seemed to have a dying wish, which I will try my best to fulfill."

"A dying wish? What was that?"

He sighed. "I only wish I knew." As he pulled his stockings on over wet feet, he recounted the innkeeper's cryptic utterings about a letter, including his own misunderstanding of the word and the sealed correspondence now residing in his own pocket. He almost wished he'd allowed her to accompany him in spite of her condition; she might have noticed something or recognized some significance to the words that he had missed.

"I wonder what it says. It must be important, for him to speak of it with his last breath." Something in Pickett's face must have given him away, for she spoke accusingly. "John! You don't intend to read someone else's mail!"

"I have to," he pointed out. "How else am I to know what he wanted done with it?"

"I see," she said thoughtfully, regarding him with narrowed eyes. "You think it was Mr. Hawkins who sent to Bow Street."

"I think it very likely. He couldn't see me at first—he was lying with his back to me—but it wasn't until after I identified myself that he began talking about the letter. In any case, I intend to try and find out. In the meantime, we'd better get back up to our interrupted picnic."

"Hadn't we ought to notify the coroner first? Or at least go back to the inn and tell Mrs. Hawkins?"

"We can't," he said with a sigh. "I know it sounds cruel to leave him there, but I can't call undue attention to myself, not until I discover who sent for me and why. I'm working in the dark here, Julia. Someone here knows who I am and why they've summoned me, but I don't know who they are, or what I'm supposed to be doing for them. Whatever it is, it was apparently sensitive enough—or dangerous enough—that it couldn't be put down in writing. Nor, for that matter, would Hawkins run the risk of putting his name to it—if it was Hawkins who wrote the letter, which is by no means certain. It's an uncomfortable position, to say the least."

"But Hawkins is dead now," she pointed out. "Whatever is going on, and whoever is behind it, they can't hurt him anymore."

"No, but they can hurt me," he said bluntly. "Worse yet, they can hurt me the most by hurting you. That's why I can't let anyone know I've been down to the river and seen the body."

"And so poor Mrs. Hawkins will be left to wait and worry, and wonder why her husband hasn't come back home."

"I'm afraid so. It seems harsh, I know, but by keeping mum now, I might be able to discover who did this and why. Could you describe him at all—the man who pushed Hawkins, I mean? I'm afraid I didn't get a very good look—it was all over by the time I woke up, and the fellow was already making his escape."

"No—I didn't even recognize Hawkins, and I'd been watching the pair of them for some time, trying to decide whether or not to include them in my drawing. But I was seeing them only in silhouette, you know, for the sun was behind them."

"You couldn't say whether he was short or tall, thin or fat?"

"I should say Mr. Hawkins and his attacker were much of a size, but that is only an impression. It stands to reason, doesn't it, that a frail man could not have pushed Mr. Hawkins hard enough to send him over the edge? After all, he is— was—somewhat stout himself."

Pickett made no reply beyond a noncommittal noise, and Julia, focused on putting one foot in front of the other as they climbed the steep path, failed to notice anything unusual in this. Eventually they reached the gentler slope at the top of the path, and returned to the inn. Still, Julia thought nothing of his uncharacteristic silence beyond assuming that he must be pondering the unexpectedly tragic twist their outing had taken. Upon entering the public room, Julia was relieved when they entered the room to find no sign of Mrs. Hawkins behind the counter; resigned as she was to yield to her husband's wishes in the matter of informing the widow, she was glad she didn't have to look the woman in the face while withholding the information.

Upstairs, she removed her bonnet and spencer while Pickett, still apparently chilled from his wade in the river, kindled a fire in the grate. Once the flame had taken hold, he stood up, dusted off his hands, and turned to face her, and suddenly the direction of his thoughts became clear.

"Julia," he said with the air of one coming to an unpleasant but necessary decision, "I think you had best go back to London."

"Go back without you?" she asked, dismayed. "But why?"

He stared at her in stunned disbelief. "Sweetheart, a man

has been murdered."

"I've helped you on murder cases before," she pointed out reasonably.

"Yes, but on those occasions, you weren't a witness to the murder. This time you saw it happen, and the murderer obviously saw you, else he wouldn't have shot at you."

"But it doesn't necessarily follow that he knows who I am. After all, I couldn't identify him; how do we know he could identify me?"

"You couldn't recognize him because the sun was behind him; it wasn't behind you."

Julia could not dispute this home truth, but neither was she ready to give in. "We're supposed to be on our honeymoon," she reminded him. "How are you going to explain your staying behind while I return to London?"

She had the satisfaction of seeing him pace the floor for a few minutes while he pondered the question. Alas, her satisfaction was short-lived.

"We'll have to quarrel," he said at last. "Tonight, in the public room downstairs, where there will be plenty of witnesses. That way you can leave on the mail coach first thing tomorrow."

"But I don't want to quarrel with you," she said bleakly. "Not even just for show."

He stopped pacing and took her in his arms. "I don't want to quarrel with you, either," he said, knowing she was thinking, as he was, about their one and only quarrel, which had not been "just for show" at all, and which had resulted in the longest—and very nearly the last—thirty-six hours of his life. "But I don't want you to be shot, either. God, Julia, if anything were to happen to you—" He broke off, bending his head to bury his face in the curve of her neck.

"And does it never occur to you that I feel the same way about you?" she asked, stroking his hair. "That I should be utterly miserable, sitting all alone in the Curzon Street house not knowing if you were at that very moment on a London-bound coach coming back home to me, or lying dead in a ditch somewhere?"

"All right," he said resolutely as they drew apart. "You can stay, on one condition."

"Anything!" she declared fervently.

"You're not going to like it," he cautioned her.

"Try me."

He took a deep breath. "Turn around."

She turned her back to him, and he went to work on the laces at the back of her gown.

"John, this is hardly the time—"

"I'm going to burn it."

"You're going to *what?*" If anyone had asked him, Pickett would have sworn it would be impossible for anyone to exude offended dignity while clad in nothing but their undergarments. He would have been wrong. Julia, standing in only her shift and stays with her gown lying in a puddle of fabric at her feet, fairly quivered with outrage. Her bare shoulders appeared creamy in the afternoon sunlight, inviting his touch, but a finely tuned instinct for self-preservation warned Pickett that he would make advances at his peril.

"I have to, sweetheart," he said in a conciliatory tone that moved her not at all. "He's seen you in it—whoever he is—and if he sees you wearing it again, he'll know beyond any doubt who was the only witness to his crime. I won't risk it."

"I don't see you offering to burn *your* clothes!"

"No, for I was lying down, so if he saw me at all, he couldn't have got a very good look at me. And even if he had, well, I'd taken off my coat, and one man's shirt looks very much like another's, especially from a distance."

"I won't wear this dress again until we return to London," she promised. "I'll hide it in the bottom of my portmanteau."

"And if someone searches the room? What then?"

"But—but I *like* this dress!"

"You won't even be able to wear it in a couple of months," he pointed out with unassailable logic.

"All the more reason for wearing it now, while I have the chance! John, it's new," she said coaxingly. "It only just came from the dressmaker."

"I know, sweetheart, and I'm sorry. When we get back to London, you can have another one made."

"What's the use?" she asked bitterly. "By the time it was ready, I wouldn't be able to wear it—as you so generously reminded me."

"All right, then," he said, grasping at straws, "how about this? Whatever reward I get for this case is yours, to do with as you please, no matter the amount."

She regarded him speculatively. It wasn't a matter of money; her widow's jointure from her first husband was sufficient for her to replace the gown, and purchase one or two others as well. But she knew it galled him, the fact that he could not support her as her first husband had done; in truth, that had been the crux of their first, bitter quarrel. If he was willing to surrender what independence he had, without even knowing the sum that independence might amount to, then he was more worried for her safety than she'd realized. That being the case, she could not spurn such a gesture. Nor, for that matter, could she let him know that she realized the offer was worth far more than money. "You promise?" she asked, pretending to think only of pounds, shillings, and pence.

"I promise."

She said not a word, but looked down at the pool of cloth at her feet and slowly, deliberately, stepped out of it. Pickett grabbed it and bundled up both it and its matching spencer before she could change her mind. The fabric blackened and disintegrated as soon as the flames touched it.

"What about your bonnet?" He glanced about the room and found it lying on the foot of the bed. "Did you take it off at any point while I was asleep?"

"No."

He snatched it up by its plaited straw crown. "Thank God for that, anyway."

"Why? What do you mean?"

"Only that no one seeing you with the sun in your hair would ever forget it," he said, and added her bonnet to the blaze.

He'd spoken the words with no trace of flattery, and, ironically, they moved her as no amount of effusive praise would have done. "John Pickett!" she chided him. "Keep saying things like that, and soon you'll have me *begging* you to burn my clothes!"

Her voice held a mixture of annoyance and affection, and he had hopes of being forgiven—not at this moment, perhaps, but eventually. Emboldened, he cupped his hands over her bare shoulders. "I am sorry," he said.

"I know you are," she retorted, but kissed him nonetheless.

5

In Which John Pickett Joins a Search
and Makes a Surprising Discovery

T he letter, when it was opened and read, proved to be a disappointment.

My dear James, (it said)

I trust this Letter finds You and your Family Well. I have been Much Troubled of late by an Attack of Catarrh, which has left me with a Sorely Abused Nose and a Lingering Cough, but I trust my Sufferings will soon be a Thing of the Past, the Good Lord be Willing. Thankfully, none of the Children have contracted their Father's Illness, and I am confident their Good Health will continue long enough for them to Enjoy their Sire's 55th Birthday Festivities on Thursday Next. I am only Sorry that George, my Eldest, may not Join us, as his new Position requires that he Remain in Edinburgh, at least for the Nonce. It is difficult to Believe he will soon be celebrating his own 34th

Natal Day. My poor first Wife, Elizabeth (God rest her soul), would certainly be Proud of the Man he has Become.

As for the Rest of the Family, Penelope is to have her Come-Out next Spring, if she does not drive us all to Distraction long before then. Nor is my Good Lady much Better, as she can only Expound upon the Need for hiring a Suitable House in Mayfair, to say nothing of the Mantua-Makers, Florists, and various Others whose Talents must be Enlisted, doubtless at Exorbitant Cost, in order to see our Girl suitably Launched. I have always fancied myself a Warm Fellow, but I may be Bankrupt by the time the thing is Finally Done. I only hope she may attach an Eligible Parti in her First Season; I fear I have neither the Finances nor the Patience to give her a Second.

My good Wife informs me that you cannot yet know of the Blessed Event that took place on the Sixth of June. Lest she accuse me of being an Unnatural Father, I must tell you forthwith that my elder Daughter Lavinia was safely brought to Bed of a Son, to be named Evelyn after his Mother's proud Papa. My Wife predicts that I shall become so Puffed Up in my own Conceit that there will be No Living with me. As I should Hate to disappoint her Faith in me by Neglecting to carry out my Role, however Humble, in her newly discovered Talent for Prophecy, I shall do my Poor Best not to Fail her in this Regard.

And now, having Bored you to Distraction with my Familial Boasting, I have a Confession to Make. It concerns (as you might Expect, having previously made his Acquaintance) my Youngest Son, Edward. Edward is presently at Eton, but it may, I fear, be Wrong to Assume that he is receiving an Education there. Although I am presently paying 50 pounds per Annum, never mind an additional 22 for Incidentals, it would be an Exaggeration to call the hapless lad a Scholar. I suspect he spends more time on Juvenile Pranks than on Greek or Latin. But then I am reminded of the Larks you and I once Kicked Up, and I cannot be too Hard on him. He is a Good Lad at heart, and I Suspect there is nothing Wrong with him that Time will not Mend. Until then, I have Only to Resist his determined Efforts to send his Longsuffering Papa to an Early Grave. In the meantime, I Remain, as Ever,

Yr very Obedient Servant,

E. G. B.

Pickett was not quite certain what he'd expected, but he had certainly hoped for more than this.

"If he is only now turning fifty-five and already has a thirty-four-year-old son, he must have married his first wife—Elizabeth, was it?—very young." Julia had crossed the room to where Pickett sat at the table beneath the window, and read the letter over his shoulder. Following the destruction of her dress, she'd slipped a pink satin wrapper over her shift and stays, although she made no noticeable effort to prevent this garment from gaping open as she leaned forward. Pickett suspected she was deliberately tormenting him, and did her the justice to own that he probably deserved it.

His own thoughts—his thoughts concerning the letter, anyway—were running along very different lines. If the writer's complaints about the expense of launching a young lady into Society were anything to judge by, it appeared any daughter of his and Julia's was destined to remain unlaunched. In the meantime, he had less than twenty years to come up with a suitable dowry and a respectable lineage. The dowry was just within the realm of possibility; the lineage was likely to be a bit more problematic. Thankfully, it might yet prove to be unnecessary: If the daughter in question looked anything like her mother, suitors would very likely beat a path to her door, her questionable antecedents notwithstanding.

And on the subject of antecedents . . .

"E. G. B.," he said, reading aloud from the signature. "The 'E' must stand for 'Evelyn,' since he says his grandson is named after him, but what about the other initials? Do you know of any such family with a surname beginning with B? Husband Evelyn, wife Elizabeth—but no, that was his first wife, wasn't it?—a son named George and a married daughter named Lavinia? No mention of her married name, more's the pity, or any clue as to who the second wife might be."

"No, and I daresay I would not be familiar with the younger children in any case, as Penelope isn't yet out and Edward is away at school. Poor Edward! He does seem to get rather short shrift, does he not? But what is his father 'confessing,' do you think? I don't see any confession beyond an admission of Edward's shortcomings compared with the accomplishments of his siblings."

"Perhaps that's it," Pickett suggested. "He's confessing to have fathered a child with the temerity to be less than perfect."

"Poor Edward!" Julia said again, filled with righteous

indignation on the unknown Edward's behalf. "I feel quite sorry for him. I'm sure his brother George must be the greatest prig imaginable, while Penelope obviously cares for nothing but fashion and flirtation."

"Oh, obviously," agreed Pickett, entering into the spirit of the thing. "But what of the other sister—Lavinia?"

"Lavinia is the worst of all," Julia replied promptly. "Ever since her marriage, she has become quite puffed up with her own consequence. Now that she's had a baby, there will be no bearing her."

"I'm going to remind you of those words in, oh, about six months," Pickett promised. In a very different tone, he added, "This is all very amusing, but it isn't getting us anywhere, is it? I'll admit, when I realized Hawkins was talking about a letter, I'd hoped it might offer some clue—something, *anything* to go on."

"It hardly seems worth wasting one's dying breath on," Julia agreed.

"No. And yet . . ." He stared pensively at the correspondence in his hand, noting the liberal use of capital letters.

"John!" Julia's eyes grew round as the same thought occurred to her. "Could it be in code, do you suppose?"

"That's what I'm wondering. Can you spare me a sheet of paper from that writing desk of yours?"

She went to the desk in question, returning a moment later with a single sheet of paper, a quill pen, an ink pot, and a slightly guilty expression which under other circumstances would have instantly aroused his suspicions. Having, firstly, no reason to suspect any clandestine behavior on her part and, secondly, a brain firmly focused on what he believed to be a promising lead, he had no thought to spare for his wife's guilty secrets, but instead spent the next few minutes transcribing every capital letter used by the unknown E.G.B., while Julia watched over his shoulder.

She was struck by the realization that he had rather beautiful hands which must have been a great advantage to him in his earlier profession, with long, slender fingers. Still, there was something unusual about the way he wrote, something that took her a moment to identify.

"You write with your left hand," she said with the air of one making a discovery.

"You've seen me write before," he reminded her, a bit defensive concerning this clear evidence of his lack of formal education. "Taking notes on the morning after Lord Fieldhurst's murder."

"Did I? Yes, I suppose I must have," she conceded. "I never noticed. I daresay I was more concerned at the time with avoiding the gallows. But I'm surprised your schoolmaster didn't make you switch to your right hand."

"Oh, he tried," Pickett said, glancing up at her. "He told me there were those who claimed that left-handedness was the mark of the devil's spawn. He wasn't telling me anything about my father that I didn't already know, so I saw no reason to change, and I wasn't in school long enough at any given time for him to force the issue."

"I am becoming more and more curious about this father of yours," Julia said, making a mental note to visit the stationer across the street and purchase half a dozen quills from the cheaper and less desirable (for most writers, anyway) right side of the goose for her husband's exclusive use, as these would curve over the back of his left hand so as not to block his view of his own writing. "I hope I have the opportunity to meet him someday."

"That makes one of us," Pickett said without enthusiasm.

Having reached the end of the letter, he laid the quill aside and looked down at the paper on the table before him:

MJILYFWIMTACSANLCISTPGLWTCFIIGHESBFT
NISGEJPRENIBNDMWEGPMBARFPCOSDNGLBENSH
MMMFOTEECGLIWFIBFDIEPFSIIFPSMWBESJLUFIDLB
SEMPMWIPUCNLAIHFNRHTPIPBFRABDFBICMIEAYS
EEEWAEAIAIENSIPGLBLIKUIHHGLISWTMUIORELPE
GIIREYOSEGB

Pickett slumped back in his chair. "Well, that's informative," he said in a voice that communicated quite the opposite.

Julia tilted her head as if studying the string of letters from a different angle might shed some light on the puzzle. "Perhaps the words are scrambled."

"In that case, the possibilities are practically endless. I can already see 'My cat eats friendly mice' and 'Scant figs grow west of Hampshire,' and that's just off the top of my head. You could sit here for hours and find a hundred different messages. If someone were sending a coded letter, it stands to reason that he would want to make sure it couldn't be misinterpreted."

"No, I daresay one wouldn't want to inadvertently set off a run on figs," Julia acknowledged with a sigh. "I suppose it must be exactly what it appears: a chatty letter which, for whatever reason, Ned Hawkins wanted to be sure reached its destination—Mr. Sullivan, did you say?"

"Mr. James Sullivan of Dublin," said Pickett, consulting the opposite side of the letter, the side which, when folded, would have been to the outside. "Mountjoy Square, to be exact."

"Will you go to the receiving office, then?"

He gazed thoughtfully at the paper in his hand. "No," he said at last. "That is, I suppose I'll have to go to the receiving office and post a letter to Mr. Colquhoun back at Bow Street, letting him know what's happened and asking for more time to investigate. But I'm afraid Mr. James Sullivan of Dublin won't be getting this, at least not yet. I'm not quite ready to give up on the code theory."

Half an hour was enough to change his mind. He tossed the letter down on the desk and leaned back in his chair with a heavy sigh, raking his fingers through his recently cropped brown curls.

"If it's any sort of hidden message, it's beyond my ability to decipher. I've looked at every other letter—reading backward as well as forward—every third letter, every fourth letter—need I go on? There are other, more complicated codes, but they require a key, which I haven't got."

"What sort of key?"

"It depends on the code. Usually it's based on a book, or some such—" He broke off abruptly, seeing again the worn Bible on Robert Hetherington's desk.

"You've thought of something," she said.

"No, not really." He shrugged dismissively. "I just remembered that Bible of Mr. Hetherington's."

"You don't suppose it was he who sent to Bow Street, and not Ned Hawkins after all?"

He shook his head. "I think it very unlikely. If he needed a Runner, he need not have written to Bow Street at all. He could have sent a letter directly to Mr. Colquhoun and asked as a favor to an old friend. Then, too, he surely would have mentioned it this morning, when I called on him. No one else was present, so there was nothing to prevent his confiding in me. In any case, he'll have another opportunity in a few days. We've been invited to dine with him and his wife." He hesitated over a question of protocol. "I don't suppose that will have to be canceled once Hawkins's body is discovered?"

"I shouldn't think so," Julia said thoughtfully. "It's not as if Mr. Hawkins were a relation, or even moved in the same social circles. And speaking of dinner," she added, "are you ready to go down? I'm hungry."

He smiled at that. "You're always hungry."

It was true. Now that the nausea of the first few weeks had passed, her appetite had returned with a vengeance, apparently determined to make up for lost time. She was not yet noticeably pregnant, but her trim waist was not quite so well-defined as it had been. As they changed for dinner, Julia studied with disfavor her uncorseted reflection in the mirror.

"I don't look like I'm in the family way; I just look like I'm growing fat," she complained. "What do you think?"

Pickett subjected her to a long, appraising look. "You want the truth?"

"Please," she said, bracing herself for the worst.

He drew a deep breath, and slowly let it out. "Sometimes I look at you, and I can hardly believe you're mine."

Julia turned quite pink with pleasure. "You mean it?"

"Shall I prove it to you?" he offered, taking her into his arms and drawing her close.

"Yes, please. But"—she splayed her hands against his chest—"not until after dinner."

They came down to dinner (roast mutton, as promised) to find Mrs. Hawkins alternately furious with her husband for his defection and frantic with thoughts of what might have happened to him.

"He's never been gone this long before," she grumbled, setting plates of mutton and potatoes before them. "Can't think what's got into him, but when he gets home, I'll be giving him a piece of my mind!"

Julia, who knew better than anyone that the innkeeper's wife had cause for concern, looked pityingly up at her. Across the table, Pickett frowned warningly at her, to no avail.

"Is it possible that he went down to the river and—and fell in?" she suggested.

Pickett gave her a pained look.

"I've been thinking the same thing myself." Mrs. Hawkins propped her empty tray on one ample hip, apparently prepared to expound upon this theory. "I'm wondering if we should organize a search."

"It'll soon be nightfall, and there's not much of a moon," protested a man at the next table who had the look of a solicitor, or perhaps a bank clerk, on holiday. "Too dangerous to attempt that cliff path in the dark."

"Give him 'til morning," recommended another man, this one most likely a farmer. "If he still hasn't made it home, we'll go out at dawn looking for him, every able-bodied man among us."

A chorus of wagging heads confirmed this pronouncement, Pickett's among them. Julia's eyebrows rose, but she did not address the issue until after dinner, when they were alone in their room.

"You'll go out with the search party?" she asked, reaching behind her back to untie the tapes of her stays.

Pickett moved behind her to assist in a task at which he had grown quite accomplished over the past three months. "It's the least I can do—especially since you might say it was my wife who raised the suggestion."

"And now you're angry with me," she observed contritely.

He sighed. "I'm not angry with you. I could wish you hadn't mentioned the river, though."

She removed her loosened stays, and turned to face him. "I know, and that's why I suggested that he'd gone down to the water on his own, rather than falling or being pushed. But I can't let the poor woman wonder and worry for days on end. I know what it's like, waiting for one's husband to come home, not knowing if he's dead or alive—"

Her voice broke, and he took her in his arms. Not for the first time, he wondered exactly what she knew, or had guessed, about just how far he had fallen during those two days they had been estranged.

"I know, sweetheart, and I'll never put you through that again, at least not if I can help it," he promised. "But it's important that no one suspect you actually saw the murder, or that I've seen the body. I don't want to put ideas into the heads of anyone who might happen to be listening."

"All you have to do is act sufficiently shocked when you come across him in the morning."

Pickett shook his head. "I don't plan to be anywhere near when the body is found. I intend to attach myself to a group going in the opposite direction. But that's for tomorrow morning. Tonight, there's something else I want to do."

"Oh?" Julia asked, smiling coyly at him.

"I want to have a look at the inn register, and see if any of the signatures in it match the handwriting in either of the letters—the one to Bow Street, or the one in Hawkins's pocket."

"Oh," said Julia, in quite another tone.

"Sweetheart, it has to be done tonight. Once the body is found tomorrow, the public room downstairs will be filled with people come for the wake, and I won't have another chance. Still, I dare not make the attempt until the inn is quiet and everyone has settled down for the night. In the meantime," he added, regarding her speculatively, "have you any suggestions as to how I might pass the time until then?"

"Hmm." She made thoughtful noises, but came willingly into his arms. "Let me think . . ."

* * *

Some time later, Pickett donned his shirt and breeches (eschewing any footwear lest the soles of his shoes make too much noise on the stairs), then secreted the two letters up the cuff of his shirtsleeve and picked up the brass candlestick beside the bed.

"Shall I come with you?" purred Julia, pleasantly sleepy.

"Thank you, but no. You'll be more useful as my excuse."

"Oh? In what way?"

"If Mrs. Hawkins or Lizzie should happen to catch me, I'll tell them I came down to fetch you a drink of water."

"Just so long as you won't expect me to drink it." Julia grimaced. "I have to get up in the night often enough as it is."

Pickett assured her no drinking would be necessary, then kissed her and adjured her not to wait up for him. A moment later, he closed the door softly on his drowsy wife and made his way quietly down the stairs with candle in hand. Having reached the ground floor without mishap, he set his candle on the counter, positioning it so that its feeble flame cast a yellow circle of light onto the page of the open register. His own name was the last on the list, written in Julia's flowing script—he'd learned to recognize her handwriting even before they married, having kept and treasured every note she'd ever written to him, no matter how brief or businesslike the message it contained—so apparently no new guests had arrived since yesterday.

Pickett, however, was less interested in the inn's guests than he was in its proprietor. He looked at the carefully printed headings over each column: Name, Place of Residence, Date of Arrival, Date of Departure, all written in the painstaking hand of the semi-literate. He unfolded the short Bow Street missive and laid it on the counter alongside the inn register. He might have wished for a rather longer sample for comparison, but as far as he could tell, the two looked identical. It appeared, then, that Mr. Hawkins was the one who had sent the anonymous request to Bow Street. Which meant Pickett was on his own in finding out why, for he would get no further information from that source.

Nor, for that matter, would he be reimbursed for his expenses, to say nothing of being paid any kind of reward if he should succeed in resolving the case, whatever it proved to be. He remembered he'd promised Julia that reward, and only hoped she wouldn't feel betrayed when it never materialized.

Having identified the author of one letter, Pickett spread out the other, the one the innkeeper had carried in his pocket. He didn't really expect to find a match—surely someone staying at an inn in the Lake District would be more inclined to describe the beauty of the fells than an attack of catarrh—but as he'd told Julia, he was unlikely to have another chance.

He turned back page after page, all the way back to the beginning of January (strange to think that the Drury Lane Theatre fire and the aftermath that had changed his life so drastically had not even been dreamt of at that time), but there was no match for the bold scrawl addressed to Mr. James Sullivan of Dublin. Nor was there any guest with the initials E.G.B., although hope had flared briefly when he'd come across the name of one Edward Gape, who had arrived a fortnight earlier from Norfolk. But there was no name to correspond with the "B.," so Pickett was forced to concede that there was probably no connection between this guest and

Mr. James Sullivan's correspondent.

Having learned all he could from the hotel register, Pickett tucked the letters back into the cuff of his sleeve, picked up the candlestick, and climbed the stairs, determined to get what sleep he could before dawn and the grim business of searching for the body he could envision in his mind's eye, lying at the bottom of the cliff in the dark with the black water of the river rushing past.

* * *

More than twenty men assembled in the public room of the inn at dawn the next morning, their faces gleaming in the yellow pools of lamplight as they prepared to carry out the somber task of searching for the man who had, his wife tearfully informed them, never come home. Pickett was not the only one of the inn's guests to take part in the search; Lizzie Hawkins's poet was there, as was the artist Pickett had noticed in the public room on the day he and Julia had first arrived from London. Among the locals were Hawkins's son, Jem (the same one who had delivered Pickett's message to Mr. Hetherington on that first day); Jedidiah Tyson, owner of the rival inn across the street; and the young farmer who was the poet's chief rival for Lizzie's affections.

By unspoken agreement, Mr. Hetherington was placed in charge of the proceedings. "We'll let the younger men navigate the path down to the river, while we older fellows keep to easier ground. Ben," he said, turning to Lizzie's rustic admirer, "you, Mr. Pickett, and Mr. Hartsong take the river path as far as the falls."

Somehow Pickett was not surprised to discover that "Mr.

Hartsong" was none other than Lizzie's poet. As for himself, it was not the assignment Pickett could have wished—in fact, he would have preferred to have been sent to search almost anywhere else in the village or its environs—but to raise any objection could only attract the sort of attention he most wanted to avoid.

"The vicar and I will hike up to the fell," continued Mr. Hetherington, "while Mr. Tyson and Mr. Armstrong follow the main road that leads out of town. If you should happen to meet any wagons coming in, Tyson, be sure and ask the drivers if they've seen anything."

Tyson agreed to this plan with a curt nod, but his eyes gleamed with excitement, and Pickett found himself wondering if the man was thinking of the search they were about to undertake, or of what the absence of his rival might mean for his own establishment.

Soon every man present had been paired off with another and assigned an area to search. Pickett's was the only group of three; he suspected his primary task would be to keep the other two from trying to shove one another off the cliff.

By the time all the arrangements were in place, the sky had lightened enough that most of the men chose to leave their lanterns behind. Ben Wilson proved to be the exception.

"Sun won't reach the foot of the cliff for some time," he noted, glancing toward the east where the rising sun just peeked over the horizon. "Best take a light."

Lizzie's poet agreed rather grudgingly, as if reluctant to concede his rival even this small point. Was his name really Hartsong? Pickett wondered. It seemed too absurd—and too apt, given the man's occupation—to be real, and Pickett could not recall seeing the name recorded in the inn's registry.

Mr. Hetherington looked about the solemn little group. "Are we ready, then? Let's go." He turned to clasp the woman's hand in both of his own. "Never fear, Mrs. Hawkins. We'll bring your man home."

Dead or alive. He hadn't said the words, but they hung in the air, unspoken but understood all the same.

The search party shuffled out of the inn and split into groups. Pickett and his two companions rounded the corner of the inn and set off down the same path he'd traversed with Julia less than twenty-four hours earlier. Alas, it soon became apparent that he would derive very little pleasure from the trek, even quite apart from the grisly discovery awaiting them at the bottom of the cliff, as the poet lost no opportunity to score an easy point or two on his rival. However dreadful his poetry might be, Percival Hartsong had a clear advantage in any verbal exchange with his inarticulate foe, and he fully intended to make the most of it.

"I'm surprised to see you here, Wilkins—"

"Wilson," the young farmer corrected him.

"Yes, of course." The poet waved one white hand, clearly considering the name of a farmer—or perhaps only the name of this particular farmer—a matter of no importance. "But as I say, I'm surprised to see you here. I thought you would have cows to milk or sheep to shear, or some other such occupation."

"Shearing was two months ago," Ben Wilson said, declining to take the bait.

"But the cows!" protested Percival with exaggerated concern. "I have always thought there is no sound more plaintive than the lowing of a cow."

"Mayhap you'll want to go milk 'em yourself, then, while I help search for Lizzie's da."

"Faugh! Depend upon it, we'll find the fellow in bed with some doxy—a fitting subject for a comic ballad, perhaps, but—"

He got no further, for Ben Wilson dropped his lantern and seized his rival by the knot of his flowing cravat, twisting it until the poet's face turned red. "Get a little respect in your voice when you speak of Lizzie's father, or I'll give you a taste of the home-brewed!"

As he showed every intention of making good on this threat, Pickett judged it time to intervene. "Stop it, both of you! If either one of you cares for Miss Hawkins at all, you'll not want to have to tell her you wasted all your time in squabbling with each other when you should have been searching."

Perhaps Pickett's marriage had given him some measure of confidence which he had been lacking before, or perhaps it was simply due to the fact that he found himself in the unusual position of being some two or three years older than either of his companions; whatever the reason, Ben rather shamefacedly released his hold on the poet's cravat, and Percival muttered something that might have been an apology. Still, he positioned himself between the two young men as they began their descent along the cliff's edge, lest the temptation to eliminate his rival should prove more than either one could resist.

They reached the foot of the cliff without mishap, having moved at a brisker pace, even in semidarkness, than Pickett had done with Julia. Percival looked first one way and then the other, then voiced the pertinent question. "Which way do we go now?"

Since it appeared he was destined to find the body whether he wished it or not, Pickett would have preferred to do the thing quickly, while there was sufficient darkness to cover him in case he should betray by some careless gesture or expression that he had seen the body before. Still, he willed himself not to propose they go upriver, where he knew it lay. Great was his relief when Ben put forward the same suggestion.

"There." The young farmer pointed in the direction of the waterfall. "Pool at the bottom of the falls offers the best fishing. If it's fish he was after, he'll have gone that way."

Percival shot him a resentful glance, and for a moment Pickett feared he would counter this recommendation by insisting they go downriver, leaving Pickett himself to cast the deciding vote. But apparently the poet could think of no compelling opposition, for he gave a grunt which Pickett supposed indicated agreement, and stepped into the water, boots and all; whatever his speculations as to Lizzie's bare feet, he apparently had no intention of exposing his own. Pickett wondered whether the poet actually earned enough from his verse that he could afford to be cavalier with his footwear, or if he had a generous patron. Of Ben Wilson, he had no such doubts: the young farmer scrambled out of his sturdy brogues, just as Pickett had done with his own boots the previous day. As for Pickett himself, he followed the same procedure, leaving his boots beside Ben's shoes on the narrow strip of riverbank.

Soon the three young men were sloshing their way against the current. They had not gone far before Percival was bemoaning the fact that the cold water poured in over the tops of his boots, drenching his stockings and freezing (as he claimed) his feet. Pickett, all too conscious of his own cold feet—and the fact that at so early an hour they should by rights have been entwined with Julia's amongst warm bed linen— had no sympathy to spare for him.

When at last they came upon the body, Pickett did not have to feign surprise. He distinctly remembered turning the innkeeper onto his back and making sure his head was clear of the water, but Ned Hawkins now lay face down at the river's edge, his graying hair drifting in the current like some exotic species of aquatic plant. Although his clothing was disarranged, there were no marks on the body that might indicate disturbance by a wild animal. And since Mr. Hawkins had clearly been incapable of moving himself when Pickett had last seen him, his change in position could only mean one thing.

Someone else had searched the body.

6

In Which John Pickett Testifies at an Inquest

T he trek back up the path was much slower than their descent had been. Pickett and Ben carried the innkeeper's body between them, while Percival held the lantern aloft to light their way. The only sound to be heard over the rushing of the water was the labored breathing of the bearers and occasional snatches of the poet's newest tragic ode, "The Hair That Floateth Outward on the Stream," which he saw fit to try out on a captive (if inattentive) audience.

It was not until they approached the inn that he emerged from the grip of his muse long enough to consider the practical matter at hand. "I say! Who's going to tell the widow?"

Ben Wilson set his jaw. "I will. Known her all my life."

Pickett was not sorry to be relieved of this task. At some point he would have to talk to Mrs. Hawkins and discover what she knew of her husband's summons to Bow Street—if she was aware of it at all—but for now he was only a guest at the inn, a visitor enjoying the beauty of the Lake District with his bride.

His bride, who was no doubt watching from the window as they approached the inn with their burden—and who would certainly expect a full accounting upon his return.

Nor was Julia the only one watching. As they rounded the corner of the inn and approached the front door, it flew open and Mrs. Hawkins ran toward them, skirts flapping.

"Ned, Ned!" she shrieked. "Speak to me!"

"Alas, those lips will never speak again," pronounced Percival, then counted the syllables of this sentence on his fingers, pleased to discover that he had spoken in perfect iambic pentameter without even trying.

"If you'll show us the way, ma'am, we'll lay him on his bed," the farmer told the widow gently, then turned to address the poet in quite a different tone. "Make yourself useful, Hartsong, and give her your arm."

To his credit, Percival rose to the occasion, offering the innkeeper's widow his escort with all the solemnity the occasion demanded. The odd little processional entered the inn and passed through the public room to the family's rooms in the rear, where Pickett and Ben were at last able to lay their burden down. By unspoken agreement, they did what they could to straighten the crooked limbs while blocking Mrs. Hawkins's view of the body, preventing her from seeing the full extent of her husband's injuries.

"Thank you for bringing him home," Mrs. Hawkins said, dignified in her grief. "I know it wasn't easy, fetching him up from the river."

Pickett didn't have to ask how she had known they'd come from the river; her husband's drenched hair and clothes, to say nothing of his own and Ben's sodden sleeves and breeches, told their own tale.

"I'm sorry," Ben said simply. "Sorry we couldn't have brought him back to you alive."

She nodded. "Thank you, Ben. You were always a good lad."

Percival glanced around the room. "Where's Lizzie?"

"She's still abed. I'll have to wake her now and tell her that her da is—gone—but I'd rather do it in private, if you lot don't mind."

The poet appeared inclined to linger—hoping for the opportunity to console Lizzie, no doubt—but he could hardly remain when Pickett and Ben were already moving toward the door, especially when they had been specifically asked to go, so he shuffled off in their wake. Pickett, for his part, was more than ready to return to his wife.

"At last!" she exclaimed when he opened the door and entered their room. "I've been waiting forever!"

"Don't touch me," he cautioned, holding out a hand to forestall the embrace she appeared to have every intention of bestowing upon him. "I'm soaking wet, and I've been lugging a dead body."

"Yes, I know. I watched from the window." She watched as he picked up the poker and stirred the banked fire to life. "I thought you were going to avoid searching along the river."

"I was. But Mr. Hetherington took charge of the search— I suppose he considered it his duty as squire—and he had other ideas." Having finished tending the fire, he shifted his gaze to the bowl and pitcher on the washstand. "Is that still warm?"

"Tepid, perhaps." She poured some of the water into the bowl and stuck a finger in to confirm this theory. "I got out of bed not long after you left, so it's been sitting for some time. Shall I ring for hot water?"

He shook his head. "They have more important things to do downstairs. I can make shift with a tepid bath."

Suiting the word to the deed, he shrugged off his coat and waistcoat, then pulled his shirt over his head. While Julia observed this operation appreciatively, she nevertheless directed the subject back to the matter at hand. "Why did he send you down the cliff path? Did he say?"

"He said something about assigning the younger men to the rougher terrain. As it turned out, it was a good thing he did."

"Oh?"

He paused in his ablutions and looked at her. "The body had been moved, Julia. Someone else had been there. If I hadn't been there at the discovery to see the body in situ, so to speak, I never would have known."

"Are you certain? It might have been a—an animal, you know." Her voice trembled slightly over the words, and Pickett knew she was thinking of her sister, who had gone missing a dozen years earlier and was assumed to have fallen prey to a wild animal, until she was discovered quite recently, alive and well and living with the man who had rescued her from a cruel and violent husband.

"The thought occurred to me, too, but it didn't look that way." He gave her a highly expurgated description of the innkeeper as he'd first discovered him, and as he had seen the body that morning.

"Was someone searching for the letter, do you suppose?" she asked at the end of this recitation.

"I think it very likely. Unfortunately, I couldn't look as closely as I would have liked, since Lizzie's rival suitors were there. Although," he added, "now that I think of it, they might not have paid any attention to me at all. I only wonder that neither of them seized the opportunity to shove the other off the cliff."

"Perhaps the letter doesn't have anything to do with it," said Julia, much struck. "Perhaps one of Lizzie's suitors killed her father. If Ned Hawkins made it plain that he favored one of them over the other for his daughter's hand—"

"If marriage to Lizzie was the motive, then I'm thinking Percival would be our man. I can't imagine many men would be pleased with the idea of their daughter rejecting a yeoman farmer with his own land in favor of a poet, even one of good family. Of course, that's assuming it's marriage Percival has in mind, which I don't for one moment believe. A pastoral mistress might be all very well, but when it comes time to take a wife, Percival will want a lady of his own class, and one with a dowry that will enable him to write that high-minded drivel of his without his being obliged to trouble himself with such mundane matters as earning his bread."

"And yet he cannot be entirely without resources," Julia pointed out. "After all, he can afford a prolonged sojourn in the Lake District."

"Funded by his father, no doubt. But I suspect Hartsong Senior would clip the purse-strings quickly enough if Percival were to return home with an innkeeper's daughter on his arm." He grimaced. "I haven't forgotten to what lengths your first husband's family was prepared to go, in order to prevent you from making just such a misalliance."

"There you have it, then! If it was seduction, rather than marriage, that Percival had in mind, then he would have all the more reason to want Ned Hawkins out of the way. It would certainly be to his advantage not to have his paramour's irate papa at hand to protect his daughter's virtue," Julia deduced, then frowned thoughtfully. "No, that can't be right. Mr. Hawkins must have outweighed him by six stone or more— far too much for Percival to have thrown him off balance."

"Oh, it can be done," Pickett assured her. "You just have to catch your man unawares and hit him low. Take his legs out from under him, you know."

She stared at him. "Do I even want to ask how you know this?"

He gave a sheepish little laugh. "Let's just say I've had to make my share of hasty exits."

"Well, don't think you can escape from me so easily," she said, wrapping her arms about his bare torso.

This time he made no effort to avoid her embrace. "Not even if I take your legs out from under you?"

"Especially not if you take my legs out from under me," she replied, and the bleak activities of the dawn were temporarily forgotten.

* * *

The coroner's inquest, a requirement in the case of any death not resulting from illness or old age, was held the following afternoon in the inn's public room. It seemed to Pickett as if the entire village had turned out, and Julia agreed that this was very likely the case.

"They all must have known him, and besides, rural villages offer so little in the way of social occasions that no one will want to pass up such an opportunity. I know it sounds rather cold-blooded," she added apologetically, no doubt thinking of the rural village where she had grown up, and where they had both been obliged to testify at just such a proceeding, "but there it is."

"I suppose there will be even less entertainment now," Pickett remarked.

"Oh? How so?"

"The assemblies at the Golden Feather," he reminded her. "I shouldn't think Mr. Tyson would have the cheek to host a dance while his rival lies dead right across the street."

"Very likely not," she agreed. "And there lies the solution to the mystery," she added, lowering her voice to a conspiratorial whisper.

"Where?" Pickett asked, baffled.

"You killed Ned Hawkins yourself, so you wouldn't be obliged to escort me to an assembly."

"My guilty secret is discovered at last," he murmured into her ear, sending her into a fit of giggles which she quickly turned, not very convincingly, into a cough. "Although I hope you will tell me how I managed to do the deed while lying sound asleep on a blanket in full view of my accuser. It seems a useful talent to cultivate."

"Then, too, I wonder at your killing our host and obliging Mr. Tyson to cancel one assembly, or perhaps two, when you might have killed Mr. Tyson and put an end to them altogether."

"Speaking of Mr. Tyson," Pickett said thoughtfully, "there's another one who probably won't shed any tears to have Hawkins gone. I might have to send you across to the Golden Feather to do a bit of investigating."

"Do you mean it?" Julia asked, surprised and gratified to be entrusted with such a task. "Are you certain you wouldn't prefer to do it yourself?"

He shook his head. "I'm afraid appearing crestfallen at the cancellation of the assembly is beyond my acting ability."

The coroner entered the room at that moment, rendering further conversation impossible. In Pickett's experience, coroners were a mixed lot: sometimes physicians experienced in medical matters but ignorant of the law; sometimes solicitors who relished the opportunity to ape their superiors in the judicial hierarchy, the white-wigged barristers who presided over cases before the Old Bailey or the rural assizes. The coroner who presided over the inquiry into the death of Ned Hawkins was a solicitor, and seemed to be one of the more capable members of the species, for which Pickett was thankful; as one of the three purported discoverers of the body, he would be obliged to testify. This in itself was not unusual, for he had testified at numerous inquests in the past, and would no doubt testify at many more in the future. But never before had he been obliged to deliberately withhold information, and so fearful was he that he might inadvertently describe some detail from his first, private viewing of the innkeeper's remains that he had rehearsed his testimony the night before, with Julia serving as coroner—a procedure he had not performed since his earliest days at Bow Street. Not, of course, that Julia had participated in these sessions (he had not yet known of her existence, much less that she would one day be his wife), but he still had memories of himself as a terrified nineteen-year-old member of the Foot Patrol, pacing the floor of his small Drury Lane flat while he recited the pertinent facts of the case and framed answers to any question which his magistrate had told him the coroner might be likely to ask. As he recalled, this exercise had lasted so late into the night that his landlady, who lived in the back of the chandler's shop below, had finally pounded on the ceiling of her own bedchamber with a broom handle and demanded that he be quiet and go to bed so that a body could get some rest.

The coroner pronounced the inquest in session, and after hearing Mrs. Hawkins's account of how her husband had not been seen since about noon two days previously, and how a search party had been sent out only the day before, sent the widow back to her seat and summoned the first witness.

"Will Mr. Edward Gape please take the stand?"

The name was not unfamiliar; Pickett recognized it from his midnight search of the inn's register. Great was his surprise, however, when Percival Hartsong rose and made his mincing way to the front of the room, where he took the chair his hostess had just vacated.

"Your name is Edward Gape?" the coroner asked somewhat skeptically, giving voice to Pickett's question as well as his own.

"It is," the poet admitted tersely.

"And yet you have been calling yourself Percival Hartsong."

"I write poetry," the young man said, bristling. "Whoever heard of a poet named Gape?"

The coroner apparently found nothing to dispute in this rhetorical question. "You are visiting from Norfolk?" Receiving a nod in the affirmative, he continued, "And what do you do there?"

"As I said, I write poetry."

"This is how you make your living?" the coroner asked in some surprise.

"No—at least, not yet." Apparently resigned to the fact that the coroner would require the information, he confessed rather grudgingly, "I receive an allowance from my father, Sir Richard Gape."

"How long have you been in Banfell?"

"I arrived a fortnight ago."

"And your business here?"

Edward Gape might have been called to testify, but it was Percival Hartsong who waved an expansive hand and answered rhapsodically. "Inspiration, my good man! Inspiration for my Art: the lakes, the becks, the fells"—he cast a leering glance at Lizzie Hawkins, seated white-faced and numb beside her stepmother—"the other natural beauties—"

"Yes, we know all about you poet fellows," the coroner

said, unimpressed. "Tell me, were you acquainted with Ned Hawkins?"

"I wouldn't call it an 'acquaintance,' but I could hardly fail to know the man, as he was my host. I'm putting up at the Hart and Hound," he added unnecessarily, as everyone in the village must have seen him in its public room, tossing back tankards of ale and flirting with the innkeeper's daughter.

"And yet you interrupted your holiday to join in the search for a man who was essentially a stranger," the coroner observed. "A kind and thoughtful gesture, Mr. Gape."

"Not at all," the poet demurred. "Experience is as meat and drink to the poet, for how is one to write about Life unless he first experiences it? And what better way to understand Life than to come face to face with Death?"

"Oh?" The coroner looked up sharply from his notes. "You knew you were going to find your host's dead body?"

"No, of course not! But Death stalked the public room of the Hart and Hound that morning, its horrid image stamped indelibly on the face of every man gathered there. In short, we all knew what we were about to find. The only question that remained was where the Grim Reaper might have deposited his bitter harvest."

"Ugh!" Julia murmured into Pickett's ear. "I hope his poetry doesn't sound like that."

Pickett nodded. "More or less," he said, but his thoughts were elsewhere. Setting aside the poet's florid expressions and mixed metaphors, Pickett distinctly recalled his predicting that the missing man would be found in bed with some doxy. Had he been deliberately lying at the time, or had

105

he reworked the events of the previous day in his memory to cast himself in a more favorable light?

Pickett had not long to consider the matter, for the coroner was asking his next question. "Tell me, if you will, what you found on your search."

"I took the path down to the river, and then trekked back upstream some distance. The bank is so narrow in places that I was obliged to walk in the river itself part of the time." He glared down at his abused boots, and Pickett no longer had to wonder at the poet's mincing steps; he was surprised Percival Hartsong could squeeze his feet into his boots at all, after their wetting the previous morning. "After some little ways, I saw the body of Ned Hawkins lying on the bank, half in the water and half out."

"Which half?"

"I beg your pardon?"

"You say the body was half in the water and half out. Which half was in, and which half was out?"

"Oh, I see. The upper half—the head and upper torso—was in the water, and the legs were on the bank, splayed in so ungainly a manner that I knew they must be broken."

"Unless you count surgery amongst your talents, Mr. Gape, you may leave any speculations as to the medical condition of the body to the doctor."

At this rather mild rebuke, the poet flushed a dull red. "Yes, well, it didn't take a doctor to see that the fellow was dead. We could hardly leave him there in that condition, so we brought him back up the cliff path."

" 'We,' Mr. Gape? Up to now, you have given us the

impression that you were alone in your quest."

"There were two others," the poet admitted rather grudgingly. "A farmer—Wilson, I believe his name is—and another guest at the inn, a fellow from London."

"Thank you, Mr. Gape. I believe we will hear what this 'fellow from London' has to say. Mr. John Pickett, will you please take the stand?"

Pickett gave Julia a nervous glance that was not entirely feigned, and rose from his chair, doing his best to look like a holidaymaker who had never appeared before a coroner's jury in his life.

"You are Mr. John Pickett of London?"

"Yes, sir."

"And how long have you been staying at the Hart and Hound?"

"Three days."

"The nature of your business in Banfell?"

"I'm on my honeymoon."

"I see," said the coroner, his knowing look shifting from Pickett to Julia and back again. "Not so much business as pleasure."

Pickett blushed so vividly at this observation that anyone inclined to question his presence in Cumberland would have been entirely satisfied.

"And yet you left your bride and took part in a search for a missing stranger."

"It seemed like the right thing to do. When we—my wife and I—were at dinner last night, one of the men in the public room promised Mrs. Hawkins that if her husband hadn't returned by morning, every able-bodied man in the village would go out and search for him. I'm an able-bodied man"— he willed himself not to think of this assertion in the context of his honeymoon or, worse, the Harley Street physician's examination intended to confirm (or not) his impotence in order to annul the marriage, but Julia's mischievous smile told him that she, at least, had not missed his unintentional double entendre—"so when dawn came, I went downstairs to inquire, and when I learned there had been no sign of Mr. Hawkins, I joined in the search."

"Accompanied by Mr. Wilson and Mr. Gape, as he claims?"

Pickett nodded. "Yes, sir. Mr. Hetherington"—he glanced about the crowded room, but saw no sign of his magistrate's friend amongst the rural thrill-seekers—"thought it safest for the older men not to attempt the cliff path, as it was not yet light when we set out."

"Describe your findings for the jury, if you will."

Pickett relaxed somewhat, realizing the question he dreaded the most—what he did in London for a living—was not going to be asked; apparently the coroner had mistaken him for a gentleman. Pickett silently blessed Julia for tricking him out in fashionable clothing, however uncomfortable he had been with the gesture at the time. He breathed a sigh of relief and launched into the narrative he had rehearsed the night before. "We found the body—Mr. Hawkins, that is— very much as Mr. Gape said, lying face down at the edge of the river. His legs were bent at an awkward angle and his face was bruised, but there was no sign of an animal having disturbed him."

He directed this last toward the innkeeper's widow in a reassuring tone, and was not at all surprised when the coroner said somewhat condescendingly, "I know you mean well, Mr. Pickett, but perhaps such speculations are best left to the doctor."

"I beg your pardon," Pickett said meekly.

Having confirmed the poet's observations, Pickett was soon dismissed and Ben Wilson was summoned. The yeoman farmer proved to be just as reticent in the witness stand as he had on the cliff path, and the coroner soon dismissed him, realizing that he would get nothing from this third witness that he had not already heard in greater detail from the previous two. For his next witness, the coroner called for the doctor, and there was a stirring of interest from the spectators as a short, stout fellow with thinning gray hair and wire-rimmed spectacles answered the summons.

"You have examined the body of Ned Hawkins?" the coroner asked him.

"I have," said the medical man, inclining his head.

"And what is your professional opinion?"

The doctor pushed his spectacles up on his nose. "First of all, Mr. Gape is quite correct when he supposes the man's legs were broken."

"Did the man drown, then, being unable to lift himself out of the water due to his injuries?"

"Good heavens, no!" the doctor exclaimed in some surprise. "You seem to be laboring under the mistaken belief that Ned Hawkins had gone down the cliff path and somehow fallen into the water from the riverbank. It is my opinion, however, that the kind of injuries he sustained could only be the result of landing abruptly after descending from a great height. It is my professional opinion that he fell, or else leapt, from the cliff above."

At the suggestion of suicide, the room erupted in a babble of voices, the most prominent of which was that of Mrs. Hawkins.

"He never jumped!" she declared. "My Ned was a good man! He wouldn't do such a wicked thing!"

It appeared that every resident of the village had something to say on this subject, and everyone seemed to determine to air his views at the same time. Eventually, the coroner found it necessary to call the crowd to order before continuing with his questioning.

"Yes, Mrs. Hawkins," he addressed the widow, not unkindly, "you will be allowed to speak in a moment, but first let me finish with the doctor. You suggest the deceased might have leapt to his death, Doctor. Have you any reason to believe he may have done so?"

"I meant no slur against poor Ned's character," the physician quickly demurred. "I only meant to make a point of his injuries being consistent with his having descended, by whatever means, from the cliff above, rather than the bank alongside the river."

"And yet you have been his physician for some time, have you not?"

"Aye, these last twenty years and more."

"I believe men and women sometimes confide in their

doctor issues that have little to do with their health, in much the same way they might confide in a clergyman. Did Ned Hawkins ever tell you anything that might, in retrospect, have suggested that he was considering taking his own life?"

Mrs. Hawkins sobbed her objections to this line of questioning, leading Lizzie to put her arm around her stepmother and glare at the coroner. Whatever their differences over the character and intentions of Percival Hartsong, it seemed they were united in protecting the reputation of Ned Hawkins.

"Certainly he had no medical problems that might lead him to consider so irrevocable a solution, for his health was good for a man in his forties, with nothing beyond the usual aches and pains to be expected at that age. As for anything beyond medical issues, I could not say. Although Ned was a friendly and convivial man, his was not a confiding nature."

"I see. Let us return for a moment to this drop from the cliff which, in the absence of evidence to the contrary, at least for the nonce, we shall refer to as a fall. Would you say that death would have been instantaneous?"

The doctor frowned thoughtfully. "I should think it would be very unlikely for a man to survive such a fall, especially in the light of the injuries he sustained."

Pickett let out the breath he hadn't realized he had been holding. At least if anyone—the murderer, for instance—had had any knowledge of the letter in Ned's pocket, and any suspicion that this letter had been removed by a third person before the killer had been able to take possession of it himself, he would have no reason to believe that Ned had lived long enough to communicate anything to anyone before he died. Not that he had communicated much, in any case; still, if Ned was not of a "confiding nature," then the fact that he tried to tell Pickett something—never mind the fact that he had written to Bow Street in the first place—became all the more significant.

The coroner thanked the doctor and dismissed him, then summoned Mrs. Hawkins to describe for the jury her husband's state of mind the last time she had seen him. Pickett was not surprised to hear her hotly deny any suggestion that her husband might have had the slightest care in the world. His opinion of the coroner rose exponentially as that canny practitioner of the legal arts skillfully extracted the information that Ned had been a bit worried about his daughter of late, she having recently attracted the attention of the Wrong Sort of man, which was hardly surprising, for the girl was as pretty as a morning in May (thus mollifying Lizzie, who appeared ready to take exception to this disparagement of her beloved), and one couldn't be too careful these days, could one?

"And," she continued, "I'll admit my Ned has been a bit worried about money of late, too, what with that Jedidiah Tyson who never had two shillings to rub together suddenly setting himself up as a fashionable establishment right across the street, with dancing and cards and who knows what-all going on under his roof, in the hopes that these gentle-born holiday-makers will pack their bags and move across the street from our place to his. But that don't mean he was ready to do away with himself over it, for if he were to do away with anyone, it would be Jedidiah Tyson."

Pickett had been listening with only half an ear to this testimony, as he knew quite well that Ned Hawkins had not committed suicide, but at this assertion, his ears pricked up, and he sat a bit straighter in his chair.

There followed a number of utterly tedious testimonies from various persons who gave it as their opinion that Ned Hawkins had had no thought of suicide, from his daughter Lizzie ("It's true that Papa did not much like Mr. Hartsong, but only because he didn't understand about poetry") to his son Jem ("Oh, we didn't always see eye to eye—what father and son do?—but to think he'd do away with himself over such a thing don't even make sense—it would be like he was giving in to me, wouldn't it?") to the vicar ("I'm sure no parishioner of mine could consider, much less commit, such a sin against his own body").

At last the coroner invited the last of these to step down, then issued instructions to the jury, whose task, he reminded them, was to determine whether Ned Hawkins' death was the result of natural causes, suicide, accident or misadventure, or unlawful killing. It took them only a few minutes of deliberation before they returned, and a tall, thin man with a receding chin delivered a verdict that, while incorrect, was hardly surprising: "The men of the jury are convinced Ned Hawkins died when he accidentally fell from the cliff. Our verdict is death by misadventure."

7

*In Which John Pickett Displays
a Hitherto Unsuspected Talent, albeit under Duress*

I 'm glad that's over," Pickett said, shutting the door and leaning against it. After the jury had announced its decision, most of the crowd had adjourned to the Golden Feather across the street to discuss the proceedings, a rudimentary sense of decency preventing them from doing so while still under the roof of the deceased. Pickett and Julia, on the other hand, had escaped up the stairs to the privacy of their own room for essentially the same purpose.

"I thought you did rather well," she assured him. "It can't have been easy for you, deliberately misleading a jury—"

"I didn't lie to them," he put in defensively, moving away from the door. "I didn't say anything that wasn't true. I just— didn't tell them everything I knew. More to the point, I kept you well out of it. Make no mistake, Julia, I intend to seek justice for Ned Hawkins, but I'll do it without putting you in further danger. What Mrs. Hawkins said about Mr. Tyson, though—could he be our man?"

She sighed. "I knew you were going to ask me that. I don't think it was he. I think I must have noticed his being so gaunt, but I can't be certain." She pressed her hands to her face. "If only I could remember exactly what happened! It was over so quickly, and since then I've tried so hard to recall it that I'm no longer sure what I actually saw, and what my imagination has colored in after the fact."

"All the more reason for you not to have testified," Pickett said. "The coroner would have made mincemeat of you, and in the meantime whoever pushed Hawkins off the cliff would know exactly who had seen him."

"You think he was there at the inquest, then? The murderer, I mean."

"I think he would want to know exactly what had been seen, or deduced, about Hawkins's death. Then again, I expect the news will be all over Banfell within the hour, so he'll hear about it in any case."

"Yes, for the inquest probably offered the villagers the most excitement they've seen in years." She gave him a mischievous smile. "And a very good show they will have found it! I thought Mr. Hartsong—or should I call him Mr. Gape?—in any case, I thought he was a surprisingly good witness, if a bit florid. Still, my favorite part was when you assured the coroner that you were an able-bodied man."

Pickett blushed anew at the memory. "I didn't mean it that way!"

"I know you didn't, which is what made it so funny. And

now"—she put a hand to the small of his back and gave him a nudge in the direction of the washstand—"you'd best see about getting that able body of yours dressed. We're promised to the Hetheringtons tonight, you know."

The subject of the murder was dropped, at least for a time, as they prepared for dinner. Pickett's cravats had acquired significantly more starch in the few months since his marriage, and consequently required more time (and often more than one neckcloth) before he achieved a respectable result. Then, too, their room boasted only a single mirror over the washstand, meaning that he and Julia, in the absence of her dressing table, were obliged to take it in turns.

"You can't know how pleasant it is to wear colors again." Having arrayed herself for the occasion in lilac silk, she stood before the small square mirror and affixed pearl and amethyst teardrops to her earlobes. "When I think of all those months I spent in unrelieved black, I wonder you ever gave me a second look."

"I wonder you ever gave me a first," he said, marveling anew at how far they had come in the fourteen months since they had met quite literally over her husband's dead body. He had hardly appeared to advantage on that occasion, as he'd been so stunned by the lady's beauty that he could barely form a coherent sentence.

"John?" Her eyes met his in the mirror, and it soon became evident that her thoughts were running along similar lines. "What would you have done if you'd discovered proof positive that I had killed Fieldhurst?"

He shook his head. "I knew you hadn't. I knew you

couldn't have."

"For which I am eternally grateful, as your confidence in me was very likely the only thing that kept me from the gallows! But just for the sake of argument, what would you have done if you'd discovered you were wrong?"

He gave her a long, considering look. "I think," he said at last, "that poor Lord Fieldhurst's murder would have remained unsolved."

"Hmm." She subjected his reflection to a long, appraising look. "I wonder if you could have."

Coming up behind her, he wrapped his arms around her and buried his nose in her violet-scented hair. "You think I could have let you go to the gallows, if I might have done something to stop it?"

"I don't think your conscience would have let you do anything else, no matter how much you might have wished to," she said, leaning back into his embrace. "You have more personal integrity than anyone I know—when you're not withholding information and misleading juries, that is."

* * *

Robert Hetherington's carriage called for them promptly at half past seven. Pickett handed Julia inside, then climbed in after her. The distance to the Hetherington residence was not great, and he might easily have walked it himself, but among the many small facets of Lady Fieldhurst's life which he had glimpsed during his investigation of her first husband's murder was the fact that ladies' evening slippers were not crafted to withstand walking long distances. Nor, he supposed, were gentlemen's; he had worn boots on his first visit to Mr. Hetherington, but tonight he sported soft leather pumps that might have done very well for dancing (had he known how), but would very likely have fallen to pieces had he attempted to trudge there and back on foot.

In any case, the carriage ride was certainly accomplished more quickly than the walk would have been, and it seemed no time at all before they were set down before the Hetherington abode. A matched set of footmen (there was really no other way to describe them) flung open the double doors, and as they entered the hall, Robert Hetherington himself came to meet them.

"Ah, Mr. and Mrs. Pickett! So pleased you could come. I can't recall, Mr. Pickett, did you meet my wife on the occasion of your earlier visit? No? Come and let me introduce you, then."

He steered them through a door opening off the hall to the left, where a still-handsome woman of about sixty sat on a sofa upholstered in cherry-striped satin brocade. She rose and shook out her plum-colored skirts as they entered the room, and Pickett noted that she was tall and so thin as to appear gaunt. Still, her smile was sweet, and when she spoke there was a pleasant, almost musical, lilt to her voice.

"I'm so pleased to meet you, Mrs. Pickett, Mr. Pickett," she said, offering white-gloved hands to Julia. "My husband tells me you are newly married."

"Three months," Julia said, taking Mrs. Hetherington's hands in hers. She felt the older woman flinch, and immediately loosened her grip.

"Allow me to wish you both very happy," her hostess

said. At that moment the dinner gong sounded, and she turned to Pickett. "Well! That was very prompt, was it not? If you will give me your arm, Mr. Pickett, we will go in to dinner. I have an excellent cook—a French émigré, you know—but he can be quite temperamental if his masterpieces are allowed to grow cold."

"That's always the way of these geniuses," observed Mr. Hetherington as he offered his arm to Julia. "They all have their weaknesses. Don't you find it so, Mr. Pickett?"

The look which the man fixed on him was so fraught with meaning that Pickett wasn't sure if he was being invited to confide something unflattering about Mr. Colquhoun, or if his magistrate's letter had somehow given his host the impression that he fancied himself a genius, and was thus in need of a setdown. Not for the first time, he wished he knew exactly what Mr. Colquhoun had written in his letter of introduction. "I don't think I can claim acquaintance with any geniuses," Pickett confessed. "I shall have to take your word for it."

Whatever the cook's quirks of temperament, it soon became evident that his abilities had not been exaggerated. Pickett, accepting a second serving of green turtle soup, took the liberty of saying so.

"I was very fortunate to get him," Mrs. Hetherington said. "He had fled France at the beginning of the Terror, and escaped to Dublin. Mr. Hetherington found him there while we were visiting family, and we brought him back with us."

"You are Irish, then?" Julia asked her host in some surprise.

"No, no, I'm Cumberland born and bred, but Brigid

there"—he pointed his fork in the general direction of his wife, seated at the opposite end of the table—"hails from the Emerald Isle."

"What a lovely name for your home country," Julia told her hostess. Both ladies had slipped their hands free of their gloves in order to eat, and Julia noted with shocked pity that Mrs. Hetherington's fingers were so racked with arthritis as to look like claws. Small wonder the poor woman had flinched when Julia had pressed her hands!

"It is indeed a lovely name, and fitting as well, but it isn't original with my husband," she replied, smiling at him down the length of polished mahogany.

"No, some poet fellow said it first," Mr. Hetherington confessed with unimpaired good cheer.

"It figures," Pickett said, giving Julia a wink.

"Eh, what's that?" Mr. Hetherington asked.

Coloring slightly, Julia resolved to have a word with her husband regarding the propriety of winking at one's spouse over the dinner table. "There is a young man staying at the Hart and Hound who claims to be a poet," she explained. "As I am not familiar with his work, I can offer no opinion as to its quality, but he does have a tendency to express himself in rather florid terms."

"Aye, since that Wordsworth fellow moved to Grasmere—what, ten years ago?"—receiving confirmation from his wife, Hetherington continued—"every ha'penny rhymester in England has taken up residence near the Lakes. But I think I know the fellow you refer to. Testified at the inquest today, didn't he?"

"He did," Pickett concurred, somewhat surprised. "Were you there, sir? I didn't see you."

"No, I wasn't there. I reckoned I'd done my bit by organizing the search. Besides, it was plain as a pikestaff what the verdict was going to be. Misadventure, falling off the cliff, am I not right?"

Pickett nodded. "You are. Does it happen often? People falling off the cliff, I mean."

"Aye, it's a fairly common occurrence, but not usually amongst the locals. They have better sense than to stand on the edge. Most of 'em, anyway," he amended darkly, then picked up his wineglass and drank deeply.

"Robert, try to be charitable, my dear," his wife chided him. "Ned Hawkins has never seemed to me to lack for sense. Who knows what he might have had on his mind that day?"

"Aye, I suppose you're right. I'll wager just reining in that daughter of his would be enough to drive any man to distraction."

"I'm afraid Lizzie Hawkins is a bit of a coquette," Brigid Hetherington explained for the sake of her guests. "A young farmer has been courting her, but I fear the girl's head has been turned by this sudden influx of poets."

"Yes, we've seen one of them flirting with her at the inn," Julia said. "The same one who testified at the inquest, in fact. He calls himself Percival Hartsong, but as it turns out, his real name is Gape."

"For my money, she'd do best to take young Wilson," put in their host.

"That has been my impression, too," Julia agreed. "Much

as I enjoy reading it on occasion, I fear writing poetry would not provide the steadiest of incomes on which to support a wife—unless, of course, he possesses an independence from some other source." She discreetly left unsaid the suspicion, shared by herself and her husband, that marriage was not the poet's primary object in wooing the innkeeper's daughter.

The butler and two footmen entered the dining room at that moment, bearing the dishes that comprised the meat course, and conversation was suspended while the first course was removed and a joint of roast beef was placed before Pickett.

"Will you carve, Mr. Pickett?" asked Mrs. Hetherington, regarding him expectantly.

It was with some trepidation that Pickett took the large knife the butler offered, for this was a skill he had acquired only in the months since his marriage. Before that time, he'd lived alone in a small flat in Drury Lane, and on those rare occasions when he could afford a cut of meat for his dinner, he'd torn the roasted flesh from the bone with his teeth in order not to miss a single shred. Shortly after he had moved into Julia's Curzon Street town house, her kindhearted butler, Rogers, had recognized his dilemma, and had taken him aside for a private lesson in the art.

Still, this was the first time he had been obliged to demonstrate his skill (or lack thereof) before an audience. Mentally rehearsing Rogers's instructions, he identified the grain and sliced across it with sufficient firmness that he was not obliged to hack the meat to pieces by sawing back and forth on it. He glanced up at Julia and, finding her beaming at him in approval and, yes, even pride, let out a sigh of relief, marveling anew that she had known exactly who—and what—he was, and had married him anyway.

The roast having been successfully carved, the Hetheringtons' butler took charge of serving a slice of the meat to each person at the table. To the slightly embarrassed surprise of both Picketts, one of the footmen took up a position at Mrs. Hetherington's elbow and began cutting her meat into much smaller pieces.

"Pray, pay me no heed," she implored them. "I suffer from a stupid arthritic complaint which makes it impossible for me to perform such simple tasks as cutting my own meat. It makes me feel so very childlike, I half expect my long-departed governess to appear at any moment and drag me back to the schoolroom. You will say I should spare my guests' blushes and restrict myself to foods I may manage on my own, but I confess I enjoy André's cooking too much to make the sacrifice."

"Nor should you be expected to do so!" cried Julia, appalled by the very suggestion.

"For my part, I would be far more embarrassed to be eating while you did without," Pickett concurred.

"What excellent young people you are!" exclaimed their hostess. "I can see Mr. Colquhoun did not exaggerate."

She thanked the footman and dismissed him, and after the servants had left them alone, her husband picked up the strands of their abandoned conversation. "Tell me, Mr. Pickett, will you attend the funeral tomorrow?"

"I don't know," Pickett confessed. "I suppose I ought to,

since I was one of the three men who discovered the body."

"Rather macabre way to spend your honeymoon, don't you think? I should say—"

Mrs. Hetherington raised her gnarled hands. "No more, please, Robert! I refuse to have dinner haunted by the ghost of Ned Hawkins. Tell me, Mrs. Pickett, is this your first visit to the Lake District?"

With this query, the conversation grew more general. The Hetheringtons, upon discovering that neither Mr. nor Mrs. Pickett had visited the area before, were quick to recommend such pastimes as might be of interest to a newly married couple, from hiking in the fells to hiring a boat and rowing on the lake. Pickett held his breath when Mr. Hetherington suggested an especially picturesque spot in which to enjoy a picnic, recognizing it as the very place where he had dozed while Julia had witnessed murder most foul, but here he did his wife less than justice: nothing in either her expression or her manner conveyed anything beyond polite interest.

"We usually have assemblies on Wednesday nights, just like they do in London," Mrs. Hetherington continued. "I daresay the one two nights hence must be canceled. What a pity! I'm sure it must go sorely against the grain with Jedidiah Tyson—he owns the Golden Feather, you know, right across the street from the Hart and Hound—but I should think they will resume next week, if you intend to stay in Banfell that long."

"Our plans are not fixed," Julia told her, darting a quick glance at Pickett for confirmation, "but we will certainly bear it in mind. Your husband had told Mr. Pickett about the assemblies, and we have already stopped by the Golden Feather to sign the subscription book."

"That seems to be quite a rivalry," Pickett remarked to his host.

"Came up at the inquest, did it?" Mr. Hetherington asked in some surprise. "Surely no one thinks Tyson shoved Hawkins off the cliff?"

Since this was much too close to the truth for Pickett's liking, he was only too glad to be able to deny any such supposition. "No, of course not. But the question arose as to whether Ned Hawkins might have leapt to his death, with loss of revenue to Tyson's rival establishment being a potential motive for suicide."

"I can see why the possibility must be considered," Hetherington conceded, albeit grudgingly. "It must have been hard on poor old Ned, seeing a new inn open up practically on his doorstep."

"And a very elegant one, at that," Julia agreed, "if the little we saw when we went inside is anything to judge by. But Mrs. Hawkins said Mr. Tyson had never had two shillings to rub together. How, pray, did he contrive to open an inn at all, especially one catering to a fashionable clientele?"

"I believe he inherited a considerable sum from a relative, a merchant in Penrith," their host recalled. "It was two years ago, maybe three, so I can't remember all the details. He used his legacy to purchase the Feather—it wasn't an inn at the time, but a private residence that had fallen into disrepair—and set about converting it into a commercial establishment. Mind you, it has no yard, being up against the street as it is, so the mail coaches and the stage from Penrith still use the Hart and Hound. Still, it's near enough that fashionables who prefer the Feather aren't inconvenienced, provided they have no objection to hauling their own bags across the street." He chuckled at one of the more amusing aspects of the rivalry. "And haul 'em themselves they must, for Ned Hawkins wouldn't let any of Tyson's staff set foot in his inn yard, nor allow any of his own people to fetch bags for his rival's patrons."

"And so Tyson conceived of the assemblies as a form of revenge," Pickett deduced.

"I should say the shoe was on the other foot! Tyson started hosting assemblies the first summer he was open. He's got a big room one floor up that's particularly well-suited to the purpose. Ned Hawkins, on the other hand, has no place to host such things even if he wanted to, and don't think Tyson doesn't know it!" He leaned forward, lowering his voice conspiratorially. "A word of warning, Mr. Pickett. If you and Mrs. Pickett should happen to attend next Wednesday's assembly, you'd best steer clear of any drinks on offer. Tyson has been known to slip something into the wine, something that incapacitates his guests—not seriously, mind you, just enough so that they're obliged to put up at the Feather for the night—even holds rooms vacant for the purpose."

"He told us about the rooms, and I suspected the rest," Pickett said thoughtfully. "He sounds like the sort that wouldn't stick at much."

"No, but the idea that he should drive Ned Hawkins to

suicide is absurd, and I'm pleased that the coroner's jury recognized it as such," Hetherington said. "In fact, I should have said if Hawkins was inclined to kill anyone, it wouldn't have been himself, but Tyson—or perhaps that poet who's trying to give his daughter a slip on the shoulder."

"That does it!" Mrs. Hetherington laid aside her serviette and pushed her chair back. "If you are determined not to let poor Ned Hawkins rest in peace, I shall leave you to your port. Will you accompany me, Mrs. Pickett?"

Julia was conscious of a reluctance to abandon her husband, well aware that he was uncomfortable with many of the social conventions that were second nature to her. Still, it would be the height of bad manners to refuse her hostess, so she gave Pickett an apologetic smile, assuring herself that surely a friend of Mr. Colquhoun's would be inclined to look favorably upon him, and allowed Mrs. Hetherington to lead her from the room.

"Here we may have a comfortable coze," this lady pronounced, ushering Julia into a withdrawing room at the rear of the house. Once the door was closed behind them, she added, with a twinkle in her eye, "Besides, I thought by now you might be in need of the chamber pot. When I was in your condition, I could hardly get through dinner without making my excuses and escaping to relieve myself. How Robert used to tease me about it!"

"My—my condition?" Julia echoed.

"You are increasing, are you not?" Mrs. Hetherington asked in some consternation. "Pray forgive me if I was mistaken—"

"No, you are quite correct. But how did you know?" Julia cast a furtive glance down the front of her gown. "I thought it was not yet obvious."

"It is not yet evident in your figure," the older woman assured her. "But some women have a particular glow about them when they are in the family way. Add to that the fact that you have been married for three months to a young man whom you obviously love very much, and it is easy to deduce the rest. In any case, I have been in that condition too many times myself to fail to recognize it in another. Never fear, Robert will not keep your handsome Mr. Pickett from you for long. Tell me, how did the two of you meet?"

Which was a tactful way, Julia thought, of saying they appeared to be an oddly matched couple. She began to see why her husband wished he knew exactly what Mr. Colquhoun had said about them. Seeing her hostess was awaiting her answer, Julia chose her words with care. "We—we met very shortly after the death of my first husband. He was murdered, you see, and Mr. Pickett was—was very helpful—to me during the weeks that followed, although of course I had no thought at the time of marrying again. But you say you have been in the family way yourself," she added, seizing the opportunity to turn the subject. "Pray, how many children do you have?"

"Alas, none," Mrs. Hetherington said with a sigh of regret. "At least, none that survived. I was unable to carry a child to term." As Julia's eyes grew round with alarm, she added quickly, "It was the result of an injury suffered when I was very young. I am sure there is no reason to suppose you will not safely deliver a healthy child."

Julia had considered the possibility that she herself might not survive the birth (hence her furtive letter to her sister, which still resided at the bottom of her portable writing desk) but it had not yet occurred to her that she might lose the baby. Suddenly she wanted a moment alone to compose herself while she considered this new and frightening possibility. Fortunately, her hostess had provided her with a convenient excuse.

"You—you said something about a chamber pot?"

"Yes, of course. I'll show you."

Mrs. Hetherington led the way up the central staircase to her own bedchamber. The poetic phrase "emerald isle" rose unbidden to Julia's brain, for the room was furnished in shades of green, and the space over a very fine fireplace of green marble was dominated by a framed painting of a stately house set amidst the lush green of its parkland. Julia could not identify either the artist or his subject, and wondered if this was her hostess's family home, committed to canvas by some local talent unknown to the wider world.

"My dressing room is through there," the older woman said, indicating a door set in the far wall. "The chamber pot is in the cupboard."

Alone in the dressing room, Julia made no move to open the cupboard, but regarded her reflection in the cheval mirror with a long, appraising look, pressing a hand to her abdomen as if by doing so she might impart strength to the infant within. *You have nothing to worry about*, she told herself firmly, and tried hard to believe it. After all, her sister, following the drum with her husband in Spain, had given birth to a healthy baby under the most primitive of conditions. Even her mother, frail as she was, had managed to deliver two girls without mishap. Julia's own physician said everything was progressing exactly as it should up to this point—and in the meantime, while she fretted over nightmarish scenarios that might never come to pass, the gentlemen would be joining the ladies in the withdrawing room, and John, finding her gone, would wonder where she'd got off to and worry about her protracted absence. Now, about that chamber pot . . .

She returned to the withdrawing room to find the gentlemen there before her, just as she had predicted, and gave Pickett a small smile and the slightest of nods to reassure him, then cast about in her mind to find some unobjectionable topic of conversation.

"What a handsome instrument," she said, spying a pianoforte of carved rosewood in the corner. "Do you play?"

"Alas, no, not for many years," Mrs. Hetherington said with a sigh, lifting the gloved hands in her lap and letting them fall. "It has been very difficult, giving up activities in which I once took such pleasure. If you would like to play it, do pray indulge us, Mrs. Pickett. I fear my poor instrument has been far too long silent."

Julia needed no urging. She leafed through the music stacked on top of the pianoforte, made her selection, then seated herself at one end of the bench and patted the other invitingly. "Will you turn the pages for me, John?"

Pickett was more than eager to oblige, as this freed him from the obligation of exchanging polite nothings with his host and hostess. The next few minutes were spent quite pleasurably, with Julia focused on her music and Pickett focused on her, lest he miss his cue to turn the page. And then, in the middle of "Did You Not Hear My Lady," Julia, having noticed for the last few minutes a faint sound near her ear, abruptly lifted her fingers from the keys.

"John!" she exclaimed, half accusingly, half delightedly. "You can sing!"

"I—I—I can't!" he protested, finding three pairs of eyes fixed upon him. "I don't know one note from another!"

"You have never studied music, perhaps, but you have a very pleasant singing voice," she insisted. "Do not try to deny it, for I've been listening to you."

"Pray do not be so modest, Mr. Pickett," Mrs. Hetherington urged. "Sing loudly enough that we may hear, too."

Pickett threw Julia a look that somehow combined *Help me* with *Just wait until we get back to the inn.* "I can't, really," he said again. "I used to live near the theatre, and anything I know—which is not much—I learned from listening to the performers on stage."

Mr. Hetherington inclined his head. "Very well, then, we shan't expect a professional performance." Seeing Pickett was unconvinced, he added, "Come, Mr. Pickett, surely you would not deny my wife this small favor."

One need not have grown up amongst polite society to know that there was no way to deny such a request without appearing boorish in the extreme. Pickett stood up (albeit not without some reluctance) and cleared his throat while Julia played the introduction. After a bit of a shaky start, he found his voice by the time they reached the lines that had inspired him to sing under his breath: "Though I am nothing to her / Though she must rarely look at me / And though I could never woo her / I love her till I die."

He glanced down at his accompanist, and found Julia looking up at him with misty eyes. Emboldened, he continued, and soon reached the final lines: "But surely you see My Lady / Out in the garden there / Rivaling the glittering sunshine / With a glory of golden hair."

When he finished, there followed an eternity of such total silence (although it could not have been more than two seconds) that he feared he had utterly disgraced himself. Then Mrs. Hetherington, beaming at him, began to clap her gloved hands.

"Bravo, Mr. Pickett!" her husband said, joining his wife in applause. "Bravo!"

At the pianoforte, Julia wiped a tear from her eye.

* * *

"I can't recall when I've enjoyed an evening more," Mrs. Hetherington said some time later, as she and her husband accompanied their guests as far as the door. "How I wish you might stay longer!"

For his part, Pickett was only too relieved to escape, having been kept at the pianoforte by his hostess's insistence until the tea tray arrived, by which time he had been obliged to sing two more songs and to join his wife in an impromptu duet.

"Aye, it's a pity you must leave so soon," Mr.

Hetherington concurred. "Still and all, I don't blame you for wanting to get back to the inn. Smuggler's moon and all that, you know," he added, casting a glance up at the moonless sky.

"Smuggling?" Julia said in some surprise, recalling the kegs that had occasionally appeared outside the kitchen door of her childhood home, and her father's surprisingly vehement reaction when she, at the age of nine, had innocently inquired about them. "I should have thought we were too far inland for smuggling."

"Wherever there is taxation, there will be smuggling," was her host's practical observation. "But you haven't far to travel, so I don't doubt you'll reach the Hart and Hound without mishap."

With these assurances, goodbyes were said all around, and Pickett handed Julia into the Hetherington carriage.

" 'Smuggler's moon,' " Julia remarked, once the coach-man had shut the door, enclosing them in darkness. "Is that why Ned Hawkins sent for you, do you suppose? Because he had discovered a smuggling ring?"

"No," Pickett said without hesitation.

"You seem very certain."

"I am. Bow Street isn't responsible for policing potential smuggling operations. That falls to the customs office—or, once the goods have been landed, the riding officers."

"Oh," Julia said, somewhat disappointed at the loss of what she had thought might be a promising lead.

"Mind you, I'm not sorry to be excluded. It's a thankless task—and a dangerous one. They haven't enough men or funding to do the job effectively, and most of the locals are sympathetic to the smugglers, if not actively aiding and abetting them. If Ned Hawkins was aware of a smuggling ring, it's doubtful he would have lifted a finger to stop it. In fact the inn, public as it is, might well have served as a meeting place."

"And so we're right back where we started," Julia said with a sigh.

Pickett saw nothing to debate in this observation, and so the rest of the short drive was accomplished in silence. They entered the inn to find the public room empty and dark; apparently whatever crowd might have been there had dispersed early in deference to Mrs. Hawkins, whose husband was to be buried the next morning.

Upon reaching their room, Pickett opened the wardrobe and removed the black tailcoat he usually reserved for court appearances. "What do you think?" he asked Julia. "Will it pass, or should I send it downstairs for ironing?"

"You brought your black coat?" She knew, of course, that it had been the best he owned at one time, but she'd done her best to correct that, purchasing for him a completely new wardrobe—a gesture that had not been received with unadulterated joy. "But why?"

"None of the new ones seemed quite sober enough for a funeral."

She regarded him quizzically. "And how, pray, did you know you would need to attend a funeral?"

He had been occupied in laying out suitable clothes for the solemn occasion, but looked up at her question. "I'm a Bow Street Runner," he pointed out. "I attract funerals."

"Oh," she said, rather daunted. "Just so long as they're

not your own . . ." Her voice trailed off on the thought, and when she spoke again, it was on another subject entirely. "John, about the singing—I didn't mean to embarrass you. It just—it surprised me, you singing under your breath, and so well, at that. I'd never heard you sing before. I didn't know you could."

He gave her a reproachful look, but said nothing.

"Anyway," she continued, "it might make for a pleasant way to pass the time when my condition requires me to stay at home. Tell me, do you know MacHeath and Polly's duet from *The Beggar's Opera?*"

Pickett grimaced. "Oh, I know it. Everyone at Bow Street knows it—and we all hate that thing."

"The duet?" she asked, surprised.

He shook his head. "The whole blasted opera."

"Do you? But why?"

"Because it presents highwaymen and pickpockets in so romantic a light that crime always goes up during its run."

Julia gave a delighted crow of laughter. "Are you serious?"

"I'm quite serious. Fifty years ago, the magistrate at Bow Street tried to have it banned."

"Oh, I'm very glad he didn't succeed. If it had never been performed, certain young men of my acquaintance might never have taken up the profession."

"It wasn't by choice, believe me," he said emphatically.

"And fifty years ago would have been rather before your time, would it not?" she conceded. "Let us say, then, that your father might not have been inspired to take up the profession,

135

nor to establish his son in the family business. Then you never would have been discovered and rescued by Mr. Colquhoun, nor ever have crossed my path. And the worst part would be that I would never even know what I had missed."

Leaving the mirror over the washstand for her husband's use in untying his cravat, Julia set her jewel case on the writing table in order to remove her pearl and amethyst earrings with the assistance of the small glass affixed to the inside of its hinged lid. Or such, at least, was her intention. But when she reached behind her to pull up the chair so that she might sit down, her fingers closed, not over the top rung of the ladder-backed chair as she had intended, but over the fall of her husband's breeches, as evidenced by the sharp intake of his breath.

Startled and a bit embarrassed (for she had supposed him to be still occupied in laying out clothes for the funeral, or else untying his cravat before the washstand mirror), she turned to apologize for this quite unintentional intimacy, and suffered a still greater shock. Pickett's face had gone white to the lips, his expression stricken.

Julia's apology died a-borning. Granted, Mama's gently-bred daughter had never been so audacious as to grab her husband by his privates, but surely there was no call for so excessive a reaction to this purely accidental contact.

"John?" she asked, regarding him uncertainly. "Darling, what is the matter?"

"I—I—I'm sorry," he stammered as the blood rushed back into his face, turning it as crimson as it had been white. "I just—I wasn't prepared for—I wasn't expecting you to—

to—"

"I wasn't expecting it either, but surely if one of us should be blushing and stammering, it ought to be me! But it cannot be so very bad, can it? After all, we are married."

"Of course it isn't. In fact—but never mind that. Did you want the chair? Here, I'll get it."

Julia watched in dawning suspicion as he turned away with an alacrity suggesting relief. Although he had certainly been inexperienced when they had married, he had never been prudish. She could think of only one possible explanation for such a reaction.

"John, does this have anything to do with the annulment?" Whatever humiliation the annulment process had demanded of him, she had assumed he'd got the last laugh, if not when they had abandoned the proceedings in favor of remaining married, then surely when she was found to be increasing after only three months, following six childless years of marriage to her first husband. But it appeared she had been mistaken in this assumption. "It's all over now," she said reassuringly. "It was nothing but a piece of paper—a piece of paper that has long since been burned to ash."

"Is that what you were told?" he asked, and something about the tone of his voice lent credence to her worst fears. "That it was nothing but a piece of paper?"

"My solicitor told me that a physician would supply falsified documents stating that you had been examined and found to be impotent—both of which claims, as we very well know, are not true."

"The part about the impotence wasn't true. The other—"

He broke off, shaking his head.

"Did you really have to see a physician, then?" she asked in some bewilderment. "You said something yesterday about the lengths to which the Bertrams would go in order to—John, what did they do to you?"

"I—I went to the physician's office in Harley Street, and he had two—two women waiting for me. Prostitutes, in fact. Named Electra and Persephone."

Julia's eyes grew round with dismay. "They—you—you didn't—" But even as she struggled to frame the question, she knew the answer. His rather endearing clumsiness on their wedding night had been no sham; of that much she was certain.

"No, no," he assured her hastily. "Nothing like that."

"Then what—?"

"Don't ask, sweetheart. Please," he begged. "It was necessary at the time, in order to annul the marriage, but it's all in the past now, so let's just leave it there."

"Yes, it's all in the past—and yet more than six months later, an accidental touch has the power to turn you white as a ghost." He had nothing to say to this, and so she added, more gently, "If you suffered some indignity on my behalf—some *further* indignity, that is, even worse than I knew—then I was the unwitting cause of your distress. Does that not give me a right—an obligation, even—to know, so that I might make amends?"

"No amends are needed," he insisted. Still, her argument carried some weight, and so at last he told her, haltingly, of his experiences that day in Harley Street at the hands (quite literally) of Electra and Persephone, experiences all the more humiliating because he'd been aware the entire time that under different circumstances—and with a different woman —such an encounter might have been quite enjoyable.

Julia listened in growing indignation. Her unsophisticated young husband might have been told it was necessary, but he was not so familiar as she with her first husband's family. She suspected the solicitor who made the arrangements had been acting under instructions to ensure the annulment procedure was so degrading that the presumptuous Bow Street Runner would want nothing more to do with her. Good heavens! Had everyone but herself known, or at least suspected, that she was falling in love with him?

Any consternation she felt on her own behalf, however, paled beside the outrage she felt on his. As he concluded his narrative, she pointed imperatively toward the bed behind him.

"Sit!" she commanded.

Miserably, Pickett sat.

"I took no active part in the proceedings at all," he assured her hastily, having observed the dangerous glitter in her eyes and reached an entirely erroneous conclusion as to its cause. "At least, no active part except what was—what was completely involuntary."

If Julia heard this speech at all, she gave no sign. "If anyone is going to do such things to you, it's going to be me," she said, advancing purposefully upon him.

"My lady!" Much shocked, Pickett instinctively reverted to her former title. "You—you shouldn't—it wouldn't be—"

Julia paid not the slightest heed to his protests, but subjected him to so thorough and so passionate an assault upon his person that he had no choice but to submit—and, eventually, to reciprocate. By the time they lay bonelessly entwined in the middle of the bed an hour later, that afternoon in Harley Street had become nothing more than a distant memory, having lost forever its power to shame and humiliate.

"Julia?" Pickett said, when he could rouse sufficient energy to speak.

"Mmm?" Julia asked, finding the formation of actual words too much of an effort.

"I'm glad you're not *too* much of a lady," he said, and drifted into a deep and dreamless sleep.

8

*In Which May Be Seen
a Poet's Delicate Sensibilities*

M uch as she loved him, Julia was not sorry to see
Pickett depart for the funeral the following day; she
had an errand of her own for which his presence was neither
needed nor desired. She kissed her soberly clad husband and
bade him a fond farewell (coloring a little at the memory of
her own boldness the previous night), then waited only long
enough to assure herself that he was well and truly gone
before fetching her portable writing desk. As this necessitated
passing in front of the washstand, she paused before it long
enough to deliver a stern admonition to her reflection in the
mirror hanging above it.

"What a brazen creature you are!"

The image in the mirror smiled smugly back at her. It was
heady stuff, possessing this power over her husband, and she
wondered fleetingly if her first marriage might have been

more successful had she discovered it sooner. But no. To the late Lord Fieldhurst, conjugal relations existed solely for the purpose of begetting an heir; pleasure was to be found in other beds than his wife's. An empowered viscountess was the last thing he would have wanted. Even her second husband, she acknowledged, had his limits—and the letter secreted away in the bottom of her writing desk might well put them to the test.

She retrieved the letter, then lit the candle that stood on the table. As it warmed sufficiently to melt the wax, she searched first her bags and then Pickett's for a shilling to place beneath the seal, thus freeing her sister from the cost of paying for receipt of the missive. Should the worst come to pass and she not survive the birth, Julia reasoned, she would be asking Claudia and Jamie for funds enough; let her spare her sister and brother-in-law what expenses she could.

Alas, there was no shilling, nor any other coin, to be found anywhere in the room: Apparently it all resided in her husband's coin purse, which resided in his coat pocket, which was even now en route, along with its wearer, to Ned Hawkins's funeral. With a little huff of annoyance, Julia unfolded her letter, dipped a quill into the inkpot, and added a post scriptum at the bottom.

It appears my Husband has gone off and left me Destitute, else I would have placed a Shilling beneath the Seal of this Letter to cover the Cost of its Delivery. I hope you will Forgive the Omission, and place the Blame squarely on the Shoulders of my Lord and Master, where it Belongs.

Having disposed of Pickett, she refolded the letter, picked up the candle, and tipped it over the letter, allowing the melted wax to drip onto the paper in a small puddle which, when cooled and hardened, would form a seal. She fanned her missive to and fro in order to hasten this process, then blew out the candle and carried her clandestine correspondence downstairs.

She was not surprised to find the public room empty, as most of the village would have gone to the funeral of one of its best-known citizens; she was, however, somewhat taken aback to discover Mrs. Hawkins and Lizzie absent as well, and a lad who smelled faintly of the stables behind the counter in their place.

"Yes, ma'am?" The boy snapped rigidly to attention. "May I help you?"

"I was hoping for a word with Mrs. Hawkins," Julia said, glancing past him at the door which led to the kitchen.

"She's gone to the funeral."

He sounded a bit puzzled by her request, as if anyone ought to have known this. And so she should have, Julia supposed; it was only women of her own class who eschewed the burials of even their nearest and dearest kin.

"She's left me in charge," he continued, with a hint of pride in his voice. "Is there anything what I can do for you?"

Julia hesitated only a moment. She had hoped to entrust her correspondence to Mrs. Hawkins. But when the inn-keeper's widow returned, so too would her own husband. If she wanted to dispatch the letter without his knowledge, she was unlikely to have a better opportunity.

"I have a letter which I should like to send to my sister in Somersetshire," she said. "Can you tell me how to get to the

143

receiving office?"

The stable lad relaxed as if easy to be presented with a problem so easily solved. "Oh, aye. If you'll leave it with me, ma'am, I'll see it goes out with the next batch."

"Thank you," Julia said, and surrendered her contraband correspondence.

"That'll be a penny, it will." The lad slipped the letter into a canvas bag beneath the counter, then held out his hand expectantly.

"A penny?" echoed Julia in some consternation. "Why should I give you a penny now, when my sister will be obliged to pay a shilling to accept delivery?"

"Oh, but she won't have to," the stable hand assured her. "And what's more, it'll get there quicker, too. That's the beauty of it, see?"

Julia rather thought she *did* "see," and she did not like it one bit. She knew there were peers and Members of Parliament who misused their franking privileges, but paying a penny in order to have one's letters franked seemed the outside of enough; she doubted even her late husband's clutch-fisted heir, George, could have concocted so mercenary a scheme. She also failed to see how this might allow a letter to reach its destination any faster, as it would be traveling in the same post as its unfranked fellows.

She was not quite sure who in Banfell or its environs might enjoy franking privileges, as she could not recall having been introduced to any Members of Parliament, much less any aristocrats. She was forced to admit that this might be a good thing, else she might have been sorely tempted to tell the man just what she thought of a venture that was, if not precisely illegal, then certainly unethical. At the moment, however, she had a more urgent problem—and one, moreover, that rendered all the others moot.

"I don't have a penny," she confessed. "That is, I do, but my husband has gone to the funeral and taken his coin purse with him."

The lad gave her fashionable gown an appraising look. "Never mind, I can see you're good for it. I'll tell Mrs. Hawkins what's in the wind, and you can pay her next time you see her. In the meantime, least said, soonest mended, aye?"

As this echoed Julia's sentiments exactly (at least where her letter to her sister was concerned), she readily agreed. She turned away from the counter and was about to return to her own room when the door to the inn was flung open and Percival Hartsong strode into the room in a state of high dudgeon.

"Why, Mr. Hartsong! I thought you would be at the funeral."

He gave her a curt nod that was half agreement, half greeting. "Just came from there."

"Is it over so quickly, then?" she asked, relieved to have concluded her business, and apparently not a moment too soon.

"No," was his terse reply.

"Then why—?"

She got no further. "*I* know when I'm not wanted!" the poet said indignantly. "*I* know when—you there!" he barked at the stable hand turned barkeep. "Give me a pint of your best, and be quick about it!"

The boy jumped to obey this command, and once the poet had received his tankard and taken a long pull from it, Julia ventured to ask, "Mr. Hartsong, what has happened?"

"What has happened? What has *happened?* I'll tell you what has happened! I started to recite my poem—'The Hair that Floateth Outward on the Stream,' you know—and that dam—er, dashed farmer stood up and told me that if I didn't shut my mouth, he'd shut it for me! Well, I'd like to see him try!"

Julia, having seen the farmer in question, suspected he would make very short work of the willowy poet, but recognized that Mr. Hartsong would not appreciate having this fact pointed out to him.

"If Miss Hawkins asked you to recite the poem at her father's funeral, then it was very wrong of Mr. Wilson to interrupt you," she agreed warmly.

Mr. Hartsong had the grace to look ashamed. "She didn't ask me, precisely," he confessed. "Still, I thought she must be gratified, to think of her father being immortalized in such a fashion."

Julia suspected that gratification might not have been the uppermost emotion in Lizzie Hawkins's mind at the pre-emption of her father's funeral service by an attention-seeking poet. Still, she doubted Mr. Hartsong would view his own actions in such a light; in fact, Julia was beginning to believe he was the most narcissistic young man of her acquaintance.

"Perhaps such a work as you have composed would be

better shared in another setting," she said with as much diplomacy as she could muster.

To her surprise, the poet was not only receptive to this tactful observation, but enthusiastic about it. "A public reading! What an excellent suggestion!"

In fact, Julia could not recall having suggested any such thing. Still, she remembered that Jedidiah Tyson occasionally hosted poetry readings at the Golden Feather, and wondered if she might be forgiven (by her husband, if not by the Hawkins family) for bringing them up now. It soon became evident, however, that Mr. Hartsong had his own ideas about how his genius should be unleashed upon an unsuspecting world.

"It could be held here in the public room," he pronounced. "Tonight, so it would still be part of the festivities—er, observances—and I could stand there, before the fireplace, and recite it from memory. Do say you will come! After all, one might say the whole thing was your idea."

"Oh, I, that is, er—*John!*" When the door opened to admit Pickett, Julia all but fell on his neck, her own guilty conscience forgotten. "Is the funeral over, then?"

"Only just." He acknowledged her companion with a nod. "Mr. Hartsong."

"Mrs. Pickett has just put forth the most excellent suggestion," declared the poet, whose spirits had undergone so dramatic a transformation since Pickett had last seen him that his eyebrows rose slightly as he glanced at his wife. "Tonight I shall give a public recitation of my poem. Has Mrs. Hawkins returned yet? No? I must speak to her at once."

He made as if to head for the door, but Pickett took hold of his sleeve. "Don't."

"I beg your pardon?"

"When I last saw her, Mrs. Hawkins was deep in discussion with the vicar. I don't think she would appreciate the interruption."

"*Interruption?*" echoed the poet, bristling. "Let me remind you that we are speaking of Art! Surely a work of this importance—"

"—deserves Mrs. Hawkins's full attention," Julia put in soothingly. "She might be more receptive to the idea if you approach her when she is not distracted by the vicar's conversation."

Pickett's skeptical look suggested that she might be doing it a bit too brown. In this he had much mistaken his man, for there was no flattery too blatant for the poet to swallow.

"Very true," exclaimed Mr. Hartsong, much struck. "Holy orders do tend to make a fellow run on, do they not? As if every word they utter comes straight from the mouth of God! Very well, I shall wait until she returns, and put the idea to her then."

"Do I really want to know," Pickett asked Julia some minutes later, having adjourned with his wife to their own room, "how you came to suggest to that fellow that he do a public recitation of that god-awful poem?"

"I didn't actually suggest any such thing," Julia insisted. "I merely offered a tactful suggestion—*too* tactful, it appears—that Mr. Hawkins's funeral might not have been the best place for his verse."

"No, that would be the fire," was Pickett's bluntly stated opinion.

"I only meant that he should whisper it in Lizzie's ear, or some such thing. As for my reasoning, I wonder you should have to ask! Tell me, did Ben Wilson really inform Mr. Hartsong that if he didn't sit down and shut his mouth, he—Mr. Wilson, I mean—would shut it for him?"

"Oh, yes, he did." Pickett grinned mischievously at her, and Julia was conscious of her heart doing strange and wonderful things in response. "I'll admit, I almost hoped Hartsong would continue, just to see Wilson make good on his threat."

"You would see poor Ned Hawkins's funeral turn into a donnybrook, just for your own amusement? For shame!"

"Not 'just' for my own amusement," Pickett protested. "Who knows what interesting accusations might have been made during a brawl?"

"What an interesting life you must have led!" Julia marveled. "What, pray, were you hoping to find out?"

"If I knew that, I wouldn't have to hope for a brawl," he pointed out. "But it's interesting, our poet saying at the inquest that he'd arrived a fortnight ago—about the same time Ned Hawkins would have written to Bow Street."

"Writing bad poetry isn't a crime. Nor, for that matter, is seducing one's host's daughter, so long as she has no objection to being seduced."

"No, but as you said at dinner last night, poetry doesn't sound like the steadiest way to make a living. What if he decided he needed more money than his poetry could provide, and found a less than legal means to acquire it? Or what if his poetry is just a pretext for some more nefarious purpose?"

"And when Ned Hawkins found out and confronted him, he—Mr. Hartsong, I mean—pushed him off the cliff? But if Mr. Hawkins had reason to distrust Mr. Hartsong, why would he choose the edge of a cliff to stage a confrontation?"

"Maybe he wanted to spare Lizzie the discovery that her swain wasn't what he seemed. Or maybe he didn't 'choose' the cliff at all. Maybe Hawkins and Hartsong were in it—whatever 'it' might be—together, and he was obliged to keep up the pretense until someone from Bow Street arrived. But Hartsong discovered he'd been betrayed—remember, he was in the public room when we arrived, and would have heard me give our direction as Bow Street. It wouldn't take a genius to put two and two together and arrive at four. He could have got the wind up and decided he had to get rid of Hawkins before the fellow could tell what he knew. Hawkins might have agreed to meet him somewhere away from the inn, not realizing his secret was out and his life was in danger."

"Smuggling," pronounced Julia, recalling her host's parting words the night before. "Depend upon it, Ned Hawkins was embroiled in a smuggling scheme."

"It's possible," Pickett conceded. "But where, then, does Hartsong come in?"

Julia shrugged. "You're the Bow Street Runner; you tell me." As Pickett acknowledged this hit with a grin, she continued. "But no, I suppose it's up to me to see what I can discover, since Mr. Hartsong seems to regard me as the only one—apart from Lizzie, anyway—who appreciates his literary efforts."

"Do you think he would tell you anything?"

"It's worth a try." Her smile was deceptively demure. "After all, most men don't find me repulsive."

"That," Pickett muttered under his breath, "is what I'm afraid of."

* * *

The public room was unusually full that night at dinner. The poet was conspicuous by his absence—still sulking over his dismissal from the funeral, Pickett assumed—but the rest of their fellow guests were there, including the middle-aged sisters who usually didn't return from their treks until dark, and the artist who, as far as Pickett could tell, preferred to have his evening meal sent up to his room on a tray. As for the other diners, Pickett supposed everyone wanted to discuss the funeral with those most nearly concerned. His own efforts in that direction had not been entirely successful. When he and Julia had first come down to dinner, he had taken the opportunity of offering his condolences once again to the widow.

"It seems strange that your husband should have taken such a fall, familiar with the landscape as he was," he'd remarked innocently enough, or so he had imagined. "Has anything been troubling him lately?"

To his surprise, Mrs. Hawkins had all but gone for his throat. "My Ned was as good a man as ever drew breath!" she declared hotly. "So if you're thinking he done away with himself, like that coroner said—"

"No, no!" Pickett protested hastily. "I never thought any

such thing. I only wondered if perhaps he was distracted by some problem, and was not as careful as he would normally have been."

"I see," said the widow, the wind quite taken from her sails. "Truth to tell, I've wondered about that myself. But I suppose I'll never know," she concluded, dabbing at her eyes with her handkerchief.

Alas, no delicate probing on Pickett's part as to exactly what might have disturbed her husband had yielded the slightest results, and at last, realizing she was beginning to regard him with some suspicion, he was obliged to drop the subject. He only hoped Julia's attempts with the poet might yield better results.

He had not long to wait to find out. He and Julia had scarcely finished their dinner when a faint stirring of interest amongst his fellow diners announced the arrival of Percival Hartsong, clad in such funereal garments that any casual observer might have been forgiven for thinking it was his own father, rather than his inamorata's, who had died. Any suggestion that the poet had abandoned his bohemian manner of dress for a more staid appearance, however, was dispelled by the unstarched cravat that fell in floppy loops from a bow knot, and the artfully disarranged black locks that flowed from his brow. As he entered the inn's public room, Lizzie—who had obviously been posted as a lookout—began clanking a spoon against the side of a pewter tankard until she had the attention of everyone present.

"Stepmama and I would like to thank you all for coming," she announced solemnly. "And now, Mr. Percival

Hartsong will recite a poem he wrote about poor Papa."

While it might be true that Ned Hawkins had inspired Mr. Hartsong's ode, it would have been a stretch to say that he was its subject. It was not about the innkeeper so much as it was about the poet himself: his shock and horror at discovering the body, his sudden realization of the brevity of life, and his melancholy speculations regarding when he himself might meet "that fate to which all mortals must succumb"—an event which, if the glowering expression on Ben Wilson's face was anything to judge by, might occur sooner rather than later.

After the recitation was over, Pickett held Lizzie at bay while Julia seized the opportunity to congratulate its proud author.

"I found it very—very moving," she told him. This much, at least, was true: it had moved more than one listener right out the door. "I can see you are possessed of a keen sensibility, Mr. Hartsong."

"I believe you are right," acknowledged the poet, unencumbered by false modesty. "I do seem to feel things more deeply than most men."

"Has any of your poetry been published?"

He sighed. "Alas, no. But I fear it is only to be expected. Men who think of nothing but numbers entered into a ledger are incapable of understanding, much less appreciating, Art. I speak of publishers in particular, of course," he added hastily, "not of such ordinary men as your husband, who I am sure must possess other excellent qualities in spite of a lack of finer feeling or emotional expression."

Julia might have informed Mr. Hartsong that her husband

had no difficulty expressing his very fine feelings to the complete satisfaction of them both. But as such an outburst would serve no purpose beyond mortifying one and offending the other, she resisted the urge.

"I believe it is often the case," she said, choosing her words with care, "that true genius is not recognized except in retrospect. Still, to become famous after one is dead is not much good when one craves recognition and, yes, payment for one's efforts during one's lifetime."

"If I could but achieve the recognition my talent deserves, I would gladly forgo worldly wealth!" Mr. Hartsong declared fervently. "I have no shortage of funds, for my father gives me a handsome allowance. Not that he approves of my poetry, but my mother, I do not hesitate to say, takes great pride in my talent, and it is she who champions me. Then, too, I am Papa's only son and heir, and it would look very bad in the eyes of the world if he were to let me go begging."

"Clearly, notoriety is what is needed," Julia declared, thinking of Pickett's theory that Mr. Hartsong might be involved in some unsavory scheme. "What a pity you cannot engage in some outrageous action which might shock Society, yet not result in your being imprisoned or hanged!"

Alas, the poet failed to take the bait. "That might work in Paris or Rome, but not here," he said sullenly. "The English are too fond of dull propriety to embrace scandal, no matter how gifted its subject."

Julia, recalling the readiness with which Society had seized upon the scandal of her first husband's murder, could not agree. "Oh, they might express shock, even revulsion, but depend upon it, they will clamor to hear more. Believe me, I know whereof I speak: when my husband—my first husband, that is—died under mysterious circumstances, it was not long before my name was on everyone's lips. Be careful of what you wish for, Mr. Hartsong. You may find that fame is not so pleasant as you might suppose."

"Oh, I'm sure it would be worth any—"

He was interrupted at this point by Lizzie, who had escaped Pickett and came hurrying forward to reclaim her poet. "Oh, Mr. Hartsong! I'm sure your poem was very clever, but—well, for it to be all about Papa, it didn't really talk about him very much, did it?"

"I'm afraid you don't understand poetry," its author told her with a condescending smile. "Your father was not only your father, you know. He was a metaphor."

"A what?" asked the innkeeper's daughter.

"A metaphor," the poet said again. "A symbol of Life, Death, and Mortality."

"Oh," said Lizzie, clearly still baffled.

Seeing Mr. Hartsong preparing to launch into lengthy explanation, Julia made her excuses and escaped with her husband up the stairs to their room.

"Well?" Pickett prompted once they were alone. "What did you think of our cultural experience?"

"I think Mr. Hartsong is the most egotistical young man I have ever met!" Julia declared with feeling. "No compliment was too blatant for him to swallow, no praise too fulsome for him to accept as anything more than his due. You'd best keep a safe distance from me, for I should not be at all surprised if a bolt of lightning strikes me down for telling such taradiddles!"

But the attack, when it came, proved to be from a very different source.

9

In Which Mr. and Mrs. Pickett Find Themselves
between a Rock and a Hard Place

T he crash of splintering glass shattered the silence of the
room where Pickett and Julia lay sleeping.

"What the—-?" Awakened abruptly from a sound
slumber, it took Pickett's sleep-fogged brain a moment to
identify the noise even as he threw back the covers and leapt
from the bed. The chill that struck his bare legs was enough
to inform him, even without the moonlight streaming through
the gaping hole that had once been the window, of its source.
"Julia? Are you all right?"

"Yes, but—John, what was that?"

"The window. No, don't get up—there's broken glass
everywhere." He thrust his feet into his shoes and crossed the
room to the window, the crunching sound underfoot lending
proof to his warning. Bracing himself on the wooden window
frame, he stuck his head through the opening and leaned out.

157

Neither man nor beast stirred below, and no wind blew—there was nothing, in fact, that might account for the breakage. He groped on the writing table for the candlestick, and finally located it lying on its side; apparently it had been knocked over by whatever had shattered the window. He fumbled with the flint until the spark caught and the wick flared to life, then lifted the candlestick and turned toward the center of the room. The bare boards of the floor sparkled with a thousand tiny points of light as the flame was reflected in each shard of glass. It might have been a beautiful sight had its cause been less ominous. For there in the middle of the wreckage lay a rock about the size of Pickett's clenched fist, a rock partially covered with a narrow strip of paper which had been wrapped around it and tied in place with string.

"John?" Following his example, Julia slipped her feet into the shoes she'd worn to dinner earlier that evening, and came to stand beside him. "What is that?"

"I don't know, but I'm about to find out."

He picked up the coat he had discarded when he'd changed for dinner, and groped in it for the pocketknife he carried there. He slashed through the string that held the paper to the rock. The note contained only half a dozen words, but their meaning was plain:

Go back where you came from was scrawled in ink across the torn foolscap.

"Who would do such a thing?" Julia asked, staring in shocked disbelief at the paper in his hand.

"I think it's safe to say it isn't Mr. Colquhoun ordering me back to Bow Street."

"It isn't funny!"

"Believe me, I'm not laughing," he said, tight-lipped. "Julia—"

He got no further, for a clatter of footsteps sounded on the stairs, and a moment later someone pounded on the door.

"Mrs. Pickett?" a female voice called through the thick wooden panel. "Mr. Pickett? Are you all right?"

Man and wife hastily donned their dressing gowns, then Pickett opened the door to reveal the innkeeper's widow, also clad in a dressing gown and with her graying hair in a thick braid down her back, holding a brass candlestick in her hand.

"We're unharmed, Mrs. Hawkins," he assured her. "Unfortunately, I can't say the same for your window."

Her gaze shifted past them to take in the gaping window and the fragments of glass littering the floor. "Oh, my! Who could have done such a wicked thing?"

"Someone who doesn't like tourists, apparently," Pickett suggested, offering her the note.

"Well, I won't deny there are some folk who feel that way, but you can be sure I'm not one of them!" declared Mrs. Hawkins. "You're welcome to stay at the Hart and Hound for as long as you please, but although I'll sweep up the glass first thing in the morning, I don't know when I can have the glazier in to replace it. Of course, in the meantime, you'll want a different room. I'm afraid that poet has the second-best, but the room down the corridor has the same view as this, although it's a mite smaller. The room, that is, not the view. Oh dear, oh dear, I'm that sorry! I wouldn't have had this happen for anything!"

The next few minutes were busy ones, as Pickett and Julia gathered their belongings and followed their apologetic hostess down the corridor to a much smaller room that nevertheless had the advantage of an intact window.

"She wasn't lying when she said it was smaller," Julia observed, after Mrs. Hawkins had left them, with still more apologies and a not very confidently expressed hope that they would sleep soundly for what remained of the night. "Still, I suppose it will have to do."

"It's plenty large enough for one." Seeing her puzzled expression, Pickett added, "Julia, you're going back home first thing in the morning."

At any other time, in any other circumstances, her heart would have rejoiced to hear him refer to her house on Curzon Street as "home," for he had not always felt that way about it. Now, however, all she could think was that he intended to send her back to London without him.

"Pray don't make me," she pleaded. "John, don't—"

"Sweetheart, hear me out. Self-absorbed poets and bucolic love triangles are all very amusing in their way, but there's something more sinister at work here. Someone wants you gone—one way or the other."

"How do you know it was meant for me?" she challenged. "Perhaps he—assuming it is a 'he'—has discovered your connection with Bow Street, and wants *you* gone?"

"Who saw Ned Hawkins pushed off a cliff?"

"Yes, but I couldn't tell who did it!"

"But he doesn't know that, does he? He's tried to kill you once already, and now—this." He made a vague gesture in the direction of the ruined room at the other end of the corridor. "What if that rock had struck you? What if it had been intended to do exactly that? Please, Julia, if you love me, go back to London."

Put that way, of course, there was only one thing she could do.

* * *

It was a wan and heavy-eyed pair who waited for the Royal Mail coach to depart the next morning, for neither of them had slept much, having spent most of the night in the rather desperate lovemaking of two people who didn't know when, or if, they would have the chance again. In that regard, it reminded Julia of the night they had consummated their accidental marriage as Pickett had lain on what they both had feared might be his deathbed. The memory brought tears to Julia's eyes, and she fumbled in her reticule for a hand-kerchief.

"Please, pay me no heed," Julia said, seeing Pickett regarding her in some alarm. "I've become a veritable watering pot of late."

Privately, Pickett wondered how any man could "pay no heed" to a woman—particularly *this* woman—sobbing her heart out at the prospect of separation from him. "Julia— sweetheart—"

"I know," she assured him, stanching the flow of tears with an effort. "I don't like it, I don't want to go, but I do understand. You will write to me, will you not?"

He nodded. "I promise."

"Every day?"

"I don't know that I'll have anything to say every day," he confessed, somewhat taken aback by this request, "except to tell you how much I love you and miss you." He immediately wished the words unsaid, for they set off her tears again.

At last the Royal Mail coach drew into the yard, its maroon and black body gleaming in the morning sun. As the sweating horses were unhitched and a fresh team led out, the sack of incoming mail was tossed down and the mail bound for London and points south was lashed to the baggage platform in its place—an operation that, in the opinion of at least two of its observers, was accomplished far too quickly. Pickett handed up Julia's considerable luggage, and this too was tied fast.

They had said their goodbyes earlier, and in private, so when the step was lowered and the passengers began to board, Pickett merely took her gloved hands and pressed first one and then the other to his lips. "Take good care of these hands," he told her. "You hold my heart in them, you know."

"I'll take very good care of it," she whispered, and allowed him to hand her up into the vehicle.

The door was closed, the coachman touched the whip to the horses' flanks, and the carriage lurched slowly forward. Julia, seated against the window, gave Pickett a brave little smile and wiggled her fingers in farewell.

It was the smile, and the effort it obviously cost her, that undid him. Suddenly he was moving across the stable yard in the coach's wake, walking faster and faster until he drew abreast of the carriage at a dead run. In the meantime, Julia had disappeared from the window, and a moment the carriage door swung open and she leaped out of the vehicle and into his arms.

The coachman sawed on the reins, cursing fluently. "Damn fool woman, jumping from a moving carriage!" Still muttering imprecations under his breath, he untied the rope holding Julia's bags and threw them down, then secured the rope once more, whipped up his horses, and was once again on his way, albeit not without one last, disgusted glare for the couple whose antics had put him almost three minutes behind schedule.

Neither Julia nor Pickett, kissing passionately in the middle of the yard in full view of half a dozen grinning stable hands, paid him the slightest heed.

* * *

"All right, then," Pickett said as he returned with Julia to the inn, holding her tightly to his side as if he feared the Royal Mail coach might return and attempt to carry her off by force, "the first thing we're going to do is find out who threw that rock."

"So how do we do that?"

"I want to take a closer look at that paper. Not at the words written on it, but the paper itself. If we're lucky, it will give us some clue as to who wrote it."

"And if we're not?"

He sighed. "If we're not, then it's back to trying to find a match for the handwriting. It won't be easy," he added hastily, before she could point out his lack of success in this area thus far. "I'm going to have to search farther afield than just the inn's guest register."

"Where, then?" she asked. They had entered the inn by this time, and she had to raise her voice slightly to be heard over the two indignant middle-aged women at the counter.

"—won't stay another minute in an establishment where we might be murdered in our beds!" one of them railed at Mrs. Hawkins, who tried without success to sooth her ruffled feathers.

"I'm sure no one is going to be murdered, Miss Featherstone," she said placatingly, although Pickett might have disabused her of this notion, had he been so inclined. "My poor Ned's death was a tragic accident—"

"*She* is Miss Edith Featherstone; *I* am Miss Feather-stone," the elder of the two ladies put in. "And say what you will about your husband, that commotion last night was no accident!"

"No, it was a cruel prank. But no one was hurt," the innkeeper's widow insisted.

Julia regarded Pickett with eyes wide, but he silenced her with a look and gestured with a nod of his head toward the stairs. They would have made a discreet escape to their own room, but alas, discretion was difficult to achieve while burdened down with two portmanteaux and a couple of bandboxes. Pickett accidentally bumped one of the latter against the newel post.

"Why, look here!" Mrs. Hawkins exclaimed eagerly. "Here's Mrs. Pickett deciding to stay after all, and if *she* has no fears of remaining under my roof, I'm sure *you* can have no cause for worry! It was her window that was broken, you know."

"What Mrs. Pickett does is entirely beside the point," returned Miss Featherstone, unimpressed. "She may do as she pleases, for she has a Man to protect her. But as for my sister and me, traveling without the Protection of a Man's Presence, we intend to remove to the Golden Feather for the remainder of our holiday. Pray send someone up to fetch our things."

Having no other choice, Miss Hawkins summoned her stepson and gave him the necessary orders. He obeyed with obvious reluctance, but not before making a point of relieving Pickett of Julia's bags and carrying them up the stairs.

"Poor Mrs. Hawkins!" Julia exclaimed once Jem had left them for the far more disagreeable task of fetching the bags of the departing guests. "I had never considered that her other guests might be frightened off."

"It's interesting that their imaginations should leap to murder," Pickett said thoughtfully. "Or perhaps not their imaginations, after all. I couldn't help remembering all those capital letters and thinking here was a person who spoke that way."

"That in itself doesn't mean anything. I write with a fair amount of capitals myself," Julia said, thinking rather guiltily of her own letter, which was even now on its way to her sister in Somersetshire. "It was the fashion when my governess was young, and so that was the way she taught Claudia and me. But as for the Misses Featherstone, I should think their mention of murder was no more than the megrims of a pair of spinster ladies traveling alone," Julia said. "Although it would seem to suggest that they suspect Ned's death was something more than the accident the coroner's jury ruled it."

"If that were the case, they would be wise to keep their suspicions to themselves, else they might find a rock thrown through their own window," Pickett said. "Although it's not a bad idea, moving across the street to the Golden Feather. I'm tied to the Hart and Hound for the duration, since my instructions specified it, but if you would prefer to—"

"I'm staying with you," Julia said, tugging on the lapel of his coat in a gesture half possessive and half protective. "Whatever is happening here, we'll see it through together."

Pickett could find nothing to dispute in this very admirable sentiment, so after sealing this pact with a kiss, he turned his attention to the writing table (considerably smaller than the one positioned beneath the window of their previous room) and the three missives that sat on it, weighted down by the rock that had been the means of delivery for the most recent one. As he had expected, the one summoning him to Bow Street was written in a very different hand, but as for the other two—

"It's a match," he told Julia, holding them side by side for her inspection. "The note tied to the rock and the long letter, the one to James Sullivan of Dublin from the mysterious E.G.B. Look at the capital 'G's and the lowercase 'm's and 'a's."

She leaned closer for a better look, then nodded. "They're the same, or very similar."

"Too similar to be a coincidence, I think," he agreed. "Then, too, the paper is the same. Hold it up to the window, and you can see the watermark. There's just a bit of that same mark on the note, where the scrap of paper was torn from a larger sheet.

"John, you don't suppose we might find the rest of this sheet of paper lying about somewhere, do you? After all, the note didn't require much, and paper is too expensive to waste."

He shook his head. "Expensive or not, if I were going to tear off a strip, write a threatening note on it, tie it to a rock, and throw it through a window, I would consign the rest of that sheet to the fire at the earliest opportunity, and never mind the cost."

"Yes, but not everyone is as clever as you, darling."

"If I were as clever as all that, you would be on a mail coach halfway to Penrith by now," he grumbled. "Still, searching for a torn piece of paper that might belong to anyone would be a bit like looking for the proverbial needle in the haystack."

"I suppose so," she conceded with a sigh. "All right, then, what do we do next?"

"We try to determine whose paper this is."

"But you just said—"

"I said it would likely be a waste of time trying to find the sheet of paper that the note was torn from," Pickett reminded her. "But it has a watermark, and watermarks can be traced."

"And there's a stationer's shop just down the street!" exclaimed Julia, getting into the spirit of the thing.

"Exactly! All we need is an excuse to call there."

"Oh, but I have one," she informed him smugly.

"You do?"

"I do. When I noticed you writing with your left hand, I thought I needed to purchase a few quills for you. I had thought to wait until we returned to London, but it will serve as a good excuse now—provided, of course, that a village stationer's shop carries quills made from the feathers on the right side of the goose."

Pickett frowned. "There's a difference?"

"There is—as you will soon see."

With this confident prediction, she took his arm and they set out for the shop of Mr. Hiram Copley, Stationer. The proprietor of this establishment proved to be a tall, wiry man of about forty, with round spectacles perched precariously on the end of a rather beaky nose. Like the other shops along the High Street, Mr. Copley's establishment offered a selection of items far beyond what one might expect to find in a village the size of Banfell. Besides the right-wing goose quills (which, at Julia's request, the stationer produced from a shelf behind the counter, there usually not being a demand for quills from this side of the bird), there were the more specialized quills favored by those artists who worked in pen and ink: swan quills for broad lines and crow quills for fine ones, as well as the goose quills from the left wing which were the writing instruments of choice for most penmen.

As Julia conducted her business with Mr. Copley, Pickett wandered farther into the deep, narrow showroom. He found one of his fellow guests from the Hart and Hound, the artistic fellow with the sketchpad, inspecting a selection of colored inks in red, blue, yellow, and green; apparently his artistic efforts were not limited to the charcoal he'd been using in the public room on the day of their arrival. He gave Pickett a nod of recognition but showed no sign of desiring to engage him in conversation, for which Pickett could only be grateful. Beyond the artist, a number of stretched canvases in varying sizes stood propped up against the wall, and beyond them—

Beyond them was what Pickett had come for. Here was a selection of foolscap of varying quality, which might be bought in quantities ranging from the quire (for those customers whom two dozen sheets would suffice) all the way up to the bale (for those patrons wealthy enough to purchase almost five thousand sheets at once). On a shelf above them, and in significantly smaller quantities, was a rather smaller selection of parchment and vellum, for patrons such as solicitors, who required the more durable (and far more expensive) hides of calf, kid, or lamb that were preferred for legal documents.

Ignoring these last, Pickett lifted one of the loose sheets of foolscap and raised it to the light that filtered to the back of the shop from its front window. This, alas, was not much, but even in the dimness he could pick out the faint cap-and-bells watermark that had given this particular size of paper its name. But the watermark on the letter, and the partial mark on the note, had portrayed not only the traditional jester's cap, but the fool himself depicted in profile. Pickett picked up a sheet from another, slightly more expensive quire, and repeated the process.

On the third try, he found what he was looking for. He'd been reluctant to take the letter he'd found on Ned Hawkins'

169

body for the purpose of comparison, even though it contained several examples of the full watermark, for fear someone might recognize it and demand to know how it had come to be in his possession. Still, he had the note with its fragment. He removed this from his pocket, and held it up to the light. The partial mark on the narrow strip of paper appeared, at first glance, to match the complete specimen on the pristine paper offered for sale. Just to be sure, he raised it to the light again, and positioned the note on top of it. The marks aligned perfectly.

His mind made up, Pickett took the quire of paper to the front of the store, where Julia was concluding her business.

"Excuse me," he addressed the stationer, "I wonder if you could tell me a little about this particular paper."

"Why, certainly," said Mr. Copley, all eagerness to sell a quire—perhaps even a ream—of one of the more expensive papers he carried. "It's an excellent quality, made entirely of linen rag—none of the cotton one sees in cheaper papers, you know."

"Do you sell much of it?"

The man's face fell. "Well, I wouldn't say 'much.' The cost is prohibitive for many, of course. Still, visitors to the Lakes often like to write letters to their friends and family, and for them, only the best will do. Then, too, I try to keep sufficient quantities on hand for the local gentry, who are pleased not to be obliged to have their writing papers sent all the way from London."

"Could this particular paper be purchased in London?"

"Of course!" the stationer boasted. "I take pride in

offering my patrons the same little luxuries they might find in London or Bath. Mind you, I have to charge a bit more, as there are the added costs of having the goods brought up from London, but for the more affluent of my customers, the convenience is worth the extra expense."

"And what customers are those?"

"Locals, or visitors?" Mr. Copley asked, his brow puckering.

Pickett shrugged. "Either. Both."

"Well, I couldn't say who the visitors are, for I don't know their names. As for the locals—" He broke off, his eyes growing as round as the lenses in front of them. "I say! Are you the Londoners whose window was broken last night?"

"How do you know about that?" asked Pickett, taken aback.

The stationer merely shrugged. "News travels fast in the country. Besides, Jem Hawkins came in as soon as I opened up this morning, wanting paper to cover the window—not that kind," he added quickly, glancing down at the linen rag foolscap in Pickett's hand. "The coarse brown stuff. Something to cover the hole until new glass can be put in. Not but what there'll be bigger holes to be filled before long, I'm thinking."

"Oh?" Pickett asked, the stationer's words having conjured up gruesome images of empty graves.

"Young Jem's been mad for his da to knock out most of the back wall and put in big windows looking out over the fells," was Mr. Copley's rather more mundane explanation. "Well, and I'm not saying he isn't right, what with the Hart

171

and Hound losing patrons every day to Jedidiah Tyson and his assemblies."

"I should think so," Pickett agreed. "What were Ned Hawkins's objections?"

"Only that his father—or mayhap it was his grand-father—had built the place, and what was good enough for Grandda Hawkins ought to be good enough for young Jem. Besides that, the wall Jem is wanting to knock out was the very spot where King Charles—not the one what lost his head, but his son, the Merry Monarch himself—once sat at a table with a tankard of the inn's best cider on one knee and Grandda Hawkins's sister on the other. Begging your pardon, ma'am," he offered as a quick aside to Julia, "but, well, you know how folks do like to talk."

"I do indeed," she assured him. "It is a very curious thing, but behavior which would be quite shocking if it were to take place today seems merely quaint when viewed from a distance of a century and a half."

"Very true, ma'am," the shopkeeper said, much struck by the truth of this observation. "If you'll pardon me for seeming to make light of what must have given you quite a fright, ma'am, mayhap in a few years this business with your window will be no more than a thrilling tale to tell your children someday."

Pickett rather doubted this, but paid a shilling for the quire of paper (he could do no less, after having expressed such an interest in it), and this, in addition to the purchases Julia had already made, rendered the stationer genuinely sorry to see them go. Not until after they had been bowed from the premises with his sincerest regrets that someone should play so shabby a trick on them—one of these tourist sorts with too much time on his hands, no doubt—along with his fervently expressed hope that they would honor his humble establishment with another visit before they returned to London, did Julia turn to her husband with a puzzled look.

"You never did press him for names."

"No," Pickett confessed. "I didn't want to appear too interested, not with one of our fellow guests in the rear of the shop."

"One of—was there? Who was it?"

"The artist with the sketchpad."

"You don't suppose *he* threw the rock, do you?"

Pickett shook his head. "I have no reason to think so, but I don't want him going back to the inn and telling anyone we're making inquiries, either. Then, too, I'm not sure I would have got any more information, even if I'd asked. You heard Mr. Copley dismiss the incident as no more than a shabby trick played by a tourist. Depend upon it, even if he suspected one of the locals, he would have felt honor-bound to protect him."

Julia conceded the point with a sigh. "The tourist trade does seem to be regarded as rather a mixed blessing, doesn't it? The locals resent them—or should I say 'us'?—even as they welcome the added custom." He made no response, and she looked up to find him staring thoughtfully into space. "John? What are you thinking?"

"I was just thinking that poets must have to buy a great deal of paper."

"Writing bad poetry isn't a crime," Julia objected. "Although it is a curious circumstance that Percival Hart-song's given name is actually Edward, for there was an Edward mentioned in the letter, was there not? Ned's letter, I mean—the long one from someone who signed himself E.G.B."

At this reminder, Pickett shook his head as if to banish the notion. "Yes, and that is the biggest point in his defense." Seeing her puzzled look, he explained, "I saw his handwriting in the inn register, remember? I didn't realize at the time that Edward Gape and Percival Hartsong were one and the same, but I do remember seeing the name and rejecting the signature as a possible match."

"Then what, if anything, did we learn from visiting Mr. Copley's shop?"

"Not much," he confessed. "It appears that the paper was very probably purchased there, but there is still the chance that it was already in the possession of some guest when he arrived in Banfell. You made sure to have a ready supply of paper in that portable desk of yours before we ever left London, didn't you?"

"My dear John!" she exclaimed, torn between exasperation and amusement, "Surely you are not accusing me of throwing a rock through my own window!"

"Not at all—merely proving my point that the paper need not have been purchased here at all."

"So where does that leave us now?" she asked, rather crestfallen.

Pickett lifted one shoulder, indicating the package of

paper and quills, now wrapped with coarse brown paper and tied with string, which he carried under his arm. "At least I can replace the writing paper I wasted in a futile effort to decipher that blasted letter. Then, too, I'll have something to use in writing to Mr. Colquhoun. He needs to know what's happened here, and that I'll need more time to get to the bottom of it. As for the letter," he continued, setting his jaw, "We're back to the handwriting. I must find a match for it."

"But you've already looked, and found nothing."

"I've looked in the Hart and Hound's register, but no further," Pickett said. "I have to cast a wider net, that's all."

"And how, pray, do you intend to do that?"

They had reached the inn by this time, and Pickett flexed his arm, tightening it about Julia's fingers resting in the crook of his elbow. The message was clear: He would say no more until they reached the privacy of their own room. She bided her time in patience as they climbed the stair, but returned to the subject as soon as the door was closed behind them.

"Well?" she asked impatiently. "What do you intend to do now?"

"I have to find a way to look at the handwriting of people who aren't guests at the Hart and Hound. The local gentry, for instance, who would be able to afford paper of this quality, and any visitors who might be staying at the Golden Feather."

"John!" Julia exclaimed, her eyes widening as enlightenment dawned. "The subscription book!"

"That, and the church registry. The guest register at the Feather might be worth a look, too, as some of the guests staying there might have no interest in attending the assemblies, or might be unwilling to pay the necessary half-guinea per person for admission." He sighed. "Although how I'm to do that, I have no idea. It's doubtful that Tyson would hand it over to me without requiring some explanation."

"The same holds true for his subscription book, I suppose," she concurred, albeit not without sympathy.

"Oh, as for the subscription book, I had hoped my clever wife might be willing to take on the task."

"Are you certain?" she asked, torn between eagerness at being given so active a role in the investigation and fear of wounding his pride by encroaching upon what had, after all, been his area of expertise long before she had met him. She'd made that mistake once before, with disastrous results.

"Absolutely," he assured her. "As I told you before, I'm afraid pretending to be disappointed at the cancellation of Tyson's assembly would tax my acting ability far beyond what is credible."

"Very well, but be warned that when the assemblies resume next week, I shall not allow you to wriggle out of escorting me."

"All the more reason to settle this case without delay," said Pickett, mopping his brow.

10

In Which Mr. and Mrs. Pickett
Search for a Fine Italian Hand

A short time later, Julia left the inn with the letter—the long one that Pickett had found in the dead man's pocket, which would, as he had pointed out, give her a larger sample from which to determine a match—tucked away in her reticule. She waited as the stagecoach from Penrith rattled into the yard trailing a cloud of dust, then crossed the High Street and entered the elegantly appointed vestibule of the Golden Feather.

"Ah, Mrs. Pickett!" cried Jedidiah Tyson. He seemed not at all surprised to see her, and Julia made a mental note to inform her husband of this curious circumstance. "Am I to deduce by your charming presence that you have decided to spend the rest of your holiday beneath my humble roof? An honor for my establishment, ma'am, and one I'm sure you will not regret."

"I'm afraid not," Julia said, allowing the merest trace of annoyance to color her voice. "Mr. Pickett is quite determined to remain at the Hart and Hound. Truth to tell, he seems to feel some sense of obligation toward Mrs. Hawkins, perhaps because he was one of the three men who found her husband's body."

"His scruples no doubt do him credit, but surely his first obligation is to see to the safety of his wife," protested the innkeeper.

Not even for the sake of an investigation could Julia allow this slight against her husband. "Oh, he tried," she said. "He put me on the Royal Mail coach the very next day and would have dispatched me back to London as if I were a sack of mail, but I"—she broke off, blushing becomingly—"well, I'm afraid I jumped off."

There was no reason not to recount this event, as it—and the very public display of affection that had followed—had no doubt become common knowledge by now. The rather knowing look with which he regarded her seemed to confirm this assumption.

"Yes, well, I'm sure London's loss is Banfell's gain. But if you won't be requiring a room, then how may I be of service to you?"

"It's about the assemblies," Julia confessed, her mouth drooping. "I was so looking forward to attending. It's such a pity the one scheduled for tonight must be cancelled."

"Oh, but it hasn't been!"

"It hasn't?"

Mr. Tyson had the grace to look ashamed. "You'll be

thinking I should have called it off, what with Ned right across the street not yet cold in his grave. But, well, his grace is in residence—the Duke of Ramsdale, you know, who usually spends the summer months in Brighton—and I wouldn't want to be behindhand in offering him the hospitality of my establishment. Besides, my noble patrons—and those of the Hart and Hound, like you and your husband—wouldn't have known Ned Hawkins from Adam, at least not in the usual scheme of things. Why should you be denied your pleasures on account of the death of a stranger? Then, too, there's the practical matter of refunding the admission fees of everyone who's bought a ticket, and paying the musicians a fee for cancelling, and I don't know what-all else. It just seemed simpler to go ahead and have the thing. Of course," he added somewhat belatedly, "if the scruples of some folks make them balk at an evening of merrymaking, well, that's their choice, and I'll not think the worse of them for it."

Drawing a bow at a venture, Julia smiled mischievously at him. "And while one might think Ned would take some satisfaction in knowing that he had forced you to cancel your assemblies, I daresay he would secretly find it galling to think he might owe you any gratitude for rendering him this courtesy."

Tyson chuckled richly at this suggestion. "Aye, you've the right of it there, ma'am. Truth to tell," he confessed, his smile fading, "I'm going to miss old Ned."

He seemed surprised by this discovery, and Julia, observing his reaction, was convinced he was telling the truth. She filed this revelation away for her husband's consideration, then turned her attention to the task that had brought her to the Golden Feather.

"I suspect he would feel the same, were your situations reversed," Julia assured him warmly. "But if the assembly is to be held tonight, it appears my errand is wasted. I had thought to have a look at the subscription book in order to see if there are any of my London acquaintances presently staying in Banfell upon whom I should leave my card. But if I am to see them tonight in any case—" She broke off, shrugging her shoulders. "Still, since I have come all this way, might I perhaps steal a peek at the book and see what friends I may expect to meet tonight? Half the pleasure, you know, is in the anticipation."

"Oh, of course!" Tyson exclaimed, as if she had come all the way from London for this purpose, instead of merely walking across the street. "If you will follow me?"

He led the way upstairs, just as he had on the day she had signed the book, and here she encountered her first obstacle: having delivered her to her destination, Jedidiah Tyson now refused to leave.

"As you can see, each person who signs the book also writes down his direction. Oh, but you already know this," he corrected himself hastily, "for you would have written down your own when you signed the book, would you not? Ah, yes, there it is!" he exclaimed, pointing with one bony finger to the line that read *Mr. and Mrs. John Pickett, 4 Bow St., London.*

"Thank you, Mr. Tyson, you have been very helpful," she said, gently dismissive. "Still, I don't doubt you are very busy, and I would not want to keep you from your work—"

"It's no trouble at all serving so charming a lady as yourself," he declared gallantly. "Now, as you can see, the Golden Feather entertains visitors from across the length and breadth of England, as well as Scotland and Ireland. As I recall, we even had a French couple staying here a few years ago during the Peace of Amiens, short-lived though it was—the peace, I mean, not my French guests' stay—"

A bell sounded somewhere below, and Julia silently blessed the stagecoach from Penrith.

"Dear me, duty calls! I'm afraid you'll have to excuse me, Mrs. Pickett," said Tyson, bowing himself from the room. "So sorry—your most obedient—"

At last he was gone. Julia fumbled in her reticule for the letter, then spread it out and quickly scanned the signatures written in the book, comparing them to the handwriting on the letter. There were a couple of bold scrawls that appeared promising at first glance, but upon closer inspection, several of the individual letters were quite different—the capital "G"s Pickett had noted, as well as the capital "L"s and lowercase letters with tails, such as "g" and "y". She did, in fact, come across the names of two or three acquaintances, but far from sending cards, as she had told Mr. Tyson, she resolved to avoid these people if at all possible, lest they publicly snub her husband and thus damage his credibility amongst the locals.

By the time the innkeeper had shown the new arrivals to their chambers and returned to the room where the assemblies were held, Julia was ready for him. She thanked him again for allowing her to examine the subscription book, expressed her eagerness to attend the assembly that very night, and took her leave.

* * *

While Julia invaded the Golden Feather, Pickett betook himself to the parish church. He found the church open, which was encouraging, but occupied, which was not: At the front of the chancel, a man dressed in rusty black arranged silver candlesticks on the altar with painstaking precision.

"Excuse me," Pickett called as he strode up the aisle.

The clergyman turned, and Pickett beheld a fellow no older than himself and quite possibly younger, with gingery hair and a scattering of freckles across his nose. Pickett found himself thinking of his brother-in-law, second husband of Julia's sister, who would have taken holy orders had circumstances not dictated otherwise.

"You're the curate?" he asked.

"Yes, indeed," the young man said, extending his hand in confirmation. "Philip Bell, at your service."

"John Pickett." He returned the curate's handshake. "I was wondering if I might have a look at the parish registry."

"Oh, I don't—that is, I suppose—" stammered the curate, clearly taken aback by this simple request. He gave a rather sheepish grin. "Truth to tell, I don't exactly know. Mr. Richardson—the vicar, you know—has gone to Penrith for a few days, and I am left in charge in his absence. It's my first time—I was only ordained a few weeks ago—and I don't want to do anything he would not like." He glanced back at the candles on the altar and made an infinitesimal adjustment to the one on the left.

"I would not ask such a thing," Pickett said, seeing some explanation was called for, "but while my wife and I are visiting the Lake District, I thought I would try and find my mother's baptismal record, as she may have been born in Banfell or hereabouts." In fact, Pickett had no idea who his mother was, much less where she had been born, but at the moment Banfell seemed as good a place as any other. "I would wait until the vicar's return, but I have no idea how long I'll be in the area." This much, at least, was the truth.

"Well, I suppose it can't hurt," conceded the curate.

Abandoning his task, he led the way to the lectern and withdrew an enormous calf-bound volume from its shelf. "The record here goes back to 1765," he said, setting it atop the lectern with an effort. "If you need the one earlier than that, I can fetch it for you."

If his unknown mother had been more than nineteen years old at the time of his birth, Pickett would have been obliged to accept this offer, for he had been born in 1784. But as he had no intention of examining records earlier than the last few months, he was able to assure the curate with perfect sincerity that this volume would be sufficient to tell him anything he might wish to know.

In this, it soon transpired, he was overly optimistic. He saw no need to trace the entries back further than, say, six months; surely if Ned Hawkins had discovered any havey-cavey dealings before that time, he must have sent his anonymous summons to Bow Street much earlier. But although Pickett examined each entry all the way to the beginning of 1809—by which time he could have recognized the vicar's spidery script at fifty paces—he found amongst the marriages (recorded not by the Reverend Mr. Richardson, but by the bride or bridegroom) and baptisms (recorded by the infant's proud parents) no match for the threatening note that had accompanied the rock thrown through the window. At length, he was forced to concede defeat. After folding the note and tucking it back into his coat pocket, he closed the registry and returned it to its shelf within the lectern, then thanked the curate for his assistance while admitting, quite truthfully, that no, he had not found the information he sought.

Alas, there were still more disappointments in store, for upon his return to the Hart and Hound he was met by Julia, who, after confessing that her efforts had been as fruitless as his own, imparted the further information that he was to have the pleasure of escorting her that very evening to an assembly at the Golden Feather.

11

In Which John Pickett Trips the Light Fantastic

A t some minutes before eight o'clock that evening, Mr. and Mrs. John Pickett descended the stairs of the Hart and Hound, Pickett clad in the dark blue tailcoat and black pantaloons which comprised the only set of evening clothes he possessed, and Julia in all the splendor of pale blue Urling's net over a satin slip dyed in the same shade and shot through with silver threads. Their appearance in all their finery was sufficient to draw the eyes of everyone in the public room— including Lizzie's, which filled with tears as she looked up from wiping down the bar with a cloth and exclaimed, "Oh, how I wish I could go!"

"Now, Lizzie," chided her stepmother, albeit not without sympathy, "how would it look, you going off dancing and your father only buried yesterday? There'll be other dances, just see if there won't."

"Not for me." She shook her head sadly. "Percival had

bought me a ticket for *this* one! Who knows if he'll ever buy me another, or even how long he'll be in Banfell at all?"

Mrs. Hawkins looked as if the poet's departure could not come soon enough to suit her, but remained stoically silent on this subject, satisfying herself with drawing a fresh tankard from one of the kegs on the wall behind her and handing it to Lizzie, saying, "Take this to Mr. Graham over in the corner, there's a good girl."

Lizzie's demeanor as she carried out this errand was so uncharacteristically docile that Pickett felt compelled to offer some word of comfort. "I should think it will be rather a flat affair, coming so soon after your da's funeral," he said, then added with perfect truth, "I wouldn't be going myself, if Mrs. Pickett didn't have her heart set on it."

If he had truly thought the funeral the previous morning would have a dampening effect on the festivities at the Golden Feather thirty-six hours later, Pickett was soon made aware of the enormity of his error. As he and Julia crossed the High Street, they were obliged to thread their way between a number of carriages cluttering the thoroughfare—obviously the local gentry would be well represented, in addition to those patrons on holiday who had taken up temporary residence at the Golden Feather. From the moment they stepped inside, Pickett could hear the babble of voices and the scraping of violins wafting down from the floor above, and could see the crush of people ascending (or attempting to ascend) the gracefully curved staircase. He and Julia took their places among these, and eventually gained the upper floor and the large room where they had signed the subscription book.

To say it had been transformed would be an understatement. Every one of the chairs along the walls was occupied, and under Jedidiah Tyson's direction, a man (hastily rousted from the kitchen, if the white apron swathing his person and the faint aroma of onions clinging to him were anything to judge by) was busily engaged in setting up more. At the far end of the room, half a dozen musicians tuned their instruments, while all about its center little clusters of people, from elegantly dressed gentlefolk to prosperous local merchants wearing their Sunday best, chatted in hushed tones. Ned Hawkins might not have approved of his rival's assemblies, but it was clear that he was the main attraction at this one, as everyone seized the opportunity to ask the questions and put forth the speculations that courtesy had forbidden at the funeral the day before.

As they moved beyond the doorway, a buzz of attention greeted them, and Pickett stood a bit taller, proud and at the same time humbled by the knowledge that he bore on his arm the most beautiful woman in the room. Gradually, however, he became aware that the object of all this attention was not his wife, at least not entirely; in fact, the hubbub seemed to be centered on some point behind her. He turned and saw a man standing in the doorway, a silver-haired man of late middle age who surveyed the company through his quizzing glass with an air of bored indifference. Clearly, Mr. Tyson's hopes had been realized: The duke was in attendance.

"Welcome, your grace, welcome!" cried Mr. Tyson, abandoning a less exalted guest in mid-sentence in order to give the new arrival his full attention. "So pleased your grace could honor our little entertainment with your presence. Will you do us the honor of opening the dancing? Lady Marchant is here, if you would care to partner her. You are acquainted with her ladyship, are you not? Good, good!"

The duke bowed over the hand of Sir Henry Marchant's wife, and as his grace led his partner into the center of the room, Julia watched with a smile, determined not to betray to her husband for a moment her awareness that not so very long ago it would have been she, as a viscountess and the highest-ranking lady in the room, who would have opened the dancing on the duke's arm, rather than Lady Marchant, the wife of a mere baronet. Thankfully, she had not long to wait for a partner; even those amongst the gentry who were un-acquainted with the late Lord Fieldhurst needed no knowledge of precedence to solicit the hand of a beautiful woman whose husband seemed disinclined to partner her.

Pickett, for his part, contented himself with prowling about the perimeter of the room, listening to what snatches of conversation he could without appearing to eavesdrop. In truth, he was less interested in the idle chatter of the gentry than he was in the thoughts of those locals of the middling classes who had paid their half-guinea for the privilege of rubbing shoulders with their betters. He had seen the coroner enter the room with his wife, a long-nosed female in purple satin, as well as the physician acting as escort to a blushing damsel of about eighteen who was clearly his daughter. The stationer, Mr. Copley, was also in attendance—talking shop, no doubt, with the bookseller whose establishment shared a wall with his own. The death of Ned Hawkins constituted the topic of more than one discussion, and once or twice Pickett overheard low-voiced speculations as to whether the innkeeper might have been pushed off the cliff, and who might have had reason to do such a thing. Mr. Hetherington might have been the first to voice the possibility aloud, but he was obviously not the only one to entertain such a thought.

As for who might have done the deed, opinions were mixed. Jedidiah Tyson's name came up more than once, but was dismissed almost as frequently; one man dressed in the full-skirted frock coat of the previous century appeared to speak for many when he gave it as his opinion that whatever their professed hatred of each other, neither Hawkins nor Tyson would have wanted to put so irrevocable an end to a rivalry which secretly brought so much pleasure to both men.

Lizzie was the object of considerable censure for her possible rôle in the death of her parent, to the point that Pickett thought it was probably best that she had been unable to attend after all. While some held that the dishonorable attentions of "that poet fellow" were behind the tragedy and others cited Ben Wilson's blighted hopes, all agreed that Lizzie's behavior was certainly no better than it should have been, and they would hate to see any daughter of their own conducting herself in such a way that she could only be deemed a shameless flirt.

As for the "poet fellow" himself, he was in attendance and, having failed to overcome Lizzie's scruples (or, rather, her stepmama's) and prevail upon her to attend, was much inclined to sulk. He did partner the physician's pretty daughter for the first set (making it clear by his demeanor what a singular honor he was bestowing upon her) and partnered Julia (with considerably more courtesy) for the second. It was during this one that Pickett's attention was distracted from the revolting sight by a late arrival. Ben Wilson stood framed in the doorway, freshly washed and shaved and looking extremely uncomfortable in his best Sunday clothes, running a finger beneath his too-tight cravat as he surveyed the crowded assembly room. He frowned at the sight of Julia going down the dance with Percival Hartsong (Pickett entered into his sentiments entirely), but it was clearly not the poet whom he sought.

Pickett, seeing an opportunity to do a service for one who might yet prove to be a valuable source of information, made his way through the crowd to join him. "If you're looking for Miss Hawkins, she isn't here," he told the young farmer. "It wouldn't be proper, with her father just buried, you know." That these sentiments were voiced not by Lizzie, but by her stepmother, was a fact Pickett chose to keep to himself.

"So Lizzie's over across the way, then," Wilson said thoughtfully, jerking his head in the direction of the Hart and Hound.

Pickett nodded. "She was when my wife and I left there."

Wilson's grim visage lightened. "Much obliged to you," he said, and left the assembly without a backward glance.

Pickett turned his attention back to the dancers, and found that Percival Hartsong had surrendered Julia to her next partner, the Duke of Ramsdale. She and his grace appeared to be chatting easily, and as they turned in time to the music, her eyes met Pickett's across the room. She gave him a little smile and said something to the duke, whereupon his grace turned and nodded in his direction. Pickett could just imagine their conversation: "I had heard of your remarriage, but truth to tell, I could scarcely credit it . . ." "Yes, your grace, it is quite true —oh, look! There is my husband now . . ." Granted, she didn't *look* embarrassed, much less ashamed of him, but then, she didn't have to; he felt it keenly enough for both of them.

In fact, Pickett was quite out in his speculations. When the duke had solicited her hand for the new set, it had occurred to Julia that here was one who, as an aristocrat with a seat in the House of Lords, enjoyed franking privileges. Determined to discover what she might of some scheme through which the duke might be making his frank available to others—for a price—she accepted his proffered arm and allowed him to lead her into the set. As his grace had been an acquaintance, if not an intimate, of the late Lord Fieldhurst, she was prepared for the usual comments regarding the death of her first husband and her remarriage, two months before her year of mourning was complete, to a man whose position in Society was so far beneath hers as to be nonexistent.

"I'm sure it will come as no surprise to you when I say that Fieldhurst and I had not been in perfect charity with one another for some time," she replied in answer to the duke's rather dubiously expressed wishes for her future happiness. "And while I would never have wished for his death—and certainly not in such a way!—I cannot but feel that to some extent he was the author of his own downfall."

"This is plain speaking!" exclaimed the duke, more than a little shocked to hear such sentiments on the lips of one who had always seemed to him a demure and pretty-behaved young lady.

"Indeed it is, for I think too highly of your intelligence to fob you off with mere platitudes. As for my remarriage, while it is true that the doors of Almack's are no doubt forever closed to me, I have very few regrets. In truth, it is something of a relief to be freed from many of the obligations that accompany a lofty position—the hosting of dinner parties to advance my husband's career, for instance."

The movements of the dance brought them into view of Pickett, and thus the exchange of glances that had so cut up his peace.

"If you were to host a dinner party to advance your current husband's career," observed the duke, frowning, "you would no doubt be obliged to throw open your home to pickpockets and cutthroats!"

"Very true," she said, smiling at Pickett as her eyes met his across the crowded room. "And he would very likely be much more at ease in such company than in that of the Russian royalty by whom he was recently honored."

"Yes, I seem to recall reading something about that in the *Times*," conceded his grace, acknowledging Pickett with a nod.

"In fact," Julia continued, "the only things I truly miss about my first marriage are quite mundane ones, the sort of things one hardly notices until they are gone. The ability to send letters through the post free of charge, for instance. I was shocked to discover that it will cost my unfortunate parents fully a shilling to accept any letters I may choose to send them from Banfell!"

If Julia had hoped to be invited to avail herself of the duke's frank for the price of a penny, she was doomed to disappointment.

"At least when you are in London, your first husband's heir would surely be willing to perform this small service for you," suggested his grace.

Julia shook her head. "I fear you cannot be much acquainted with the new Lord Fieldhurst. Even if such a generous offer entered his head—and, I must confess, I think it highly unlikely—I should feel compelled to decline. He is persuaded I have brought shame and disgrace upon the family, and claims no longer to know me. Not, I must admit, that his acquaintance is any great loss."

It was clear that the duke had some knowledge of her late husband's cousin George, by reputation if not in person, for he threw back his head and laughed. Pickett, standing forlornly along the wall, saw that laugh and regretted once more the difference in their respective stations that left him looking on as other men partnered his wife.

Gradually, however, he became aware that this assembly was not like the private ball they'd attended in London a few weeks earlier. Here the middling classes and their betters intermingled, if not with equality, then certainly with a degree of intimacy that would have been unheard of in Town: Before taking the floor with Julia, the duke of Ramsdale had been partnering the solicitor's wife, while Lady Marchant was even now going down the dance with Mr. Copley, the stationer. This democratic mix of persons was reflected, too, in the dances being performed, for those members of the merchant class had, like himself, not had the advantage of dancing-masters. Instead, they would have learned by observation, imitation, and, perhaps, trial and error. And the steps did not appear complicated . . .

Pickett wasn't aware of having come to any decision, but as the set came to an end, he found himself making his way across the assembly room to where Julia was now besieged by half a dozen men ranging from baronets to bank clerks, all soliciting her for the next dance. Shouldering his way into the crowd, he held out his arm to her and, raising his voice slightly to be heard over the importunities of her various swains, said, "Mrs. Pickett, if you would do me the honor?"

Her gaze flew to his with a silent question and, finding the answer she sought, she laid her hand on his arm with great ceremony. "The honor is all mine, Mr. Pickett." Excusing herself to her court of admirers, she allowed him to lead her out of the little group, but once they could be assured of relative privacy, she asked, "Are you quite sure, John?"

"No," he replied without hesitation. "So if you ever want to dance with me, you'd best do it now, before I have time to think better of it."

She looked up at him, her heart in her glowing eyes. "It's all I've wanted, you know, ever since we left the Hart and Hound."

"Is it?" Pickett asked, conscience-stricken by the realization that his primary reason for soliciting her hand was not any desire to dance, nor even to please his wife, but to make it plain to the pack of jackals sniffing about her that she was *his*. "You never said."

"I didn't want to make you uncomfortable."

He turned to stare at her. "You think I've been comfortable, propping up the wall while every man jack in the place makes sheep's eyes at you?"

"John! Don't tell me you were jealous!" Julia exclaimed, not at all displeased by this realization.

"Let's just say that playing the fool over you is a privilege I reserve for myself," he said, and led her into the set just forming.

While it could not be said that he performed even the simplest country dance entirely without error, only the highest sticklers would have accused Pickett of making a fool of himself. Perhaps more to the point, he actually found himself enjoying the act, and when Julia pointed out (quite correctly) that to dance with no other partner save his own wife would be seen as the height—or, rather, the depth—of bad manners, he solicited the hand of the physician's young daughter for the next set, supposing that her youth and, presumably, her limited experience might make her less inclined to despise his own efforts. In fact, the unhappy result of this invitation was that that damsel spent the better part of the night sobbing into her pillow after being informed by her father that the partner to whom she had pinned all her romantic hopes was, in fact, a married man; but as Pickett was blissfully unaware of his effect on the young lady, he was in high good humor by the time he and his lady wife returned to the Hart and Hound.

So, too, was Lizzie. "Oh, is it over, then?" she asked, her gaze darting past them to the door through which Percival

Hartsong would no doubt soon enter.

"Not quite," Julia told her. "It lacks half an hour yet to twelve, but we decided to return before the crush of carriages begins to line up before the inn."

"Was it very grand? I can see it must have been, for you look like you've had a fine time." Her voice held a wistful note, but there were none of the tears that had accompanied their departure.

"Oh, I suppose it was well enough," Julia said without enthusiasm, not wishing to set her off again.

But Lizzie seemed not to hear her. "I've had a very nice time, too," she said, blushing becomingly. "Ben Wilson had bought a ticket, but when he saw I wasn't there, he came to keep me company here instead. And after he'd spent half a guinea on a ticket, too—only fancy! He asked me to go walking along the river, if it wouldn't distress me too much, being so close to the place where Papa fell, and when we did, he helped me pick wildflowers to throw into the water in Papa's memory, and he told me all about his new lambs with their sweet little black faces. He even promised to give me one for my very own."

"Aye, and where we'll put it when that sweet wee lamb becomes a full-grown sheep, I'm sure I don't know," her stepmother put in, albeit with an indulgent smile. "We'd have to slaughter it, and what you'll say to that, after giving it a name and raising it as a pet, I can just imagine! Still, I won't deny it was right kind of Ben. He always was a good lad, and you could do far worse for yourself."

"Stepmama—" Lizzie began, and Pickett and Julia made

their exit before the inevitable argument began in earnest.

"I didn't see Ben Wilson come in, did you?" Julia asked once they had reached the privacy of their own room.

Pickett nodded. "I believe you were dancing with a certain poet at the time."

"What else could I do?" she retorted playfully. "My husband hadn't yet screwed his courage to the sticking place. But was it you who suggested that he court Lizzie behind Percival's back?"

"I didn't have to," said Pickett, all innocence. "He's no fool, you know. Once he realized Hartsong had left him a clear field, no one had to tell him what to do. Although I think he would stand a better chance of success if his prospective mama-in-law would keep her opinions to herself and let him do his own courting."

"Yes, very likely." Her smile faded as a new thought occurred to her. "John, have you considered that perhaps the rock wasn't intended for me—for either of us—at all?"

Clearly, it had not. He stopped in his tracks and regarded her with dawning comprehension. " 'Go back where you came from,' " he quoted the anonymous message. "No name and no mention of London or anywhere else. You think it might have been young Wilson hoping to frighten off his rival and choosing the wrong window by mistake? But anyone who happened to be in the public room the day we arrived must have heard Ned Hawkins say what room he was taking us to. Hawkins had a booming voice, and he was making no effort to be quiet. That would seem to eliminate any possibility of Wilson's mistaking our room for Hartsong's."

"Not necessarily," she objected. "I'm not sure Ben Wilson was paying much attention to anything but his intended bride flirting with Percival Hartsong."

Pickett could not dispute this observation, but remained unconvinced nevertheless. "It seems, I don't know, out of character for him," he said, trying to put his doubts into words. "I can't picture Ben Wilson sneaking about throwing rocks. It seems to me he'd be much more likely to darken the fellow's daylights."

To Julia, who had no brothers, the cant term was unfamiliar. "Darken—?"

"Black his eyes," Pickett explained.

"Oh. Yes, I suppose you're right."

"Still, we had best consider the possibility—just to rule it out, if nothing else," Pickett conceded. "I only wish I could think of a plausible excuse for calling at his farm in the morning."

"Lambs," Julia said promptly.

"Beg pardon?"

"Lambs," she said again. "The sweet wee lambs with their little black faces. You have only to tell him how Lizzie waxed rhapsodic about them, leaving your wife with a burning desire to see the dear creatures for herself."

Pickett stroked his chin thoughtfully. "That might work," he said at last. "Of course, if Wilson agrees, I'll have to take you to his farm, and you'll have to behave with suitable enthusiasm."

Her face fell. "But won't you take me with you tomorrow?"

"I wish I could, but Wilson might be more inclined to talk to me if I come alone."

"Yes, and if he were to say anything useful in my hearing, well, one never knows when I might be seized with an urge to indulge in a good gossip with Lizzie or her stepmama, does one?"

He gave her a reproachful look. "I didn't mean it that way. But as for Ben Wilson, we don't know him well enough to be sure how his mind works, do we? He's tight-lipped even at the best of times."

"Very well, leave me to mope about the inn all morning on my own. I shall have my revenge tomorrow afternoon, when I will require you to row me about on the lake in one of those boats Mr. Hetherington assures us we may hire."

"You drive a hard bargain," he said, shaking his head in mock sorrow. "I'll take you out on the lake, if that's what you want, but if I end up tipping us both into the water, just remember you have only yourself to blame. I've never rowed a boat before, you know."

"I have every confidence in you," she assured him.

"I'm glad you're here," he said, suddenly serious. "I shouldn't be—I should have put you on the mail coach to London and left you there, never mind your tears. What kind of man knowingly exposes his wife to danger rather than deprive himself of her company?"

She slipped her arms around his waist. "My kind," she said, and lifted her face for his kiss.

12

In Which John Pickett Visits a Sheep Farm

P ickett dared not ask Mrs. Hawkins for directions to the Wilson farm, lest Lizzie overhear and beg to accompany him. After all, Percival Hartsong had returned from the Golden Feather quite late, and was unlikely to emerge from his room before noon; in his absence, Lizzie might well decide that her former favorite was better than no suitor at all. And so, instead of inquiring directions of his hostess, Pickett went to the inn's stables, where more than one groom grinned knowingly at his approach. As these grins also held more than a trace of envy, they troubled him not at all; in fact, he suspected his very public demonstration of affection for his wife—or, rather, her affection for him—might well improve his standing among these men whose birth and breeding, however humble, was very likely better than his own.

In this assessment he was quite correct. "The Wilson

farm?" echoed one, a brawny redhead who had been engaged in repairing a harness prior to Pickett's entrance. "Aye, I know the place. It's naught but a few miles' walk. Or, if you can wait 'til I finish here, I can give you a ride—if you've no objection to riding in a wagon, that is."

"Never mind, Tom," put in a new arrival, "I'm going to old Allanby's place to fetch some cabbages for Ma. I can take you up with me for part of the way," he told Pickett, "provided, as Tom says, that you won't mind taking a seat in a wagon."

Pickett would have assured him this would not be necessary, but upon realizing the speaker was none other than Jem Hawkins, only son of the deceased, he hastily revised his plans. He accepted the offer with alacrity, and soon the wagon was rattling out of the inn yard with Jem at the reins and Pickett seated on the box beside him. Pickett waited until Jem had navigated the traffic choking the High Street—a mixture of farm wagons and tradesmen's gigs, along with the elegant equipages of the Lake District's fashionable visitors—and emerged into open country before expressing once again his condolences and concluding, "I daresay most of the expressions of sympathy are directed toward your stepmother, but I suspect much of the day to day operation of the inn has fallen on you."

"Aye, that it has," Jem confessed, surprised and gratified to meet with one who, on very slight acquaintance, had such a firm grasp of the awkwardness of his own position. "Not that I don't know all about the running of the inn, mind you. Growed up here, I did, for I was always running back and forth between the inn and the stables. But I won't lie to you, Mr. Pickett. I had ideas about making it more profitable—still have, for that matter. It's those assemblies, see—we've been losing patrons every year since Tyson started hosting them. Oh, first-time visitors to Banfell usually stay with us, since the stage sets them down in our yard. But then they go to one or two of those assemblies, and if they come back to the Lakes next year, or the year after that, it's the Golden Feather that gets their business, not us."

"What do you plan to do about it?" Pickett asked, intrigued.

Jem sighed. "Well, we don't have room to host assemblies, even if we wanted to—which I don't, me not wanting to give Jedidiah Tyson the satisfaction of thinking we've got no new ideas of our own, so to speak, but can only copy him—but no matter how many assemblies and lectures and poetry readings and what-all he may offer, he's still on the wrong side of the street from the lake and the river and the best views of the fells, and there's not a thing he can do about that. So I've been telling Da that we need to knock out that back wall—not the whole thing, mind, but holes to put in big windows from floor to ceiling—so as to make the best of what we do have, if you know what I mean."

"I know nothing about running an inn, but it seems like a sound plan to me," Pickett said.

"Aye, and I always thought that whenever I inherited the Hart and Hound, I'd lose no time in putting it into practice. But now that Da's gone and I'm in charge, I don't know whether I ought to change things up, or run it Da's way. In honor of his memory, you might say."

"I should think your dilemma is not an unusual one," Pickett said, bethinking himself of a certain weaver he had met in London just after Christmas. "Not long ago I met a fellow about your age, the foster son of a mill owner, who said he and his foster father were forever at loggerheads over the running of the business. Like you, he had—has—his own ideas about how things ought to be done, but his foster father is an old-fashioned sort, and won't hear of changing anything."

"Aye, I know the feeling," put in Jem.

"Yes, but listen: His foster father knows of his sentiments—from what I saw of the fellow, I can't imagine him keeping his thoughts on the matter to himself—but the old man has made no attempt to bring another business partner on board, or arrange for the mill to be left to someone else. And he could easily do so, especially since this fellow is only a foster son and not his own flesh and blood. But even knowing what will happen to his mill as soon as he's underground, he still intends for this young man to inherit it. I should think that suggests he trusts the fellow more than he might care to admit."

Jem turned to stare at him, much struck. "You mean," he said, finding his voice at last, "that if Da really didn't want me to knock holes in that back wall, he would have made sure to leave the Hart and Hound to someone else? But I'm his only son, you know."

"Yes, but surely you have cousins. He might even have left it to Lizzie as a dowry. Although," Pickett added, "between you and me and the lamppost, I wouldn't hold out much hope for the future of the Hart and Hound if Percival Hartsong should get his hands on it."

"Lud, no!" exclaimed Jem, grinning. "He'd very likely sell it to publish a book of his poems. Or else he'd use the public room to read them aloud, and put all our patrons right off their dinners. What Lizzie sees in such a namby-pamby fellow, I'll never know. But," he continued in a more serious vein, "you think by not arranging to leave it to someone else, Da was sort of giving me permission to try my ideas? Giving me his blessing, you might say?"

"I think it very likely," Pickett said. Of course, there was the fact that Ned Hawkins was still relatively young, and had had no reason to think that his death might be imminent, but he saw no reason to burden Jem with this observation. One might even take Ned Hawkins's anonymous letter to Bow Street as evidence that the innkeeper suspected his life might be in danger; if that were so, then it stood to reason Hawkins would also have taken the opportunity to put his affairs in order, just in case his worst fears came to pass.

"There's still that one table against the back wall," Jem said, his mind obviously still on his plans for the Hart and Hound. "The one where King Charles sat. Da was always right proud of that, and his da before him."

"Can you not commemorate the king's visit in some other way?" Pickett suggested. "A plaque on the wall, perhaps?"

"There'd be no wall there anymore, nothing but glass overlooking the fells and the path to the river. I don't see how—no, but wait! Not on the wall, but on the table itself. Better yet, a plaque set into the floor," Jem continued, warming to this theme. "That way if the tables were moved, or if we were to buy new ones someday, the plaque would still be there, and in the proper place."

"An excellent notion," seconded Pickett.

"I'll see a builder about it as soon as I get back into town," Jem resolved, and lapsed into thoughtful silence. Pickett assumed his mind was filled with plans for the Hart and Hound, until he said suddenly, "It's an odd thing, Da falling off the cliff like that."

"Oh?" Pickett asked noncommittally.

"He's warned me against standing too close to the edge for as long as I can remember. It's almost as if—" He broke off, shaking his head as if to banish a thought too absurd—or too horrendous—to contemplate.

Pickett decided he would never have a better opportunity. "Jem," he ventured, "do you know of anyone who might have had reason to do your father an injury?"

"Who might have pushed him off, you mean," deduced Jem, who was clearly no fool. "I'll admit, I've wondered about that myself. But it don't make sense. Oh, him and Tyson have quarreled back and forth for years, but it's not the sort of thing that would end with either one of them murdering the other. And I suppose mean-spirited folk might say Ben Wilson had cause for complaint, what with Da not sending that poet fellow to the rightabout as soon as he started sniffing around Lizzie, what with him and Lizzie being as good as betrothed, but Da can't afford to offend paying customers—specially one that might take it into his head to write no end of nonsense about him! Besides that, Ben's a good sort, and I'd be proud to call him my brother," he added stoutly.

"But no one else?" Pickett asked, careful not to sound too interested in the affairs of a relative stranger.

Jem shook his head. "Nothing beyond the sort of squabbles that come up from time to time in any village small enough that everybody knows a bit too much about everybody else's business, if you know what I mean. And now," he added, drawing his horses to a halt, "here's where you'll need to get down, Mr. Pickett. If you'll follow the lane there"—he pointed his whip toward a dirt track winding through open meadow on both sides—"you'll come to the Wilson place. It's naught but half a mile or so. Oh, and Mr. Pickett—"

"Yes?" Pickett prompted, when he seemed disinclined to continue.

"About—what I was saying—I beg you won't mention it to my stepmother."

Pickett assured him that burdening Mrs. Hawkins with this suggestion was the very last thing he would want to do, and having put the younger man's mind at ease, set off on his walk. A short time later, he arrived at the Wilson residence, a stout, square farmhouse made of the ubiquitous gray stone, roofed with slate tiles and flanked by chimneys on each end. A curl of smoke rose from one of these, and Pickett was encouraged to hope that the young farmer was still at home, having not yet begun the day's chores. He stepped up to a door so low he would no doubt have to duck his head, should he be invited to come inside, and knocked. A cacophony of barking hailed from inside, and a moment later the door opened. A tiny gray-haired woman stood there, accompanied by two large, growling dogs who regarded Pickett as if gauging the amount and quality of meat to be had from his calf muscles—and finding the result of their speculations very much to their liking.

"Mrs. Wilson?" hazarded Pickett, giving the dogs a wary eye.

"Aye, what of it?" she asked.

"John Pickett, visiting from London," he said, stooping still lower in a approximation of a bow. "I should like to have a word with Ben, if I may."

"He's been gone to the fields these three hours and more," she said. "You want to talk to him, you'll have to go find him."

"Very well," conceded Pickett, not at all looking forward to the prospect of finding one lone sheep farmer in an unspecified expanse of open field. "Er, if you could point me in the right direction, I would be much obliged."

"I'll have Jack and Davy take you to him."

"Thank you—" Pickett began, but when the woman spoke again, it was not to him, nor to any other human.

"Jack! Davy!" she addressed the dogs milling about her skirts. "Go find Ben! Go on, now!"

The dogs needed no further urging. They raced through the door, all but knocking Pickett down as they pelted past him in their enthusiasm to carry out this command.

The woman muttered something under her breath, the only intelligible part being "town's full of strangers these days," and disappeared back into the house.

Pickett's canine escorts showed no inclination to wait for him to follow, but he had no objection to being left behind; besides having no great desire for companions who seemed far too interested in sizing him up for their next meal, he would account himself a very poor Bow Street Runner if he could not follow the trail of two very loud dogs.

His canine guides soon disappeared over a ridge, and very shortly thereafter the bleating of a flock of agitated sheep offered evidence of their presence, along with, presumably, their master. Pickett trudged to the top of the ridge and found the flock milling about in the valley spread out below, the white of their fleece a brilliant contrast to the green of the grass on which they had been grazing before the interruption. In the midst of them stood Ben Wilson, calling the dogs to heel. His finery of the previous night had given place to a serviceable smock, breeches, and sturdy brogues. His blond head was bare, and across his shoulders he carried a lamb in much the same way as a lady might wear a tippet, its legs draped over his chest.

"Hallo, Wilson!" Pickett called as he descended the ridge. "Hallo, there!"

Ben Wilson turned and looked up, releasing the lamb's hind legs in order to raise a hand to shield his eyes. "Mr.—Pickett, is it? What brings you here?"

"I've come to ask a favor." Pickett launched into the excuse Julia had provided. "When Mrs. Pickett and I returned from the assembly, Lizzie told us all about your lambs, and now nothing will suit my wife but that she must see them for herself."

"Liked that, did she?" asked Wilson, obviously pleased. Having finished his business, whatever it was, with the sheep, he turned and started back up the ridge.

"Oh, yes," said Pickett, falling into step beside him. "She's in the family way, so I suppose it's only natural that she should be interested in babies, regardless of species—"

The farmer's reaction astounded him. "The devil she is!" he ground out between clenched teeth, as his sun-bronzed face turned an alarming shade of purple. "By God, I'll kill the fellow who's debauched her—and I'm thinking I won't have to look far to find him," he added darkly.

Revelation dawned. "No, no!" Pickett said hastily. "I meant my wife, not Lizzie." Once he could be sure young Wilson had assimilated this information, he continued. "No matter what Hartsong's intentions toward Lizzie, I believe she has too much good sense to let herself be seduced by pretty words unless he first puts a ring on her finger." He only hoped he was correct in this assessment, for Lizzie's sake as well as Wilson's. "Still, I expect you'll be glad to see the back of him."

"Aye, I will at that." Wilson gave a huff of frustration. "We were all set to marry until *he* came to town."

"I don't suppose you've considered, er, speeding his departure?" Pickett asked blandly.

Wilson frowned. "What do you mean?"

"A rock was thrown through my window two nights ago," Pickett explained. "A rock with a threatening note attached. It occurred to me that, well, if you'd thought to frighten him off, and chose the wrong window, I'm sure no one could blame you."

Far from being gratified by this show of sympathy, the young farmer set his jaw and drew himself up straight and very tall. "It's a right coward who won't look his foe in the face," he said. "If I thought that fellow had given Lizzie a slip on the shoulder, I'd give him such a beating that his own mother wouldn't recognize him. As things stand now, he knows what I think of him without me stooping to such tricks."

Looking into that stern, set face, Pickett had no doubt Wilson would make good on his threat should the need arise. The two young men walked side by side in silence for some time, until Wilson said abruptly, "So Lizzie liked hearing about the lambs?"

"She did. She was much impressed that you should have left the assembly after paying half a guinea for admission, and come instead to keep her company." Pickett gave him a sidelong look. "If I may say so, it showed a level of thoughtfulness that she's unlikely to encounter from Percival Hartsong. My wife says he's the most self-absorbed person of her acquaintance—and if you knew anything of her first husband's family, you would know that's saying something."

Wilson gave a short bark of laughter, but when he spoke, it was once again on the subject of Lizzie and his visit on the night of the assembly.

"Did she say I'd offered to give her this little fellow?" A jerk of the farmer's head indicated the lamb he carried across his shoulders. "His mother rejected him shortly after he was born."

Pickett reached out to scratch the animal behind the ears, and the tips of his fingers sank into soft and slightly oily white fleece. "I know how he feels," he said cryptically.

"Eh, what's that?"

Pickett shook his head. "Never mind. But yes, Lizzie told us you'd offered to let her have a lamb of her own. Mrs. Hawkins wasn't entirely keen on the notion, but she didn't reject it out of hand—just wondered what they would do with it once it was a full-grown sheep."

Wilson considered this obstacle in silence for a moment. "Could always take it back once it was weaned," he said at last. "Don't want to cause no trouble between Lizzie and her Ma. Thing is, been feeding it milk through a hole cut in the finger of a glove. Has to be done four times a day, though. Don't have time. Be obliged if she could help me out."

"And," Pickett deduced, "having raised the lamb herself, Lizzie would likely want to come visit it from time to time."

The farmer looked as sheepish as any of his livestock. "Aye, I won't deny the thought occurred to me."

"Why don't you come to the Hart and Hound and ask Mrs. Hawkins yourself?" Pickett suggested. "If you put it to her in those terms, I daresay she'll agree readily enough, for she much prefers you to the poet as a prospective son-in-law. If you need some pretext, you can always say you came to invite my wife to see the lambs, and to arrange a time that might be mutually agreeable."

"Aye," the farmer said again, brightening. "I'll do that this very afternoon."

Too late, Pickett remembered that he'd promised to row Julia out on the lake. "Best wait until tomorrow. In the meantime—" He broke off, unsure how to frame the question he knew he must ask in a way that would not give offense. He was well aware of the tendency of his wife's class to sprinkle vails about in exchange for any small service they received, and yet he was still not entirely comfortable with his new prosperity, "In the meantime, granting my wife's request must take you away from your work. How much do I owe you?"

They were once again in view of the house by this time, and Wilson stopped to stare blindly in its direction as he considered this question. Pickett couldn't help wondering if he were imagining Lizzie living there as its mistress, just as he himself had tried (not entirely successfully) to picture Julia in his own two-room flat in Drury Lane long before such an eventuality seemed even remotely possible.

"It seems to me," Wilson said at last, "that we'll be doing each other a favor. If you're agreeable, let's call it even."

Not being accustomed to buying his way through life, Pickett found this suggestion very agreeable indeed. They shook hands on the bargain, then Pickett set out on the long walk back to the Hart and Hound, looking forward with mixed emotions to the pleasure cruise that awaited him.

* * *

Julia, for her part, had lost no time after his departure in undertaking a mission of her own. She rummaged through Pickett's clothing and selected one of his cravats, then knotted both ends together to make a large loop. She slipped this over her head and slid her right arm inside, resting her forearm experimentally in the fold of starched white linen. Satisfied, she removed her arm long enough to gather up paper, quill, and ink, then returned her arm to its sling and, carrying her writing materials awkwardly in her free hand, descended the stairs to the public room.

It was surprisingly full for so early in the day: tourists, she supposed, as well as a few farmers and laborers fortifying themselves for the day's work with a hearty breakfast cooked by Mrs. Hawkins and served by her stepdaughter. Julia dismissed the basest of this lot as very likely illiterate, and therefore impracticable for her purposes, but chose one of the more prosperous-looking of the farmers (as evidenced by the content and quantity of his morning meal) and approached him with pretty hesitation.

"I wonder if I may ask a favor of you," she said apologetically, setting her burden on the table with perhaps a bit more clumsiness than was strictly necessary, "I need to write a letter, but it is the stupidest thing! I have fallen and sprained my wrist. If I tell you what I want to say, would you be so good as it write it down? Oh, thank you!" she exclaimed brightly upon receiving an affirmative answer. Once her mark had arranged the paper before him and dipped the quill into the ink, she began her dictation. "Are you ready? 'Dearest Mama and Papa . . .' "

Professing her unwillingness to impose on her de facto secretary, she recited only a sentence or two before gathering up her writing materials (coyly turning aside his insistence that it was really no trouble, no trouble at all), and looking about for another likely candidate. She had no difficulty in this endeavor, for by this time those sitting near enough to hear were fully aware of her dilemma, and were quick to offer their services. When at last she returned to her room with what was surely the most tedious correspondence ever committed to paper, she had collected more than a dozen handwriting samples for her husband's inspection.

* * *

Pickett, returning to the inn some time later, was dismayed to enter the room he shared with his wife and discover her with her arm in a sling.

"What's this?" he asked in some consternation, gesturing toward her incapacitated limb. "Sweetheart, what happened?"

"Nothing." She withdrew her arm from its sling and reached for the sheaf of papers on the writing table. "That is, my arm is uninjured. I did help myself to one of your cravats, though. I hope you don't mind."

He grabbed the loop of starched (albeit sadly crumpled) linen that hung from her neck and gave it a tug, pulling her closer in the process. "Making free with my clothes, are you?" he growled with mock severity.

"Yes, but never mind. I shall let you borrow my best bonnet in retaliation."

"Thank you, but I'll pass. I don't doubt it would look better on you."

"And you would very likely burn it," she put in, giving him a reproachful look.

"Julia—" he began apologetically.

"Never mind that now, for I have something to show you." She handed him the papers and explained as he inspected them. "Handwriting samples. I tried to concentrate on the locals, but when a couple of tourists offered, well, I could hardly refuse them after professing to need help, could I?"

"Can you identify all these people?" Pickett asked, looking up at her. "Which handwriting goes with which person, I mean?"

"I think so," she said. "I might not know their names, but I'm reasonably certain I could recognize them if I saw them again."

"My lady," Pickett said, falling back, as he sometimes did, on her former courtesy title, "you are a wonder! Let's see if any one of them is a match."

But the results of this experiment proved to be a disappointment. When Julia's letter was laid beside the one Pickett had removed from Ned Hawkins's body, it soon became clear that none of them matched.

"Well, I suppose that's that," Julia said, regarding the evidence before her with some disappointment. "I hope you had better results."

He shook his head. "Not really."

"At least this afternoon will be better," she remarked, brightening.

"Will it?"

"Of course! Don't you remember? You promised to row me out on the lake."

"I'm trying to forget," muttered Pickett, succumbing nevertheless to his fate.

13

Adventures on Land and Sea

P ickett's hopes for the outing were not high, his one foray onto the water being an outing on a fishing boat off the coast of Scotland—an experience that had left him shaky, nauseated, and (he recalled fondly) tucked tenderly into Lady Fieldhurst's bed to recover, although her ladyship had been regrettably absent from it at the time. Still, there were difficulties here that had not been present on that earlier occasion, the first and foremost of these being the need to plant one foot in the long, narrow boat to hold it steady while he handed his wife aboard. At least, he hoped it would remain steady; a pretty fool he would look, spread-eagled over the water with one foot in and one foot out while the boat drifted farther and farther from the pier.

Nevertheless, having paid a shilling and sixpence for the privilege, he took a deep breath and stepped over the gunwale, maintaining his balance with an effort until the rocking craft adjusted to its burden. Having accomplished this feat, he held out his hand to Julia and assisted her to board. She stepped lightly into the boat (setting it into fitful motion once more) and seated herself at one end, then unfurled her parasol and settled it on her shoulder. Having done his duty by his wife, it remained only for Pickett to shift his weight to the foot on the boat and bring his other foot onboard—an exercise that sounded simple enough in theory, but in practice ended with him sprawled across the center thwart in an ungainly heap.

But at least he was dry. He scrambled over the thwart to his own seat opposite Julia.

"You've done this before," he observed, his tone faintly accusing.

She nodded. "When I was a child, Lord Buckleigh—not *that* Lord Buckleigh, but his father—kept a little rowboat for the children of the local gentry to take out onto his ornamental lake. When I was about seven years old, Jamie rowed Claudia and me out to the middle of the lake, and then quite deliberately rocked the boat back and forth until he tipped us over. Claudia was furious—she was thirteen years old at the time, and very much on her dignity—and wouldn't speak to him for a week."

"And what did Julia think about her unexpected wetting?" he asked, entranced by this glimpse of the early life of not only his wife, but his sister- and brother-in-law as well.

Julia smiled. "I was delighted at the chance to swim without Mama present to insist that I behave like a lady! I don't remember it very well, but I've been told that I refused to climb back into the boat once it was righted, and eventually

Lord Buckleigh's head groom was obliged to threaten to come in after me and remove me by main force—or, worse, to send word back to Mama. But I paid for my little act of rebellion in the end, for I contracted a horrid cold and had to stay in bed for a week."

Pickett had been engaged in fastening the oars in the locks, but at this interesting prospect, he looked up from his task and regarded her speculatively. "In bed for a week, you say?"

"Yes, but I suffered *fits* of sneezing, and my nose was all runny and red. So if you have any idea of following Jamie's example, I give you fair warning that it will profit you nothing, and I should very likely stop speaking to you as well."

"Oh, in *that* case—" He dismissed the notion with a shrug, and took up the oars.

He had been given brief instructions from the man who hired out the boat, and although he tried to bear these in mind, the business of rowing proved more difficult than it appeared. It seemed somehow wrong, sitting with his back to the direction in which he wished to go, and when he drew his hands down to lift the oars from the water, the one on the left shot up with such force that both he and Julia were showered with spray.

"I'm sorry," he said as she wiped a drop of water from her cheek with the back of one hand, "but I did warn you."

Eventually Pickett was able to achieve some sort of rhythm, and soon they were bobbing pleasantly over the water, leaving the pier farther and farther behind. The lake was long, narrow, and slightly bowed in shape as it curved around the foot of the fell. As they rounded the bend, the village disappeared from view, leaving the impression that they were completely alone in the wild and picturesque landscape. Pickett decided his wife might have had the right idea after all.

"It is nice, isn't it?" Julia said. Safely out of sight of the inn, she had slipped her arm free of its quite unnecessary sling, and now idly trailed her hand in the water.

"So says the lady who sits under her parasol while her husband does all the work." He arched a skeptical eyebrow in the direction of her dripping fingers. "Isn't that arm supposed to be injured?"

"I daresay the cold water will be good for it. I expect I shall be quite recovered by tomorrow morning."

"Somehow I thought you would be."

"Sarcasm does not become you, darling. Are your arms growing tired? You can always stop and let us drift a bit. We can discuss the case here, where we need not fear being overheard."

"Have you remembered something, then? Keep your voice down," he warned her hastily. "Sound does carry over the water, you know."

"How do you know?" she asked in some surprise. "I thought you hadn't been on the water before last autumn in Scotland."

"I hadn't been *on* the water, but that's not to say I'd never been *around* it. I used to haul coal, Julia, loading it onto the wagons from the lighters that brought it to the quay from the ships anchored in the Thames. Even before that, I mudlarked along the river at low tide." Seeing the blank expression on her face, he explained. "It's a form of scavenging. When the tide went out and the water went down, I searched through the mud for anything that could be sold. I remember hearing quite clearly the men on the ships calling to each other, and wondering about them—who they were, where they were coming from, and where they were going." His gaze grew distant at the memory of wading barefooted in the cold mud at the river's edge, poking with his toes in search of some bit of scrap metal or bone to take back home to his father even as he watched the men on the ships and dreamed of stowing away on voyages to India or China.

"Those days are gone, John," Julia said softly. "You never have to go back there again."

He dismissed the memory with a shake of his head, but his smile was a bit forced. "But you wanted to tell me something about the case," he reminded her.

"Yes!" she said eagerly, leaning forward and lowering her voice to a conspiratorial near-whisper. "It concerns Ben Wilson."

He shook his head. "I suggested to Wilson that he might be forgiven for wanting to frighten off his rival with a rock through the window, and he told me in no uncertain terms that playing such tricks without looking his enemy in the face would be the work of a coward—and I'm not sure but what I don't think he's right. No, Julia, if you're pinning your hopes to Ben, I'm afraid you're fair and far off."

"Oh, the rock!" she said impatiently, dismissing this act

of vandalism as a thing of no importance. "I'm talking about the murder of Ned Hawkins. Suppose Ben had hoped Ned would take his part and encourage Lizzie to marry him instead of setting her cap for Percival Hartsong."

"But he did," Pickett objected.

"Mrs. Hawkins did," Julia corrected him. "But I can't recall anyone saying what Ned's views on the matter were."

"Surely any man would rather his daughter marry a farmer with his own land than become the mistress of a mediocre poet!"

"Yes, but no matter how indifferent his poetry, Mr. Hartsong—or perhaps I should say Mr. Gape—is the son of a gentleman," Julia pointed out. "You can't deny that Lizzie Hawkins is a very pretty girl—"

"Oh, is she?" asked Pickett with a marked lack of interest. "I hadn't noticed."

"Wise man!" Julia said approvingly. "But purely as a matter of scientific observation, I shall allow you to acknowledge the fact. Suppose Ned Hawkins thought Mr. Hartsong—or Mr. Gape, if you prefer—might be so taken with her charms as to offer her marriage? Might he not see the poet's interest in his daughter as an opportunity to improve his own family's social standing by marrying into the gentry?"

Pickett could not agree. "I'd rather see my daughter marry a farmer with brains than a fool with a genteel bloodline."

"I shall remind you of that statement in, oh, about twenty years," Julia promised.

He might have objected, might have told her that the

lower classes did not think like hers, prizing lineage above all else, but he was not sure he could make her understand; class standing was second nature to her, taken in with her mother's milk. Then again, he amended mentally, there had probably been no mother's milk involved; she had no doubt had a wet nurse, and would very likely expect to engage one for their own child. Moreover, he was afraid she was right, at least where his own views were concerned: If the baby should prove to be a girl, he would hope she could someday marry back into the class her mother had deliberately abandoned in order to be with him—although he hoped little Miss Pickett would have the good sense not to choose a poet who possessed neither talent nor intelligence.

"You disagree," she observed, watching the play of emotions over his face. "What are you thinking?"

"Jem Hawkins has apparently heard rumors to that effect, but he doesn't set much store by them," Pickett remarked, improvising rapidly. "Besides, Ben Wilson is what Mr. Colquhoun would call a 'braw, strapping lad.' Surely you would have noticed if it had been a fellow his size who pushed Ned Hawkins over the cliff."

She sighed. "You would think so, but the more I try to remember, the less I can recall. Consider, too, that they were standing some distance away, and uphill from our picnic spot. Surely that would have distorted my perceptions of—John, you're splashing me!"

"It's not me, at least not this time." He had been aware for some time of the gray clouds behind her, which seemed to be moving nearer even though he was rowing away from them. Now the rain was here, and although Pickett was London born and bred, he had the sense to recognize that the middle of a lake was not the safest place to be, should a thunderstorm develop.

Julia, in the meantime, had made the same discovery, and raised her parasol to cover her head. Alas, this ruffled and frilled confection was designed for protection against sun, not rain. "Do you want to get underneath with me?" she asked doubtfully. "I'm not sure it's big enough for two, but we can try."

"Both of us on one end of the boat?" Pickett asked, raising a skeptical eyebrow. "Now who's going to tip us out? No, I'm trying for that spot along the near shore, where the trees are. Not perfect, I'm afraid, but it's the best I can do."

He put his back into his rowing, but although his strength was not lacking, his fledgling navigational abilities left something to be desired. It took some doing to steer the boat into the little inlet protected by overhanging limbs. Once this was accomplished, however, it proved to be well worth the effort.

"John, look!" exclaimed Julia, pointing at something over his shoulder. "A cave!"

He turned, and saw that she was right. Beneath the trees, a dark hole opened up in the rock just above the surface of the water, an opening almost as high as Pickett was tall. While he had no desire to intrude on some wild animal (what sort of animals might one expect to find in the Lake District, anyway?), sheltering in the cave certainly seemed a better option than cowering under the trees.

The bottom of the boat crunched against the shingle, and Pickett pulled off his boots, leapt out into cold water that came halfway up to his knees, and dragged the boat up onto the shore.

"Stay here," he told Julia. "I'll make sure it's safe."

"And in the meantime, I have only to worry about being soaked to the skin."

Pickett knew this for an exaggeration, as the leaves of the trees diverted all but the most determined raindrops. Still, he took the hint. Holding the boat steady with one stockinged foot on the gunwale, he held out his hand for Julia, who scrambled over the center thwart to the end he had just vacated. Once she was within reach, he swung her over the side and into his arms, then set her on the dry shingle.

"Thank you," she said, looking up at him, "for not leaving me behind."

He knew she was not talking about leaving her in the boat—at least, not *only* about leaving her in the boat—but about his not sending her back to London while he continued the investigation alone. He still was not entirely convinced he'd made the right decision, but she, at least, seemed to have no doubts at all on that head. He took her hand and gave it a little squeeze, and together they entered the cave. Pickett had to duck his head, but beyond this minor inconvenience, it appeared to be an excellent place to wait out the rain, provided one had no objection to inky blackness.

"I wish I'd brought a lantern," he said, his voice bouncing eerily off the rock walls.

"You had no reason to think you would need one," Julia

pointed out. "I daresay it will not be so very bad, once our eyes begin to adjust."

Even as she spoke, he was able to make out more of their surroundings: a rock jutting out of the wall to their left, which appeared an excellent place for his wife to sit, and just beyond it something pale, something about the size of a man's head—

Julia gasped. "John—" She pointed one trembling finger in the direction of the pale object he had just noticed. He stepped toward it and squatted down for a closer look

"It's all right, sweetheart," he assured her. "It's only a sack."

"Oh," she said tremulously. "I thought it was—was—" She broke off, shuddering.

"A body," he said, nodding. "I know. It did look a bit like a head, didn't it?"

It didn't any longer, for he had picked it up by the drawstring that held it closed and raised it up to the light that penetrated into the cave from the entrance, and suddenly it was nothing more than a bulging bag made of some pale gray cloth. "Still, it's a strange thing to find in a cave, isn't it? Let's see what we've got here."

He stepped forward to the mouth of the cave, where the light shone in but the rain was kept out. He tugged at the drawstring, then dumped out the contents of the bag. A dozen sheets of folded and sealed paper littered the ground at their feet.

"Letters," he remarked, kneeling down to examine them. "Either the Royal Mail has taken up some very odd practices, or we've stumbled across the smuggling ring Mr.

Hetherington mentioned."

"Smuggling?" Julia echoed in some surprise.

Pickett looked up at that. "You had reached that conclusion yourself, hadn't you?"

"Yes, but I'd been thinking of kegs of brandy, or ropes of tobacco, like one finds along the coast. But this"—she gestured toward the little hoard—"you think someone is smuggling letters?"

"I can't imagine what else they would be doing here," Pickett said, turning back to leaf through his find. "These aren't going to France, though. They all seem to be headed for London or other points south. Then, too, there's the bag they're in."

"What about it?"

"It doesn't look like the sacks the Royal Mail uses. You were on the mail coach, Julia," he reminded her. "Do you remember when they threw the mail sacks down and took up the new ones?"

"I didn't notice. I had other things on my mind."

She meant, of course, that she'd been crying her eyes out. Pickett did not remind her of the fact, but his expression softened as he lifted his head to look at her. "They were a dark brown, and they had the mark of the Royal Mail."

"It's gratifying to know that while I was agonizing over going back to London without you, you were making note of what the mail sacks looked like!" she retorted with mock indignation.

"Only because I was wondering how much it was going to cost to write to you every day like you asked, for however long this case might take, at a shilling per letter."

"Oh, but you wouldn't have had to pay that much. The stable lad told me I could—" She broke off abruptly, her horrified expression evident even in the dim light.

"Julia," he said, regarding her with narrowed eyes, "what have you been up to?"

"I—I wrote a letter," she confessed guiltily. "To Claudia."

"Is that all? Sweetheart, you don't have to have my permission to write to your sister!"

"No, but it's *what* I wrote. You—you won't like it."

"Try me," he suggested.

"I asked her if, in case I should die in childbirth—"

He dropped the letters and stood up, then seized her almost roughly by the arms. "You're not going to die in childbirth," he insisted. "I won't let you."

"You wouldn't be able to stop me," she pointed out reasonably.

"You dragged me back from the point of death, after the fire," he reminded her. "Do you think I would do less for you?"

"I don't expect you will have to," she assured him. "Dr. Gilroy says he sees no reason why I should not be able to safely deliver a healthy child, but—well, women do some-times, you know, in spite of everything. And if I should, the jointure that is paid to me—to us—from the Fieldhurst estate would die with me. So I asked Claudia if, in such a case, she and Jamie would—would help you."

"Would give me money, you mean," he said in a flat

227

voice.

"John, there is no doubt in my mind that you will someday be rewarded with a magistracy, and be able to support me and any number of children," she hastened to assuage the blow to his pride which she had known would be the result of this revelation. "But I find it hard to believe that even you could accomplish the feat by December, and at only twenty-five years of age! I only wanted to be sure that, if the worst should come to pass, you would have the means to bring up our child as a gentleman—or a lady, as the case may be."

He was silent for such a long time that she began to wonder if he intended to answer her at all. "I want this baby to be raised as any child of yours deserves," he said at last. "If my agreeing to accept assistance from Jamie and Claudia if necessary will ease your mind during the next six months, then by all means, send your letter."

She stepped over the pile of letters and wrapped her arms about his waist. "Thank you," she whispered.

"But"—he took her by the shoulders and gave her a little shake—"you're *not* going to die in childbirth, you know. I'll be sponging off the Bertrams for many years to come."

He spoke lightly enough, but she knew it troubled him that he could not support her on his wages, at least not in the manner to which she was accustomed. "Wouldn't it be funny if it turns out to be a boy?" she said in the same playful tone he had used. "George will be furious with me for being so obliging as to bear you a child when I would not do the same for Frederick—as if the fault were mine!—but if it's a boy, he can't utter a word of reproach, for if I had given Frederick a son, then that child, and not George, would now be Lord Fieldhurst."

" 'George will be furious,' " he quoted her thoughtfully. "Have you not told your family, then?"

"Oh, *my* family knows. In fact, Mama is quite prepared to acknowledge that in some ways you are actually superior to Frederick as a husband—which means she is secretly over the moon at the prospect of having another grandchild to dandle on her knee. But as for my first husband's family, no, I haven't told them."

He cocked a knowing eyebrow at her. "Afraid of Cousin George ringing a peal over your head?"

She gave him back look for look. "Have you any idea how much he hates it when you call him that?"

"Of course I do! Why do you think I do it?"

"Wicked man!" she scolded, laughing nevertheless. "But no, I'm not 'afraid,' exactly, although I'll admit I'm not looking forward to the harangue I know will follow the announcement. For now, I'm content to just let it be our little secret—you and me, and our family and close friends. Oh, and Mrs. Hetherington."

"You told her?"

"She guessed. It turns out she's been in the same condition herself several times, although she could never carry an infant to full term—something about internal injuries sustained in her youth, poor woman—and she recognized the signs."

Pickett, seeing her expression grow serious, feared she would now begin to dwell on the possibility of miscarriage, and quickly turned the subject back to more immediate concerns. "But I think you were about to tell me that you had already sent your letter to Claudia, and for far less than a shilling. Am I right?"

Julia brightened at once. "Yes, you are, for the stable lad—he was minding the public room while Mrs. Hawkins and Lizzie were at the funeral—said it would only cost a penny. Can you imagine? Only a penny, to send a letter all the way from Cumberland to Somersetshire! He said it would reach her more quickly, too. I confess, I thought some enterprising aristocrat or Member of Parliament was selling his frank—although how that might hasten a letter to its destination I could not imagine. When I danced with the Duke of Ramsdale at the assembly, I said something about how I missed being able to send letters through the post at no charge, hoping that he would offer to frank any letters I might care to send for a penny each, but he didn't mention any such scheme, more's the pity."

"None of these letters bear a frank." Pickett glanced down at the little pile of letters, not one of which bore the signature that would allow it to be delivered free of charge. "Besides, I should think a penny a letter would hardly be enough for an aristocrat or M. P. to bother with. At that price, this can't be much more than a shilling's worth. No, I think what we have here is a nice little mail-smuggling operation. It wouldn't be the first time a secret mail service operated outside the auspices of the Royal Mail."

He picked up two of the letters at random, broke their seals, and scanned the crossed lines. There was nothing of any particular interest in either of them, although one bore a date at the top which indicated that it had been written two days earlier.

"Is that why Ned Hawkins sent for you, then?" Julia seated herself on a nearby rock, by this time quite resigned to the sight of her husband shamelessly reading other people's mail. "But you said smuggling wouldn't fall under Bow Street's purview."

"It wouldn't—at least, smuggling from across the Channel wouldn't. Smuggling within the country, I couldn't say. I've never been summoned to investigate such a case, but then, as half my time as a principal officer has been spent practically on retainer to a certain widow of my acquaintance—"

"Oh, ungallant!" Julia exclaimed. "And I flattered myself you'd *wanted* some excuse to see me again!"

He gave her a speaking look that promised to address this charge at a more appropriate time and in surroundings better suited to the purpose. "But I can't recall having heard any of the other Runners discussing any instances of internal smuggling, either. If I'm not sure who would investigate such a thing, I shouldn't think Ned would know, either. Still, there is the fact that he had only that one letter on his person when he died. If he wanted to prove the existence of a mail-smuggling scheme, a single letter would hardly make for compelling evidence. No, there must have been something about that letter in particular." He sighed. "I only wish I knew what it was."

"It seemed perfectly ordinary—dull, even," Julia agreed.

Pickett glanced down with disfavor at the specimens in his hand. "These don't appear to be any better."

"So what will you do next?"

"I think," Pickett said, stuffing the letters back into the bag and cinching the neck shut, "that will depend on who comes to retrieve this."

14

In Which John Pickett Encounters a Smuggler

P ickett arose at dawn the next morning and stretched his arms in a futile attempt to relieve his aching muscles. It had been a very long time since he had done anything as physically demanding as yesterday's rowing expedition, and the prospect of repeating the experience—only this time without the pleasant distraction of Julia's company—was one that filled him with dread. Stifling a groan, he reached for his clothes.

"John?"

Apparently he hadn't stifled it quite as much as he'd thought. "Did I wake you? I'm sorry. I'm just a bit sore." And that, he added mentally, was an understatement if ever he'd heard one.

"Poor love," Julia said sympathetically. "Must you take the boat out again? Surely there must be some way to reach the cave by land."

"There must be," he agreed, "but I don't know what it is, and I don't want to arouse suspicions by asking questions."

"Are you quite certain you don't want me to come with you? I'll admit, I wouldn't be much help rowing the boat, but I might help you pass the time more pleasantly."

"You would definitely do that." He paused with shirt in hand to bend and kiss her. "But I don't know what I might be walking into, or how this person—or persons—will react when they realize they've been found out."

"In other words"—she pushed back her tousled hair, the better to regard him with a baleful eye—"you won't allow me to walk blindly into danger, but you have no qualms about doing so yourself."

"Oh, I've qualms aplenty," Pickett assured her. "But I have a duty, and I must do it, no matter the risk to myself."

"At least own that I was right in trying to persuade you to bring a pistol!"

He shook his head. "I wouldn't be taking it with me today in any case. Shooting off guns in a cave isn't the safest practice, you know. Too great a chance of missing in the dark, and the bullet bouncing off the walls."

Seeing he would not be swayed, she slid out of the bed, then picked up his brown serge coat and held it open for him to slide his arms into the sleeves. "May I not go with you as far as the pier? I could bring my sketchbook and draw while I wait for you to return."

"Your arm is supposed to be injured, remember?"

"Oh, but it's much better today, just as I predicted." She pushed up the sleeve of her night rail and held up one slender arm for his inspection.

Tempting as it was to press the inside of her white wrist to his lips, he refused to be distracted. "Julia, you've been shot at once already. I'm not going to leave you sitting alone on the quay, an easy mark for whoever tried and failed the first time. I'm going to have to ask you to stay here—not in this room, perhaps, but inside the inn—until I return."

"When, pray, might that be?"

He shrugged. "Whenever someone comes to fetch that bag of mail."

"And if no one does?"

"Then I do the same thing again tomorrow, and the day after that. Not that I think it will take that long," he added quickly, silencing her protest before she could utter it. "I can't imagine anyone leaving letters in a cave so near the water for very long, not if they want them to be legible by the time they're delivered. One of the letters was dated two days ago—well, three days, now—so I should think someone will be coming for them very soon."

"And in the meantime, what excuse am I to give as to why we are spending long periods of time apart during what is supposed to be our honeymoon?"

"Fishing," he said promptly. "The man who hired out the boat also had fishing gear available. I'll hire a rod and buy some bait."

"I didn't know you knew anything about fishing," said Julia, momentarily diverted.

"I don't. But Mr. Colquhoun does, and from him I know that it's not unusual for anglers to spend all day at the sport.

Once I've rowed out of sight of the village, I'll drop a line just long enough to get it convincingly wet, dump my bait overboard—the fish should like that, don't you think?—and then continue on to the cave. You can stay here and complain to Mrs. Hawkins and Lizzie—preferably in the public room, with plenty of witnesses present—about how neglectful your husband is."

She sighed. "I can see you've thought of an answer for any argument I can put forward."

"I have tried," he admitted, picking up his hat.

"I shall ask Mrs. Hawkins for some liniment, and when you return I'll rub it into your shoulders," she promised.

"I'll take you up on that."

"John, you will be careful?" She clung to his lapel and lifted her face to be kissed.

He obliged her willingly. "I'll do my best."

And then he was gone, closing the door behind him and descending the stairs as quietly as possible to avoid waking the house. Julia stood at the window watching for him to emerge onto the path that led down to the water, conscious of a wholly illogical relief that the route to the lake would take him in the opposite direction from the spot where she had seen Ned Hawkins go over the cliff. There he was now, a tall, lean figure whose long, easy strides had become increasingly familiar—and infinitely dear—over the last three months. She pressed her hand to the window pane as if she might reach right through the glass and touch him. And perhaps she did, for he turned back for one last look, and raised one hand in farewell before the path curved away out of sight.

"Come back safely to me," she whispered, then turned away from the window and climbed back into bed.

* * *

The sun had risen by the time he reached the pier, and the same man who had hired them the boat the day before was back at his post. Pickett paid a shilling and sixpence for the hire of the boat and another sixpence for the use of fishing tackle and bait, and set out across the lake. His arms and shoulders protested these fresh demands placed upon them, and he thought longingly of the promised liniment, to say nothing of the hands that would rub it in. As he rowed, however, his aching muscles loosened somewhat, apparently resigned to their fate, and at length he reached the cave. He shipped the oars and leapt ashore, then dragged the boat out of the water with some effort and left it concealed in a thicket of trees that grew at the water's edge, where it would be (he hoped) out of sight of whoever might come for the letters.

He was relieved to find the bag just as he had left it; although he had told himself that yesterday's rain would prevent its being recovered at once, he had not been entirely certain of this, and was gratified—and to no small degree relieved—to discover that he'd been correct in this assumption.

Having assured himself of this fact, he put it back as it had been when he had first discovered it, or as nearly as he could remember. Then he moved farther into the depths of the cave and sat down with his back against the wall, awaiting events. It was likely to be a long, dull morning. He wished for a moment that he had brought a book or something else to occupy his mind, but remembered he had no lantern and would not have dared to light it even if he had. Nor could he have moved closer to the mouth of the cave where the light was better, for fear of betraying his presence.

No, he would do better to use this time reviewing what he knew of the case so far—which he was afraid wasn't much. He'd been less concerned with finding Ned Hawkins's killer than with trying to keep Julia safe: first trying to identify the man who had shot at her, then trying to determine who had thrown a rock through their window—a rock that might well have been intended to strike her. Mr. Colquhoun would argue that he was going about the thing backwards, but that was easy for him to say; Mr. Colquhoun, after all, had never been married to Julia, Lady Fieldhurst.

Save for a futile search for a handwriting to match the letter in Ned's pocket, and a once-promising lead in the rival innkeeper which had ultimately come to nothing, most of his own efforts thus far had focused on those rivals in love, Percival Hartsong (alias Edward Gape) and Ben Wilson, primarily because each had reason for hoping to gain Ned Hawkins's favor—and each had a motive, albeit a weak one, for shoving Ned off the cliff after his prospective father-in-law dashed his hopes. Additionally, both had been in the public room when he and Julia had arrived, thus hearing him give a London address that would identify him as being connected with the Bow Street Public Office, and both had later accompanied him in "discovering" the body (was it possible that he had not been the only one of the trio who had already known what they would find?), and had subsequently testified at the inquest. But none of these things in themselves constituted grounds for suspicion, and even taken together they amounted to no more than the most circumstantial of evidence.

Furthermore, some of the actions of which they were suspected seemed frankly unlike them. The poet seemed too proud of his own delicate sensibilities to sully his hands with murder—although who could tell what the fellow really was beneath that bundle of affectations?—and Ben Wilson, whom Julia suspected of having thrown the rock through their window after mistaking it for Percival Hartsong's, had been openly contemptuous of the very suggestion. And indeed, to Pickett's mind the young sheep farmer seemed more likely to communicate his sentiments more directly, and with his fists. Nor had they been the only ones in the public room who might have overheard Pickett give the direction of the Bow Street Public Office. Mr. Hetherington had been there with his Bible, as had several other men, any one of whom might have—

The crunch of footsteps on the shingle outside the cave interrupted Pickett's rather fruitless train of thought, and he instinctively pressed his back more firmly against the wall of the cave, holding his breath lest it betray his presence.

A man entered the cave, and although Pickett could see only his outline, silhouetted as he was against the sunlight beyond the mouth of the cave, Pickett recognized him at once, at least in part because of the large book he carried under his arm. The new arrival seated himself on the rock where Julia had sat only the day before, picked up the bag of letters, and tugged its drawstring loose. Then he opened his book, removed something from it, and added this to the bag. Having completed this task, he cinched the bag shut and slung it over his shoulder as he stood up and turned toward the mouth of the cave, apparently prepared to take his leave.

Pickett judged it time to make his presence known. "Mr. Hetherington, I'm afraid I must ask you where you are going with that bag."

The older man gave a start at being addressed when he had believed himself to be alone, but made a quick recovery upon identifying the speaker's voice.

"Why, Mr. Pickett! What brings you here?"

"I might ask you the same question."

"Aye, you might, but then, my presence here is not so surprising as yours; after all, I don't have a pretty young bride left alone to wonder at my absence."

Pickett made no response, and the older man heaved a sigh. "Ah well, I wondered how long it would be before you tumbled to our little scheme. Patrick Colquhoun speaks very highly of you, you know—seems to think of you as a second son."

If he had hoped to disarm Pickett with flattery after having failed to distract him, he succeeded admirably. "I wouldn't say—" Pickett stammered. "I would not presume to—"

"Nonsense! Colquhoun doesn't suffer fools gladly, so it stands to reason you must have something in your brain-box, else he'd never have taken such an interest in you."

"Mr. Hetherington," Pickett said impatiently, "you must know that what you're doing here is illegal."

"And what, exactly, do you think you've discovered here?"

"A smuggling ring whose purpose is to send letters independently of the Royal Mail."

Hetherington inclined his head, like a tutor congratulating an especially promising pupil on a correct answer. "Very good. Although to call it a 'ring' would be to put too fine a point upon it. It's not so well-organized as all that—just an agreement that anyone going into Penrith will carry any letters bound for London."

"And once they reach Penrith?"

He shrugged. "I assume someone headed south will take the letters with them. Quite simple, really."

"And quite illegal, as I'm sure you must be aware."

"Oh, yes, I'm aware. But so much in the law is merely a matter of degree, don't you think? Have you never sent a message by private courier—to save time, perhaps, or to be certain it reached its destination? I can see in your face that you have. What, pray, is the difference between that and this?"

Put that way, Pickett was hard pressed to offer an answer. "The scale of such an operation, perhaps—"

"Precisely! Only a matter of scale, and Banfell is not so large as to cost the Royal Mail that much in lost revenue. Nothing like Manchester, where it's said that four out of every five letters never sees the inside of a receiving office."

"Speaking of scale," Pickett said, unconvinced, "have you any idea what the penalty would be, if this scheme were discovered?"

Hetherington nodded. "Five pounds for each occurrence."

Which meant that the contents of the bag represented what to Pickett would be very nearly a year's wages. "Why would you take such a risk?"

"Truth to tell, Mr. Pickett, I consider it something of a public service. Do you know what it costs to send a letter from Banfell to London through the Royal Mail?"

Here, at least, Pickett was on firm ground. "A shilling."

"Precisely! Little enough for you or me, perhaps," the older man conceded, leading Pickett to wonder once again exactly what Mr. Colquhoun had said about him, "but a considerable burden for people like Mrs. Hawkins or Ben Wilson, and well-nigh impossible for the truly poor."

Pickett knew from bitter experience that abiding by the law was much easier when one had food in one's belly and money in one's pocket. Mr. Hetherington must have taken his silence for concession, for he continued to expound upon this theme.

"I could show you a woman who regularly sends a blank sheet of paper through the Royal Mail to her brother who lives in another part of the country, and frequently receives the same from him. When this letter—if one may call it that—is delivered, he declines to pay the postage to receive it, and she does the same. In this manner, each can be assured that the other is well, without being obliged to pay for the letter. I ask you, is a system fair when it forces honest citizens to commit what a strict interpretation of the law must consider mail fraud? If it is not—if it is in fact *un*fair—does it deserve obedience?"

"Mr. Hetherington, I'm afraid you're asking the wrong person," Pickett confessed, thinking quickly. "I have no interest in what you choose to do, beyond warning you of the risk should you be discovered. But I wonder if you would be willing to give me some information in return for my silence."

"What is it you wish to know?"

"I believe—that is, I have reason to suspect—that Ned Hawkins's death was not an accident, regardless of the inquest's findings to the contrary. Have you any idea why someone might wish him dead?"

"Other than those two bellicose young men with designs on his daughter's virtue, you mean?" He shook his head. "No, I can't say that I do."

"I saw you with your Bible at the Hart and Hound the day I arrived," Pickett reminded him. "I expect the inn makes a good point from which to collect and distribute letters."

"Ah yes, my Bible." With a flick of his wrist, Hetherington flipped the worn leather cover open. The insides of the pages had been cut completely away, leaving a hollow cavity. "Country folk bring their letters directly to the cave, but it can be inconvenient for those who live in the village. I arrange to be at the Hart and Hound three days a week to receive any letters they might wish to add to the bag." He gave the drawstring a jerk, hefting his burden higher onto his back.

"Did Ned Hawkins know?" Pickett asked.

"Of course."

"Is it possible that he took exception to his establishment being used for such a purpose, and that someone deemed it necessary to, er, remove the impediment?"

The older man bristled. "We are not the Hawkhurst Gang, Mr. Pickett!"

"No, of course not," Pickett assured him hastily, aware of having offended. "I only meant—"

"Few men had as much reason to wish the scheme to continue as Ned Hawkins did," Hetherington pointed out in a more moderate tone. "It brought him a steady supply of customers, for anyone hoping to submit letters for delivery would not wish to call attention to himself by visiting a public house and failing to purchase so much as a single pint of ale."

"No, I suppose not," Pickett said, conceding the point.

"Depend upon it, Ned Hawkins stepped too near the edge of the cliff and, in a moment of carelessness, he fell. Tragic, of course, but no need to make a mystery of it. Now, if you will excuse me, I must be off if I'm to reach Penrith before the fellow I'm to meet there sets out for London. Perhaps you and your charming bride can join us for dinner again soon, say, tomorrow night? Until then, I'm sure I can rely on your discretion."

Pickett assured him that he might, but remained in the cave pondering this new and unexpected development for some time after the older man had gone. At length, he shook his head as if to clear it, then exited the cave, dragged the boat from its hiding place, and began the long row back.

* * *

Julia, in the meantime, had gone back to bed after his departure, but it was some time before she drifted off to sleep. Consequently, the morning was far advanced by the time she awoke again, dressed, and went downstairs in search of breakfast. She felt a bit guilty, feasting on buttered eggs and bacon when her husband had been obliged to set out on an empty stomach, but reasoned that he would hardly be surprised; as he himself had remarked, she was always hungry these days—the result, no doubt, of Little Pickett demanding its own morning meal.

The thought of Pickett reminded her of the liniment she'd promised him, so when Mrs. Hawkins emerged from the kitchen to replenish her coffee, Julia asked if there were any to be had.

"Aye, that there is, Mrs. Pickett," the innkeeper's widow assured her. "I believe there's a letter come for you, too. If you won't mind waiting a bit, I'll fetch them for you in a trice."

These assurances proved to be overly optimistic, for Mrs. Hawkins had not yet returned by the time Julia had finished her breakfast; she wondered if the woman was quarreling with her stepdaughter again. Julia rose from the table, of two minds as to whether she should wait for her hostess or go back to her room and let Mrs. Hawkins or Lizzie bring it up to her, when the bone of contention between the two women, the poet himself, entered the public room, apparently in search of his own breakfast.

"Good morning, Mr. Hartsong," Julia said, making up her mind to wait, since the poet's arrival would very likely hasten Mrs. Hawkins's return. "It promises to be a fine day, does it not? Thank goodness yesterday's rain did not decide to linger!"

The poet, it soon transpired, had other things on his mind.

Resolutely, he crossed the room to stand before her. "I have been thinking about what you said, Mrs. Pickett."

"Oh?" Julia could not for the life of her imagine what he was talking about. "And what was that?"

"Your suggestion that I find some way to shock Society as a means of gaining the audience my talent deserves."

Julia was fairly certain she had made no observations regarding the audience his talent deserved, but she did recall making certain remarks concerning shocking behavior, in the hope—a futile one, as it had turned out—of provoking a confession. "And have you thought of some appropriately shocking action to take?"

"I have," he announced. "I shall take a mistress."

Julia frowned. "I think it would be very wrong of you to behave so shabbily toward one who is surely your greatest admirer, and an unpardonable insult to her father's memory for you to seduce his daughter while enjoying the hospitality of his establishment."

"Oh, Lizzie"—he dismissed his erstwhile muse with a wave of one slightly ink-stained hand—"why should anyone care if I gave some village wench a slip on the shoulder? No, I have in mind a *lady*—a married lady, in fact, and one rendered slightly scandalous by the fact that she was only recently suspected of having murdered her first husband—"

As Julia stared at him in speechless indignation, the poet (no doubt supposing her to be overwhelmed by the honor that was soon to be hers) seized her in his arms. "Only say you will be mine, and we shall set all of literary London abuzz!"

"Mr. Hartsong!" Julia exclaimed, struggling to free

herself from a wiry but surprisingly strong young man who seemed determined to cover her face with kisses. "Release me at once, or I shall box your ears!" She tried to suit the word to the deed, but it proved an empty threat, as he held her arms pinioned to her sides. She glanced wildly about the room for assistance, but the public room was empty of all other guests at this time of the morning.

"Why so coy, Mrs. Pickett? You would not have made such a suggestion if you were not already entertaining thoughts in that direction."

"I never"—here she was obliged to pause long enough to wrench her mouth away from his—"I never suggested any such—"

"Excuse me, Mr. Gape?"

A surprisingly meek voice interrupted her protestations, and a corresponding hand tapped him on the shoulder. The poet turned to glare at the intruder, and when he did, John Pickett's left fist met his nose with what to was, Julia's ears, a very gratifying crunch.

15

In Which a Great Light Dawns

A ny of the aristocratic gentlemen who honed their skills at Gentleman Jackson's Boxing Saloon in Bond Street would no doubt have deplored Pickett's technique, but not even the most exacting of them, or even England's Champion himself, could have argued with the results.

"My nose!" shrieked the poet, releasing Julia abruptly and clasping both hands to his abused proboscis. Within seconds, bright red blood welled up between his fingers and ran down his hand to disappear into the sleeves of his coat. "Oh, my nose!"

"Find yourself another woman," said Pickett without sympathy, pulling Julia up against his side. "This one is already taken."

"Here now, what's all this?" demanded Mrs. Hawkins, emerging from the kitchen with a jar of the requested liniment and a folded sheet of foolscap in her hand. "I never heard such a—oh, my stars and garters! Mr. Hartsong, what happened?"

"Percival?" cried Lizzie, entering the public room hard on her stepmother's heels. She stopped cold at the sight of her bloodied and disheveled lover. "*Percival!* What—? Who—?"

The answer to these disjointed queries should have been clear. Pickett had by this time released Julia, but he still glared at the poet, and with his right hand he rubbed the bruised knuckles of his left.

"Mr. Pickett!" Lizzie exclaimed, drawing the obvious conclusion. "For shame!"

"The only one who should be ashamed of himself is Mr. Gape," Julia retorted. She had been careful in the past to avoid offending the poet, using his preferred name for himself rather than the one bequeathed to him by his parents, but now felt no such scruples. To the object of this denunciation, she added, "The next time you feel inclined to honor a female with your attentions, I suggest you first be very certain she is amenable to receiving them."

Thinking to stanch the flow of blood, Lizzie snatched up Julia's discarded serviette and pressed it to her lover's nose, causing him to howl anew. "I'm sure Percival would never— you must have misunderstood," she insisted, casting a disapproving glance at Pickett over her shoulder.

Pickett took instant exception to this justification of his adversary. "It's hard to 'misunderstand' a lady struggling in the arms of a man determined to kiss her against her will— especially when the lady in question happens to be your wife."

Lizzie would have urged Mr. Hartsong to defend himself against so blatantly false a charge, had not his abused face (or what could be seen of it above the blood-soaked serviette) assumed so hangdog an expression that the poet's perfidy could no longer be denied.

"Percival!" she cried. "Oh, how could you? When you told me *I* was your Muse!"

Pickett, feeling a bit as if he had accidentally walked into a Drury Lane farce, might have felt a pang of sympathy for Mr. Hartsong/Gape, had any other woman but Julia been the recipient of that gentleman's unwanted advances. As if anything else were needed to make the melodrama complete, the door opened and Ben Wilson entered the public room.

"What the—Lizzie!" The blond giant crossed the room in three strides. "What's happened?"

"I have been Cruelly Deceived!" announced Lizzie, obviously a lover of the more lurid sort of novels.

"No wonder she took such a fancy to Hartsong," was Pickett's *sotto voce* observation to Julia.

Ben Wilson glanced from Lizzie's tearstained face to his rival's bloodied one. "Oh?"

"Percival—Mr. Hartsong, I mean—has been making Amorous Advances to Mrs. Pickett!" She cast herself onto the farmer's broad chest. "Oh, Ben! You tried to warn me, but I wouldn't listen. Can you ever forgive me?"

Ben Wilson was a man of few words, but if the willingness with which he received her were anything to judge by, he not only could forgive her, but had already done so. "If it's agreeable to you, Lizzie, I'll go to the vicarage and see the parson about having the banns read starting this Sunday." It was the longest sentence Pickett had ever heard him speak.

"Something I have to do first, though."

"Anything you wish," Lizzie declared fervently. "What is it?"

He seized Pickett's hand and pumped it vigorously, then nodded in the direction of the poet's rapidly swelling nose. "Been wanting to do that myself for the last fortnight."

* * *

The little company broke up soon afterwards. Lizzie and her intended set out arm in arm for the vicarage, while Mrs. Hawkins returned to the back bedroom she had once shared with her husband, to communicate to her departed spouse an outcome which she knew he would heartily approve. Mr. Hartsong, for his part, sought refuge in his own room, where he unburdened himself of an impassioned and embittered diatribe in iambic pentameter against the inconstant nature of the fairer sex, a work which (although he could not yet know it) would in a scant two months' time be praised by the *Edinburgh Review* (laboring under the mistaken impression that any poem of such exquisite awfulness could only be a deliberate parody, and therefore a work of genius), and one whose overwrought lines would soon be on the lips of every buck of fashion in the Metropolis.

Julia's own sentiments were most closely aligned with those of Ben Wilson, although hers assumed a rather warmer expression. As soon as the door to their room was closed behind them, she flung herself at her husband and kissed him with a passion that made Lizzie's newly discovered enthusiasm for her sheep farmer seem tepid by comparison.

"What's this for?" Pickett asked breathlessly, emerging

from an assault that set his senses reeling.

"I'm trying to wipe off that horrid poet's kisses," Julia said, reaching for him again.

He seized her by the shoulders and held her firmly at arm's length. "Well, don't wipe them on me! I don't want them any more than you do."

"In all seriousness, John, your timing was sublime. I was never more pleased to see anyone in my life!"

Thus mollified, Pickett submitted to being kissed. "Sweetheart," he said at last, "I trust you implicitly, but I have to ask: What gave that fellow the idea that you would welcome his attentions?"

"Other than sheer narcissism, you mean? I'm afraid I did suggest that he might attract attention for his poetry by doing something that Society might find shocking. Not *that*, of course," she added quickly. "Truth to tell, I thought if he was involved in anything nefarious, he might be inclined to confide in me. I could not have been more mistaken!"

"Oh, if it's nefarious you want, I can give it to you in plenty."

"John! Someone came for the letters!"

"Yes—and a very good thing, too, or I would still be sitting in a cave while my wife fended off randy rhymesters."

"But who was it?"

"Not so fast! Didn't you say something about liniment?"

"Oh, dear! There was a letter too, now that I think of it. I'm afraid I left them both downstairs in all the hullabaloo. If you'll take off your shirt, I'll go down and fetch them."

She returned a few minutes later to find Pickett naked

from the waist up and sitting in the chair beneath the writing table. Apparently he had found his exposed state somewhat chilly, for not only had he lit the fire, but also the single candle that stood nearer at hand on the writing table. She laid the letter on the table, then opened the jar of liniment and began rubbing the salve, which smelled strongly of mint, into his shoulders. Pickett closed his eyes and emitted a moan that was half pain and half pure bliss.

"Keep your voice down," she admonished him in an undertone. "Whoever is in the next room will have entirely the wrong idea about what we're doing in here!"

"That didn't bother you last night," Pickett said, and received a sharp whack across his shoulder blades.

"You were going to tell me who came for the letters," she reminded him.

"You wouldn't believe me if I told you."

"It must have been Mr. Hetherington, then."

"Julia!" He wheeled about in his chair, giving her a very pleasing view of bare chest. "How did you guess?"

"You said I wouldn't believe you, so I just named the least likely person I could think of. Although not so unlikely, now that I think of it," she added. "After all, he knew about the smugglers, for he warned us about them."

"He warned us about a smuggler's moon—that is, no moon at all—no doubt to distract our attention from the fact that the letters are removed in broad daylight."

"Still, if he hadn't brought up the subject, we might never have known anything about it."

"Oh, he was convinced I would tumble to it eventually—

me being so brilliant, and all. Emptying the butter boat over my head, as Mr. Colquhoun would say."

"So what will you do now?"

"Do?"

"Darling, how can I rub liniment into your back when you will persist in turning around? Yes, I asked what will you do. It *is* illegal, you know, and you *are* a Bow Street Runner."

"I'm not going to 'do' anything! He's a friend of Mr. Colquhoun, sweetheart, and he's invited us for dinner tomorrow night. Should I arrest him in the middle of the fish course, do you think, or can I wait until after the sweet is served?"

"Very funny," she chided, working the liniment into his upper arms with perhaps more force than was strictly necessary.

"Besides, I'm not sure he isn't right when he claims he's doing a public service," Pickett continued. "It does seem a pity that mail between Banfell and London is so expensive—and as he said, it puts an undue burden on families like the Hawkinses and the Wilsons, if they have business dealings or family members farther south."

"On the subject of letters," Julia said, "one came for us this morning. It's on the table there, if you'd like to read it."

As she continued to work her magic on Pickett's aching shoulders, he picked up the letter and broke the seal. "It's from Mrs. Hetherington," he remarked, unfolding the single sheet of foolscap. "I'll wager this didn't come through the Royal Mail."

"Very likely not," she agreed before adding, conscience-stricken, "But I should have written to her the day after we dined with them, to thank her for her hospitality. She must think me shockingly rag-mannered! I daresay this is her way of giving me a gentle reminder."

Pickett read through the usual social platitudes, which he was beginning to recognize as the common language of his wife's class, regarding Mrs. Hetherington's "sincerest gratitude" for "the pleasure of your company."

"You'll have a chance to redeem yourself after tomorrow night," he said. "In the meantime, surely some lapses can be forgiven a woman on her honeymoon." Having reached the end of the correspondence, he tossed the letter back onto the table and leaned back in his chair, giving himself up to his wife's ministrations. Suddenly he sat bolt upright, grabbed the letter again, and fumbled through the papers littering the desk until he located the one he'd found on Ned Hawkins's body. He held them up side by side so Julia could see. Behind the two letters, the flame from the candle glowed through the paper, turning the foolscap to burnished gold.

"Do you see it?" he asked over his shoulder.

Julia rested her hands on his shoulders and leaned forward, studying the letters intently. "The handwriting," she said. "It's the same."

"Exactly. Why would Mrs. Hetherington be writing a letter recounting the achievements of children she doesn't have, and signing herself as 'E.G.B.?'"

"Perhaps she was doing it as a kindness for someone else," Julia suggested. "Remember me with my arm in a sling? Perhaps E.G.B., for whatever reason, could not write, and so spoke his letter aloud while she took down his words. It is rather conversational in tone, is it not? As if someone were speaking the words instead of just writing them."

"In that case, I should think his wife or daughter—Penelope, was it?—would be the most likely person to act as secretary."

"I daresay they were unavailable—at the dressmaker's, perhaps, or attending other details of Miss—oh, but we don't know her last name, do we?—of Penelope's presentation."

"I can't say I like it, but I suppose it's just within the realm of possibility," Pickett conceded, albeit grudgingly. "Which brings us to the next question: What would Ned Hawkins be doing with one of Mrs. Hetherington's letters in his pocket?"

Julia shrugged. "Carrying it down to the bag, I suppose."

"But that makes no sense. For one thing, the path down to the pier—and, presumably, the cave—lies in the opposite direction from the inn than where Ned Hawkins was standing when he was pushed off the cliff."

"Perhaps he had called on Mrs. Hetherington to collect it."

"Why should he, when she could just give it to her husband?"

"Perhaps it was something she didn't want him to see," Julia suggested.

Pickett arched a knowing eyebrow at her. "Keeping clandestine correspondence from her husband? My lady, you shock me to the core!" Seeing her reproachful look, he quickly returned to the subject at hand. "But as far as we can tell, it's just a recounting of family news. What could he find objectionable in that?"

"Very well, you've convinced me," Julia said decisively. "It must be in code. No other explanation makes sense."

Pickett sighed. "In that case, we're back where we started, for I've tried every code I know—which I'll admit aren't many—and I can't find any hidden messages. Then, too, there's the note tied around the rock. I can't see Mrs. Hetherington sneaking out of the house in the middle of the night to go throwing rocks through windows."

Julia shook her head. "It was no woman—and certainly not Mrs. Hetherington!—who pushed Ned Hawkins off the cliff. It must be nothing more than a coincidence, certain similarities in handwriting, perhaps as a result of having learned penmanship under the same schoolmaster—"

"Mrs. Hetherington grew up in Ireland, remember? No, there's something important here that I'm missing, something I can't quite—quite—"

He broke off, staring at the letter in his hand. As the paper grew warm from the candle behind it, lines—faint lines, perhaps, but unmistakable nonetheless—began to appear beneath certain letters:

My dear James,

I trust this Letter finds You and your Family Well. I have been Much Troubled of late by an Attack of Catarrh, which has left me with a Sorely Abused Nose and a Lingering Cough, but I trust my Sufferings will soon be a Thing of the Past, the Good Lord be Willing. Thankfully, none of the Children have contracted their Father's Illness, and I am confident their Good Health will continue long enough for them to Enjoy their Sire's 55th Birthday Festivities on Thursday Next. I am only Sorry that George, my Eldest, may not Join us, as his new Position requires that he Remain in Edinburgh, at least for the Nonce. It is difficult to Believe he will soon be celebrating his own 34th Natal Day. My poor first Wife, Elizabeth (God rest her soul) would certainly be Proud of the Man he has Become.

As for the Rest of the Family, Penelope is to have her Come-Out next Spring, if she does not drive us all to Distraction long before then. Nor is my Good Lady much Better, as she can only Expound upon the Need for hiring a Suitable House in Mayfair, to say nothing of the Mantua-Makers, Florists, and various Others whose Talents must be Enlisted, doubtless at Exorbitant Cost, in order to see our Girl suitably Launched. I have always fancied myself a Warm Fellow, but I may be Bankrupt by the time the thing is Finally Done. I only hope she may attach an Eligible Parti in her First Season; I fear I have neither the Finances nor the Patience to give her a Second.

My good Wife informs me that you cannot yet know of the Blessed Event that took place on the Sixth of June. Lest she accuse me of being an Unnatural Father, I must tell you forthwith that my elder Daughter Lavinia was safely brought to Bed of a Son, to be named Evelyn after his Mother's proud Papa. My Wife predicts that I shall become so Puffed Up in my own Conceit that there will be No Living with me. As I should Hate to disappoint her Faith in me by Neglecting to carry out my Role, however Humble, in her newly discovered Talent for Prophecy, I shall do my Poor Best not to Fail her in this Regard.

And now, having Bored you to Distraction with my Familial Boasting, I have a Confession to Make. It concerns (as you might Expect, having previously made his Acquaintance) my Youngest Son, Edward. Edward is presently at Eton, but it may, I fear, be Wrong to Assume that he is receiving an Education there. Although I am presently paying 50 pounds per Annum, never mind an additional 22 for Incidentals, it would be an Exaggeration to call the hapless Ned a Scholar. I suspect he spends more time on juvenile Pranks than on Greek or Latin. But then I am reminded of the Larks you and I once Kicked Up, and I cannot be too Hard on him. He is a Good Lad at heart, and I Suspect there is nothing Wrong with him that Time will not Mend. Until then, I have Only to Resist his determined Efforts to send his Longsuffering Papa to an Early Grave. In the meantime, I Remain, as Ever,

Yr very Obedient Servant,

E. G. B.

"Julia?" Pickett didn't dare to look away, didn't dare to move lest the lines fade away and vanish as quickly as they had come. "Bring me a quill and paper, will you?"

She didn't waste time in asking questions, but hurried to obey, and Pickett silently blessed her for her perspicacity. He took the writing materials she had fetched from her portable desk and began to transcribe the underlined letters and words. He had not yet trimmed any of the new quills she'd bought him, so he was obliged to use one of her own writing instruments—the end result being that the curve of the quill prevented him from seeing what he wrote until he reached the end of the letter, laid aside the quill, and examined his handiwork:

CARLISLECASTLEUNDEFENDED55THFTREGIN
WESTINDIES34THFTBOUNDFORPENINSULATUESN
EXTMAINGATEINSWALLBATTERYIMMRTINSIDEGA
TEFACINGWESTELEVENCANNONBUTSIXONLOWER
LEVELMAYBEINOPERABLEARMOURYONFIRSTFLO
OROFKEEPGUARDEDBYFEWERTHAN50MEN22FREN
CHPRISONERSONGROUNDFLOORGODSPEEDANDE
GB

Determining the divisions between words would take some doing, as would deciphering some of the more obscure abbreviations, and Pickett had no doubt that much of the task would fall to minds more trained to the work than his. Even to a novice, however, one thing was abundantly clear.

"This is it, Julia," he said unsteadily, looking up over his shoulder at her. "This is treason."

16

In Which the Final Piece Falls into Place

C arlisle Castle undefended,' " Julia read over his shoulder. "That much is obvious, and something about the West Indies, but what does the rest of it mean?"

"Let's find out, shall we?"

The room boasted only one chair, so Julia settled herself on Pickett's knee (his right, so as not to obstruct his left-handed writing), and offered suggestions as he copied the message again, leaving spaces between any readily identifiable words. Eventually the message read:

CARLISLE CASTLE UNDEFENDED 55TH FT REG IN WEST INDIES 34TH FT BOUND FOR PENINSULA TUES NEXT MAIN GATE INSWALL BATTERY IMMRT INSIDE GATE FACING WEST ELEVEN CANNON BUT SIX ON LOWER LEVEL MAY BE INOPERABLE ARMOURY ON FIRST FLOOR OF KEEP GUARDED BY FEWER THAN 50 MEN 22 FRENCH PRISONERS ON

GROUND FLOOR GODSPEED AND EGB

"There you are, then," Pickett said. "The castle is undefended, or soon will be, because the 55th foot regiment is in the West Indies and the 34th will be headed for the Peninsula next Tuesday."

"What does 'inswall' mean?" Julia asked, frowning thoughtfully at the paper. " 'Inside wall'? No, that can't be right. 'Main gate inside wall' makes no sense."

" 'In south wall,' perhaps?" Pickett suggested. "I don't suppose you've ever visited Carlisle Castle, have you?"

She shook her head. "No, for it isn't like Belvoir Castle, you know—it was never a home. I believe it was built during the Middle Ages to defend the northern border against marauding Scots—although that seems rather hard to believe today, doesn't it?"

Pickett grinned at her. "I don't know about that. I should think a few thousand Mr. Colquhouns pouring over the wall would be rather terrifying. One can be scary enough, if he's in the right mood—or the wrong one, depending on your point of view." He raked his fingers through his brown curls and added, suddenly sobering, "And what he's going to say when I tell him the wife of his old friend is involved in a treasonous plot—"

"It was a man who pushed Ned Hawkins off the cliff," Julia insisted. "And even if it was a woman dressed in a man's clothing, it could never have been Mrs. Hetherington. She's far too frail."

"I agree with you there. But she has servants, you know, servants who could be bribed, or threatened, or who might even share her Irish sympathies. She picked up a French cook in Dublin, remember? It wouldn't be the first time the Irish and the French have joined forces against the English. Or what of that fellow who cut up her meat at dinner? I should think that degree of dependency might well lead to a bond of affection well beyond what would usually exist between mistress and servant."

"But are you quite certain it's treason?" Julia's voice rose on a note of desperation. Pickett could sympathize: he liked the woman, too. "Perhaps she only meant to express concern at being left unprotected in case of invasion by the French. The people along the southern coast live in a state of constant anxiety over that very thing—not that fear prevents them from availing themselves of the contraband tobacco and brandy that manages to cross the Channel, but still—"

"And so," Pickett said skeptically, "being worried about a French invasion, she writes a letter in code, describing in detail the layout of the castle's defenses, right down to the number and position of its cannon?"

Julia peered more closely at the paper he'd transcribed. "Where does it say that?"

"There." He pointed with the feathered end of the quill. " 'Battery immediate right inside gate, facing west.' Followed by the number of cannon, the location of the armory, and an estimate of the remaining troops. I don't like it any more than you do, sweetheart, but any way you look at it, this is treason."

"So what happens now?"

Pickett gestured toward the original missive with its faint brown underscoring. "This will have to be turned over to the magistrate—not Mr. Colquhoun, but whoever holds the position locally—along with the rock and the note that was tied to it. And then"—he slumped in his chair with a sigh—"I have to tell Mr. Hetherington that his wife will be hanged as a traitor."

She put her arm around his shoulders and gave them a squeeze of silent sympathy. "You've done this before, haven't you? Had to arrest someone's wife, I mean."

"I've had to arrest my own! Julia, have you never wondered how I happened to turn up on your doorstep at just the right moment that day? I had an arrest warrant in my hand. I'd come to your house prepared to execute it."

"But you knew I was innocent!" she protested, taken aback by this revelation.

"Oh, I knew, all right," he recalled bitterly, "but I had no proof. And although the evidence against you was purely circumstantial, I had no answer for it."

She picked up the letter and traced the incriminating brown lines with the tip of her finger. "Might this not be circumstantial, too? Some sort of flaw in the paper that causes spotting, perhaps—"

"Spotting that just happen to spell out the details of a military installation? I'm sorry, sweetheart, but no. Nothing is *that* circumstantial. Still, I'm not so callous that I can stroll in and arrest a lady after sitting at her dinner table. I'll put this to Mr. Hetherington tomorrow and see what he has to say about it."

"Tomorrow?"

"He's gone to Penrith today with the bag of letters,"

Pickett reminded her. "I won't let him come back home to discover that his wife has been taken up for treason. I spent three days in Kent investigating your first husband's murder, you know."

"Kent?" She blinked at the sudden *non sequitur*. "What were you doing there?"

He gave a humorless little laugh at the memory. "Grasping at straws. And although Mr. Colquhoun assured me he wouldn't send anyone to arrest you in my absence, I couldn't quite believe him. He knew that I—I admired you—and he didn't approve. I couldn't quite shake the feeling that I would return to London only to find you'd been clapped into Newgate, and me powerless to stop it. I won't put another man through that, Julia, no matter what his wife may have done."

Her gaze softened as she looked down at him. "I hadn't thought—I had always assumed you were merely being thorough and not jumping to conclusions in Frederick's murder. I never realized you had taken it so personally."

He gave her a rather rueful smile. "Why should you? I mean, look at you, and look at me."

"I'd rather look at us," she said, stroking his disheveled curls with loving fingers.

"There wasn't any 'us' at the time. I had no reason to think there ever would be." He looked down at the papers littering the table and sighed. "There won't be any happy ending here, though. That much is certain."

She slid off his knee with some reluctance. "I suppose I'd better let you get dressed, then. If you plan to see Mr. Hetherington tomorrow, I daresay you'll want to find the magistrate this afternoon and have him issue an arrest warrant."

"Not just yet," Pickett said thoughtfully. "I want to hear what Mr. Hetherington has to say first."

"But won't that give him time to, I don't know, spirit her away before you come back to arrest her? Take her to Ireland, perhaps, or even to France?"

"Perhaps."

Her eyes narrowed in sudden suspicion. "In fact, you hope he will."

He neither confirmed nor denied this charge, and she bethought herself of a similar conversation that had taken place only a few days earlier, in the guest chamber that had originally been assigned to them.

"I asked you what you would have done if you'd discovered I had killed Frederick after all," she said slowly. "You said you thought the case would never have been solved. That's what you're doing for Mr. Hetherington, isn't it? But won't that make you an accessory after the fact?"

"Very likely. But at least I'll be able to live with my conscience." His lips twisted in a travesty of a smile. "I never knew my morals were so elastic. It looks like I'm my father's son, after all."

* * *

There was little else that could be done that day except for behaving like the honeymooning couple they were supposed to be, although Julia suspected her husband's mind was elsewhere. They wandered arm in arm through the village, peering into store windows and stopping once to purchase an utterly useless china plate bearing in its center a painted representation of the lake and the surrounding fells.

"What do you intend to do with it?" Pickett asked upon being informed that he was to have the honor of carrying his wife's newest acquisition.

Julia shrugged. "I suppose I shall present it to Lizzie as a wedding gift. I shouldn't think Mr. Hartsong would much care for a reminder of his visit to Banfell, do you? Unless, of course, you were to offer it to him as an olive branch of sorts."

"That would only work if I was sorry—which I'm not," said Pickett, hardening his heart. "But I'm not so sure about Lizzie. Why would she need a painted plate, when she can see the real thing just by looking out her window?"

"Oh dear, I suppose you're right. I only thought we should behave like tourists while we have the chance." She gave him a sidelong glance. "I daresay we will be headed back to London very soon."

He nodded. "The day after tomorrow, I expect."

After their return to the inn, they procured another basket from Mrs. Hawkins, this time taking the path to the lake for their picnic rather than stopping at the place where Julia had seen Ned Hawkins pushed to his death. But in spite of the change of scenery, Pickett remained distant and withdrawn, his thoughts clearly on the confrontation that lay ahead of him. Julia wished for some way to relieve him of his burden, at least for a while, but although he was unfailingly polite— attentive, even—she could not seem to reach him. It was not until much later that night, long after they had retired to their room, that the opportunity presented itself.

When she had turned her back on Society by marrying beneath her class, Julia had gained in return a passionate, if inexperienced, young lover. There was no trace of passion, however, in the slightly mint-scented embrace that awakened her in the middle of the night. It was a plea for comfort, pure and simple. And she answered it in the only way she could.

* * *

Several hours later, Pickett arose and dressed, then kissed Julia lingeringly before setting out on foot for the Hetherington estate.

"Are you sure you won't eat breakfast first?" asked Julia.

He shook his head. "I couldn't eat if I tried."

"We'll both have something after you return," she promised him, forcing a smile. "Little Pickett will no doubt be demanding it by that time."

"You needn't wait on me," he said. "I may feel even less like eating by the time I come back."

He kissed her again, and she fought the urge to cling to him, knowing it was for the best that he could put the unpleasant business behind him as soon as possible. And so she smiled encouragingly at him and bade him goodbye, then dressed for the day in a walking dress of Pomona green kerseymere (noting with mixed emotions that it fit a bit more snugly through the bosom than it had previously done) and descended the stairs to partake of a light breakfast.

She returned to her room to await Pickett's return, wondering if he had reached the Hetherington manor house yet—and if so, what reception he had found there once the object of his visit had become clear. The letters were stacked neatly on one corner of the writing table, awaiting delivery to the magistrate that afternoon. Julia picked up the top one and scanned the innocuous-looking black scrawl with the faint brown lines beneath. Her brow puckered thoughtfully. Something was odd about it, something quite aside from the hidden message revealed by the candle's heat . . .

Suddenly she knew. How had they missed it? It was obvious, so very obvious . . . As she stared at the sheet of foolscap in her hand, the bold black lines seemed to take on a life of their own, writhing across the page like a serpent. *There aren't any serpents in Ireland, are there?* she thought irrelevantly. St. Patrick had driven them into the sea, where they had all drowned . . . all but one, which had crossed the Irish Sea to England and taken up residence in the Lake District . . . The paper slipped from her hand and fluttered to the floor as she fought the inky black serpents who curled themselves into spots that danced at the corners of her vision.

It had been so obvious, and yet they had missed it, both of them, and now he was walking into danger all unawares.

"Not now, little one," she murmured to the baby, banishing the black spots through sheer force of will. "Not now. First we have to try and save your papa."

17

In Which Events Take a Most Unsettling Turn

P ickett arrived at the Hetherington residence, and suffered the misfortune of having the footman throw open the door to him just as Mrs. Hetherington was crossing the marble-tiled hall. To his chagrin, she appeared genuinely delighted to see him standing on the portico.

"Why, Mr. Pickett!" Her Irish accent, which he had previously found so lilting and musical, now served only to remind him—as if he needed a reminder!—of what he was about to do. "What a pleasant surprise! But does Mrs. Pickett not accompany you?"

"No, I—I'm afraid not," Pickett said. "I've come to—I was hoping for a word with your husband on a—a matter of business."

"Of course. Do come in! You may go, James," she said, dismissing the footman with a nod. "I shall take Mr. Pickett to Mr. Hetherington's study. I believe he is recording the rent receipts," she added to Pickett, "but I'm sure he will welcome the interruption."

Pickett was equally sure he would not, but had no choice but to follow the traitress across the hall to the same room in which he had first made the acquaintance of his magistrate's friend. Unlike that earlier occasion, Mr. Hetherington was already present, seated before his desk. The brown velvet curtains covering the floor-to-ceiling windows had been tied back, but although the sun would not reach this side of the house until the afternoon, the indirect light was sufficient to cast the man into silhouette, giving him a somewhat sinister appearance that did nothing to ease Pickett's mind.

"Robert, my dear, look who's come to visit," she announced. "Mr. Pickett, my husband tells me that yesterday he offered an impromptu dinner invitation to you and Mrs. Pickett for tonight. Dare we hope you have come to deliver your acceptance in person?"

Pickett shook his head. "I—I'm afraid not."

"What a pity! Perhaps another night, then? I should so like to hear you sing again!"

"I—I believe we will be returning to London very soon."

Mrs. Hetherington made suitably disappointed noises, then concluded with, "But I must not keep you standing here when you have business to discuss with my husband! Robert, you will let me know when you are finished with Mr. Pickett, will you not? We can at least give him tea before we send him back to his wife."

Mr. Hetherington promised not to let their guest depart before she had plied him with this beverage, and she, satisfied with these assurances, took her leave. After the door had closed behind her, Mr. Hetherington addressed his unexpected caller. "Well, Mr. Pickett, to what do I owe the pleasure of your company? I believe my wife made some mention of business?"

"She did, sir, but I'm afraid it's a business that brings me no pleasure."

"Oh?"

Pickett's eyes had by this time adjusted sufficiently to the sunlight to see his host's face. Pickett wished they had not; having to look the man in the eye made the ugly business even worse. Taking a deep breath, he recounted the story, starting with the anonymous letter that had brought him from Bow Street and continuing through the letter he'd found on Ned Hawkins's body, whose secrets had only been revealed by accidental proximity to a candle flame and whose handwriting exactly matched the one from Mrs. Hetherington.

"If I may say so, sir," he concluded, "I like your wife very much, and I think it a great pity that her hospitality to me and mine should result in such unexpected and tragic consequences."

"So do I," the older man said with a sigh. He pulled open one of the lower drawers of the desk and leaned down to fumble amongst its contents. "But mayhap Patrick Colquhoun can console himself with the knowledge that his young prodigy was not nearly so clever as he supposed."

Whatever reaction Pickett had expected, that was not it. "I, er, there must be some mistake—"

"Aye, that there is—and you're the one who made it."

Hetherington straightened in his chair, and Pickett found himself staring down the barrel of a blunt-nosed pistol. A hundred, a thousand images flashed through his mind in the space of an instant: Mrs. Hetherington's arthritic hands; a footman stationed by her chair to cut up the meat that she could not; the pianoforte she could no longer play; and, worst of all, his own wife with her perfectly sound arm in a makeshift sling fashioned from one of his cravats, so pleased with her own cleverness in gathering handwriting samples by enlisting others to write her letter for her . . .

"It was you," he said, feeling more than a little ill at the realization of what he'd missed. "You're E. G. B.; your wife can't write."

"Oh, E. G. B. isn't a person," Hetherington said, giving him the rather pitying smile he might bestow on an engaging but particularly slow child. "It stands for 'Erin go bragh'—or '*Éire go Brách*,' if you prefer the Gaelic form. Roughly translated, it means 'Ireland forever,' and is a favorite expression amongst all those who support the cause of Irish independence. As for my wife, she can indeed write. But not for very long, and not without pain, so for the last several years I've handled her social correspondence. Did you never even suspect, then? Tut-tut, Mr. Pickett, I should have thought better of you, after reading your magistrate's testimonial—which was quite glowing, by the bye."

"You were Mr. Colquhoun's friend!" Pickett insisted. "You were above suspicion!"

"Like Caesar's wife?" He shook his head, but the gun never wavered. "I'm sure Patrick Colquhoun would tell you that no one is above suspicion, Mr. Pickett. I daresay a few more years at Bow Street would have taught you that. It's as I said before: You've been asking the wrong questions."

The wrong questions, indeed. Small wonder Ned Hawkins had been so reluctant to identify himself, when the Bow Street Runner he'd sent to London for had no sooner set down his bags than he was asking how to contact the very man Hawkins had summoned him to investigate!

"Unfortunately," Hetherington continued, "you won't live long enough to benefit from a lesson hard-learned."

Pickett's eyes never left the small, cold circle of metal aimed at him, but his brain took frantic stock of his surroundings. The study door behind him was closed—he remembered seeing Mrs. Hetherington shut it behind her—but even if it were standing wide open, he would never be able to reach it in time. Nor did the tall windows along the opposite wall offer any escape, for Mr. Hetherington, still seated behind his broad desk, blocked his access to them.

"If you shoot me," Pickett said slowly, "your wife will hear the gunshot and come to investigate." He wished his voice didn't sound so tremulous. If he was going to die in any case, he might as well meet it bravely, in a way that would make Julia and Mr. Colquhoun proud. The thought gave him courage, and he stood a bit taller, forcing Hetherington to adjust his aim slightly upward.

"Aye, that she will. But you provided me with the excuse yourself. That 'business' you had with me," he explained, seeing Pickett at a loss. "You had thought to buy a pistol from me. Unfortunately, it will accidentally go off while you are examining it. A pity you'll be so careless, but young people so often are, you know."

"If we're to speak of carelessness," Pickett said, "I wonder at your allowing that letter to fall into the wrong hands."

Hetherington gave a grunt of annoyance. "I have no idea what aroused Ned's suspicions, and I suppose I never will," he said pettishly.

"Perhaps he became suspicious of your willingness to take the risk of offering such a 'public service' as illicit mail delivery without some ulterior motive," Pickett suggested somewhat tartly, no longer constrained by good manners.

"Oh, the mail scheme has existed for decades," Hetherington said dismissively. "I only became involved quite recently. And if I may be allowed to boast, I made changes to the process that made it much more efficient—and much less likely to be discovered, at least by anyone in a position to prefer charges."

"Congratulations," Pickett put in drily.

Hetherington chuckled. "I do like a man who can keep a cool head in a crisis! I can see why Patrick Colquhoun took such a fancy to you. But as you surmise, I had my own reasons for not wanting to trust my correspondence to the Royal Mail. For whatever reason, Ned Hawkins became suspicious and went to the cave, retrieved my letter from the bag, and read it. It's unlikely he recognized the code—it involves writing in lemon juice or some other acidic substance, which weakens the paper and causes it to turn dark when exposed to heat. But having recognized my handwriting, he no doubt read the accomplishments of my children and, knowing I had none, realized there had to be more to the letter than appeared at first glance, and assumed the worst. In any case, he was on his way to my house to confront me with his discovery when we met on the cliff path. I daresay you know the rest; it was your wife who saw me push the fellow, was it not? I always thought so, but could never be entirely sure. That being the case, I have been extremely reluctant to eliminate the potential threat lest I be mistaken, but now—"

"Julia poses no danger to you," Pickett interjected quickly. "She knows someone pushed Ned Hawkins, but could not identify you."

"I am relieved to hear it, for her sake as well as my own. It would be a pity to be obliged to do an injury to so charming a lady. I found the very idea so repugnant that I slipped down to the inn one night and threw a rock through your window in the hopes of frightening the pair of you into returning to London, thus sparing me the necessity of taking some more drastic action. Unfortunately, you allowed your emotions to overpower your intelligence."

I should have left her on the mail coach, Pickett thought despairingly. *I should have sent her back to London, even if it killed me. Interesting choice of words, that . . .*

Hetherington shifted in his chair. "But 'Tempus fugit,' as the saying goes, and I would prefer to have this business settled before Brigid returns. Have you any last words, Mr. Pickett?"

It appeared his time was at hand. "Will you at least answer one question first?" Pickett asked, as much an attempt to delay the inevitable as it was an urge to satisfy a very real curiosity.

Hetherington gave a careless shrug, which Pickett took for an affirmative.

"Why?" he asked simply. "You have a good life here, a life many men would envy. Why would you risk it all to betray a country that has been good to you? Your wife, I could see, perhaps—"

"You know nothing of my wife!" the older man snapped, and Pickett thought the mask slipped, revealing a glimpse of the embittered man behind the affable manner. "My poor Brigid has little enough reason to love the English. Tell me, are you familiar with the battle of Carrickfergus?"

"No, I'm afraid not," Pickett confessed.

"I thought not. Few people are these days, as England hardly showed to advantage in the affair. They remember it well in Belfast, though. It was almost fifty years ago, during the Seven Years' War. A French privateer named Thurot took the Irish town of Carrickfergus and captured its castle. Held it for five days, too, until the Royal Navy showed up to drive him out. He made Belfast uncomfortable enough in the meantime, though, with his demands for supplies and ransom money."

"Oh?" Pickett was not quite certain where his adversary was going with all this, but reasoned it could only be to his benefit to keep the man talking. Perhaps by the time Hetherington came to his point, he—Pickett himself—would have miraculously thought of some way out of his present dilemma.

"My wife's father cast his lot with Thurot," Mr. Hetherington continued. "He had a grudge against the English dating back to the famine of twenty years earlier, when a late frost killed all the crops. Brigid had not yet been born, but her parents' three older children died in the outbreak of starvation and disease that followed."

"I'm very sorry to hear it," Pickett said. "Still, the English can hardly be blamed for the weather."

"No, although there were those who felt Whitehall might have done more to help relieve the suffering. In any case, the English must certainly be blamed for what followed. When the French withdrew from Carrickfergus, Brigid's father was arrested, and all his property was confiscated. But even though the English had stolen her inheritance, they weren't done with her yet." Hetherington's breath came fast and hard, and Pickett knew with a sick feeling in the pit of his stomach what he was about to hear. "He was being held in the castle pending execution when she went to visit him one day. Half a dozen British soldiers waylaid her. They kept her for four hours, and when she scratched one of them in the face, he retaliated by breaking her fingers. She wasn't yet fourteen years old."

"Oh, God," breathed Pickett. It was a wonder the man was still sane. If such a thing had happened to Julia . . .

But no, he wasn't going to think about that. It was that— asking the wrong questions, thinking first of Julia's safety and Ned's murder only a distant second, imagining what he might have done had it been Julia who was guilty of such a crime, when he was compelled by the bonds of love and the vows of matrimony to cherish and care for her—that had led to his being where he was now: on the receiving end of a pistol.

And because he had been unable to distance himself from the case enough to examine it objectively, his life would be forfeit for the sins of his long-dead countrymen. Still, Pickett refused to give the man the satisfaction of seeing him beg for a mercy he knew would never be granted. And so they stared at one another, Pickett braced for the shot that would put an end to his existence, his adversary engrossed in thoughts of injustices long past. The only sound in the room was the ticking of the clock over the mantelpiece, a noise that seemed to Pickett almost preternaturally loud as it counted off with relentless precision all the lost moments that he would never live to see: He would never see Julia again, never lie with her in his arms, never see his infant son or daughter, never watch it grow up—

Suddenly the crash of breaking glass shattered the silence. Pickett did not waste time in wondering why. He lunged across the desk, grabbing Hetherington's pistol arm and wrenching it with every ounce of strength he possessed. How long they struggled, he didn't know—it seemed like hours, but was very likely a matter of seconds—but the deadlock was broken when the door opened and a lilting Irish voice asked, "Robert, what was that—?"

The gun went off with a deafening report, and the look of utter horror on Hetherington's face made Pickett's blood run cold. The pistol fell from the man's hand, and he pushed past the desk, calling his wife's name in a strangled voice.

Pickett, still sprawled across the desk on his belly,

scrambled to his feet and turned in time to see Mrs. Hetherington slowly crumple to her knees. The expression on her face was one of utter astonishment, and across the bosom of her fashionable gown, a crimson stain bloomed like some obscene flower.

"*Brigid, a mhuirnín,*" her husband crooned, gathering her in his arms.

Instinctively, Pickett averted his gaze, then blinked as he took in the wreckage that had saved his life. One of the tall windows was shattered, and shards of glass littered the carpet. A rock the size of his fist lay in the middle of the floor, obviously the cause of all the damage, and on the terrace just outside—

On the terrace just outside stood Julia, staring at him with huge, stricken eyes set in a face drained of all color. "You—you're alive," she stammered. "You're alive."

Heedless of the glass crunching beneath his feet, he crossed the room in three strides and, not bothering to open the window, ducked through the gaping hole and stepped over the sill.

"I'm alive," he assured her, and caught her in his arms as she swayed on her feet.

She stroked his face with one trembling hand. "It was Mr. Hetherington."

"Yes, I—I know."

"He isn't the only one who can throw rocks," she said, with a trace of her usual spirit.

He had to smile a little at that. "No, he isn't—for which I am very grateful."

"John, the snakes—"

"Snakes?" echoed Pickett, all at sea.

"I can't—I can't hold them off any longer," she said, and went limp in his arms.

"It's all right," he murmured, cradling her closer. "They can't hurt you."

He slipped one arm beneath her knees and picked her up bodily, then turned back toward the window just in time to see Hetherington close his wife's sightless eyes with one gentle hand. Tears ran down the man's face, but hatred burned in his eyes as he looked up at his late adversary.

"I—I'm sorry, sir—" Pickett began.

"You're sorry? *You're sorry?* You don't know what 'sorry' is!"

"It was an accident—"

Hetherington's gaze shifted to Julia, lying insensible in Pickett's arms. "No, you don't know what 'sorry' is, not yet, but you will. You have a wife there, one you love. Shall I do to her what you did to mine? Shall I make you beg for her life, as you were prepared to make me beg for Brigid's? No, not today," he said, as Pickett darted a quick glance at the pistol lying on the carpet, mentally gauging how long it would take for Hetherington to snatch it up and reload. "But someday, someday when you're least expecting it, when you've convinced yourself that it's safe to lower your guard—"

His voice rose in volume with each new threat, and it was with no small sense of relief that Pickett noticed the butler, two footmen, and a wide-eyed housemaid, who had all come running and were now crowded in the doorway to the study.

"Send for the magistrate," Pickett instructed the butler. He glanced down at the lifeless heap that had once been the lady of the house. "This—this was an accident, but there are other charges against your master that are not. And be sure you keep him here until the magistrate arrives," he added, instinctively holding Julia closer. "Don't let him get away."

One of the footmen, the same one who had cut up his mistress's meat at dinner, glanced from the gunshot wound in her chest to the weapon lying on the floor next to his master's desk, and apparently drew his own conclusions. "He won't be going nowhere," he declared stoutly, setting his jaw.

Not that Mr. Hetherington was showing any signs of making any such attempt; with his outburst over, all the fight seemed to have gone out of him, and he sobbed over the dead woman whose head he cradled on his lap. But while they awaited the magistrate's arrival, Pickett had a more urgent priority, one who was just beginning to stir in his arms.

"John, you're all right?" Julia asked. "He didn't hurt you?"

"I'm fine," he assured her, turning slightly in order to block her view of the woman's body. He supposed he ought to set her on her feet now that she had recovered from her swoon, but in the light of Hetherington's threats, he couldn't bring himself to let her go. "But what are you doing here? Not that I'm complaining," he added hastily. In fact, had it not been for her timely intervention, it would have been he instead of Mrs. Hetherington who lay dead on the floor.

"I realized the handwriting looked too bold for Mrs. Hetherington to have managed it with her crippled hands, and thought her husband must have written it for her. I practically ran all the way from the Hart and Hound, rather than wait for Jem Hawkins to return with the wagon. And then when I got here, I found Mr. Hetherington holding a gun on you! Oh John, I've never been so frightened in my life!"

Pickett thought that was saying something, given the fact that during the one year of their acquaintance she had faced standing trial for murder, hanging from the edge of a cliff, and being trapped in a burning theatre.

"I'm taking you back to the inn to rest," he told her. "I can't stay with you—I'll have to come back here and tie up a few loose ends with the magistrate—but then you can pack your bags. Tomorrow we're going back to London." London, where he would be faced with the task of explaining to Mr. Colquhoun what had taken place here—and how his own mishandling of the case had allowed it to happen. Still, he was forced to admit that the outcome could have been worse— much worse. He breathed a sigh of relief. "Tomorrow we're going home."

EPILOGUE

In Which John Pickett Must Give an Accounting of Himself

A nd there you have it," Pickett concluded miserably. Almost a week had passed since the disastrous denouement, and now he stood before the magistrate's bench, making his report to a scowling Mr. Colquhoun. "You warned me—more than once—about the dangers of taking a case too personally, but that's exactly what I did. I botched this case in just about every way it's possible to botch one. I—I am sorry, sir."

The magistrate looked up from the written report in his hand to regard his most junior Runner over the top of the wire-rimmed spectacles he wore for reading. "No one expects you to be perfect, Mr. Pickett. You're only twenty-four years old—"

"Twenty-five," Pickett corrected him.

The bushy white eyebrows rose. "Twenty-five?"

Pickett nodded. "This past March."

"Well, in that case, you should have known better." With

Pickett momentarily taken aback, the magistrate pressed his argument. "It seems to me the fault must be partly mine, for giving you the impression that my acquaintance with Robert Hetherington was much warmer than it actually was. It's true that at one time we were upon visiting terms, and our wives were once very close. But then my Isabella came along, and James not long after, and it can be painful for a childless couple to find itself forever in the company of a growing family. We drifted apart, and it wasn't until I was about to dispatch you to the Lake District that I recalled Hetherington had bought a property there. I thought it might help you to have a contact in the area; I had not considered what decades of disappointment and bitterness could do to a man, and for that, I owe you an apology."

Pickett could not allow these self-recriminations to pass. "The fault is mine, sir, and mine alone. I couldn't stop thinking of Julia, of how I would have felt, what I would have done if I had discovered she was guilty of a crime—not treason, but the murder of her first husband. I lost all objectivity, and because of me, an innocent woman is dead."

"She might not have been so innocent, you know," the magistrate pointed out. "The plot is being investigated as we speak, and it may turn out that she was up to her neck in it."

Pickett rather hoped she was—not to assuage his own conscience (at least, not *only* for so self-serving a purpose), but because it seemed to him that the woman deserved some measure of vengeance. "Even if she was, sir, she still deserved the right to face her accusers, to offer a defense of her actions. Perhaps, after hearing her past history, a jury might have been lenient." A shadow crossed his face. "More lenient than I was, in any case."

Mr. Colquhoun flipped back through the written report before him. "Did you succeed in disarming him, then? I'm afraid I missed the part that said it was your finger pulling the trigger."

"No, but it was undoubtedly I who pushed her husband's arm so that the ball meant for me struck her instead."

Mr. Colquhoun regarded his inconsolable young Runner in silence for a long moment. "Show me," he said at last.

"I—I beg your pardon?"

"Show me," the magistrate said again. He pointed his index finger like a gun, and aimed it across the bench at Pickett. "Disarm me, as you tried to do Robert Hetherington."

"Better not, Mr. Pickett," Harry Carson, a member of the horse patrol, called impudently. "If you do, it'll make an awful mess."

Pickett turned, and saw that every member of the Bow Street force who was not actively engaged in an investigation had gathered around to watch.

"I—I can't—" Pickett protested feebly.

"That's just what we're going to put to the test," declared Mr. Colquhoun. "Do to me exactly what you did to Hetherington. Whenever you're ready, Mr. Pickett."

Something was different, something aside from the obvious, and after a few seconds' consideration, Pickett realized what it was. "He didn't have his arm stretched out. It was bent at the elbow."

"Meaning you had to reach, say, an extra foot or so," the

magistrate said with a nod, adjusting his "weapon" accordingly.

Pickett stared at the hand pointed at him. The events of that morning were never far from his thoughts, so it took only a moment for the flesh and blood to vanish, replaced by an image of the very real pistol held by a man who had threatened not only Pickett's life, but every happiness he had ever known. He took a deep breath and lunged across the bench, causing the wooden railing to groan beneath his weight and scattering his painstakingly transcribed report in all directions as he grabbed the magistrate's forearm. Mr. Colquhoun's arm immediately went limp, and Pickett fell sprawling belly-down on the desk, banging his chin in the process.

As his audience burst into startled laughter, he picked himself up with what dignity he could muster. "You weren't even trying!"

"No, I wasn't," confessed his magistrate, unrepentant. "If Hetherington had done likewise, his shot would have gone into the floor. But he didn't. He fought back, and it was his resistance, not your attempt to disarm him, that caused his wife's death. It was indeed a tragic accident, but one for which her husband, not you, must bear the blame."

"It's supposed to make me feel better, knowing that I couldn't overpower a man more than twice my age?"

Mr. Colquhoun regarded his protégé with a twinkle lurking in his blue eyes. "Do you want absolution, Mr. Pickett, or don't you?"

Pickett glanced down at the railing he clutched with both hands. "The bench is a bit higher than Mr. Hetherington's desk," he said.

"I doubt it would make much difference. Do you recall whether your feet were on the floor?"

Casting his mind back, Pickett remembered sliding off the desk to turn and identify the reason for his foe's horrified expression. "No, sir. They weren't."

"There you are, then," said the magistrate decisively. "You might have had the advantages of youth and strength, but he held the more stable position, seated behind his desk while you lay across it."

Mr. Colquhoun might consider the matter settled, but there was one element Pickett could not dismiss so easily, not while Robert Hetherington still lived. The assembled audience began to disperse, realizing the show was over, and Pickett waited until they were out of earshot before confiding in a low voice, "You should know, sir, that he—he threatened Julia. He promised to come after her—not immediately, he said, but later, after I've had time to lower my guard."

"I should think by that time he'll be six feet under—and may God have mercy on his soul," the magistrate said. "Mr. Pickett, you said yourself that he is being held in prison pending the Carlisle assizes. I'll make inquiries, and let you know when he's been executed."

Pickett let out a sigh. "Thank you, sir. I was hoping you would."

"And now," pronounced Mr. Colquhoun, glancing over his shoulder at the large clock that hung on the wall over his bench, "I intend to go home and seek my dinner. I suggest you do the same."

"Yes, sir," said Pickett, and turned away, prepared to suit the word to the deed.

"Oh, John," the magistrate called as he reached the door.

"Sir?" Pickett asked, pausing to turn back.

"Do you and Mrs. Pickett intend to make a habit of this? Taking it in turns saving each other's lives?"

A faint smile touched Pickett's lips. "One can only hope, sir."

"You're all right, then?"

"Not just yet," Pickett confessed, "but I will be."

And with this promise, he left the Bow Street Public Office and turned his steps toward Curzon Street, and the woman who had the power to make it so.

Author's Note

Warning: this note contains spoilers. If you haven't yet read the book, you might want to do so before proceeding further.

Some books require more research than others. This one required a lot. Thankfully, I had the opportunity to see the Lake District for myself when I visited the area shortly after the book was finished, which allowed me to flesh out descriptions of setting—and where I startled a tour guide by asking, "Are there places along the river where the bank is high enough that you could push someone over and kill them?"

While researching online for some reason the husband of an Irishwoman might bear a grudge against the English (sadly, never far to seek in the history of Anglo-Irish relations), I came across the second Battle of Carrickfergus, which had taken place in 1760 (there had been an earlier one in 1597), and which I incorporated into my story.

My investigations into mail smuggling proved more elusive. Much has been written on the smuggling of brandy and tobacco across the Channel à la Kipling's "five and twenty ponies trotting through the dark," but I could find very little on the domestic smuggling of letters beyond the fact that it existed, and was apparently widespread. I found no particulars, however, which forced me (or left me free, depending upon how one looks at it) to rely on informed imagination in creating my own story. Interestingly, the two anecdotes cited by Robert Hetherington in Chapter 14—that of a brother and sister working out their own method of communication, and the assertion that four of every five letters mailed from Manchester were sent by means other than the Royal Mail—were drawn from actual writings, albeit from about twenty-five years later; in fact, both constituted part of the debate that eventually led to postal reform and, in 1840, the creation of the Uniform Penny Post, which allowed letters to be sent for the same cost regardless of distance, with the postage to be paid by the sender, rather than the recipient.

Interestingly, the smuggling of domestic mail seems to be linked to the rise in literacy: When only the upper classes could read and write, the cost of receiving letters was immaterial, as they could easily afford it. As literacy spread to the middle and sometimes even the lower classes, however, it became necessary for them to look for affordable ways of corresponding with friends, family, and business associates, despite the dubious legality of those ways.

On the subject of letters, the old "lemon juice as invisible ink" trick is something every schoolchild knows today, but there was a time when it was the latest in high-tech intelligence. For instance, George Washington is known to have used it, and trained spies in its use, during the American Revolution.

Finally, one detail that might be confusing to American readers: In Regency England, one went to the "post office" to hire a post chaise, the Regency equivalent of a rental car; one took one's letters to (or fetched them from) the "receiving office."

About the Author

At the age of sixteen, Sheri Cobb South discovered Georgette Heyer, and came to the startling realization that she had been born into the wrong century. Although she probably would have been a chambermaid had she actually lived in Regency England, that didn't stop her from fantasizing about waltzing the night away in the arms of a handsome, wealthy, and titled gentleman.

Since Georgette Heyer died in 1974 and could not write any more Regencies, Ms. South came to the conclusion she would have to do it herself. In addition to the bestselling John Pickett mystery series (now an award-winning audiobook series!), she has also written several Regency romances, including the critically acclaimed *The Weaver Takes a Wife*.

A native and long-time resident of Alabama, Ms. South now lives in Loveland, Colorado.

She loves to hear from readers, and invites them to visit her website, www.shericobbsouth.com, follow her on Facebook, Goodreads, Pinterest, or Twitter, or email her at Cobbsouth@aol.com.